CW01184246

WHEN SHE SLEEPS

J. A. BAKER

B
Boldwood

First published as *The Midnight Child* in 2021. This edition published in Great Britain in 2024 by Boldwood Books Ltd.

Copyright © J. A. Baker, 2021

Cover Design by Head Design Ltd

Cover Illustration: iStock

The moral right of J. A. Baker to be identified as the author of this work has been asserted in accordance with the Copyright, Designs and Patents Act 1988.

All rights reserved. No part of this book may be reproduced in any form or by any electronic or mechanical means, including information storage and retrieval systems, without written permission from the author, except for the use of brief quotations in a book review.

This book is a work of fiction and, except in the case of historical fact, any resemblance to actual persons, living or dead, is purely coincidental.

Every effort has been made to obtain the necessary permissions with reference to copyright material, both illustrative and quoted. We apologise for any omissions in this respect and will be pleased to make the appropriate acknowledgements in any future edition.

A CIP catalogue record for this book is available from the British Library.

Paperback ISBN 978-1-83561-247-7

Large Print ISBN 978-1-83561-248-4

Hardback ISBN 978-1-83561-246-0

Ebook ISBN 978-1-83561-249-1

Kindle ISBN 978-1-83561-250-7

Audio CD ISBN 978-1-83561-241-5

MP3 CD ISBN 978-1-83561-242-2

Digital audio download ISBN 978-1-83561-243-9

Boldwood Books Ltd
23 Bowerdean Street
London SW6 3TN
www.boldwoodbooks.com

Three things cannot be long hidden; the sun, the moon, and the truth

— BUDDHA

By doubting we are led to question, by questioning we arrive at the truth

— PETER ABELARD

To all the sleepwalkers out there and the sufferers of nightmares. May your visions and journeys always be happy ones.

1

I'm freezing. It's the first thing I notice as I drag myself out of sleep's grip. The skin on my arms, my stomach, my face is icy, my entire body so very, very cold. Then I feel it – the sticky sensation on my hands, my legs. It jars, incompatible with the grogginess that clings to me like ivy on a knotted tree trunk. I sit up, pull back the bedsheets, blinking repeatedly, my eyes blurred, gritty. I wait for my vision to adjust to the darkness. The sun has yet to make an appearance. Outside is silent, dim and empty; inside remains swathed with an inky blackness. I turn on the bedside lamp, force my brain to stir itself, to come to life like an animal rousing from a deep hibernation. And then I see it.

To say it is a scream would be untrue. An exaggeration, even. Definitely not a scream. More of a guttural grunt: that's the sound that emerges from my throat as I leap out of bed, my legs weak, the floor spongy beneath my feet. A kaleidoscope of muted colours spins past as dizziness takes hold. I look down, see the vivid streaks of blood over my limbs, my torso. I clasp my hand over my mouth, stifling my shrieks.

I'm bleeding to death. I'm not bleeding to death. I can't be. I'm alive, up and out of bed. Not close to collapsing or passing out. I'm woozy. That's the shock. Shock at discovering a thick coating of sticky crimson streaked over my flesh, over my legs, across the upper half of my body. Even my face. I can feel it, smell it – that pungent, metallic odour. The smell of ageing bodily fluids. The stench of decay.

My head pounds. My breathing is laboured. I have no idea what to do, my brain failing me. I flail about the room, naked and shivering then stop and try to take stock. This is not menstrual blood. This is different. Very different.

Lungs fit to burst, I inspect my body for cuts and lacerations, my fingers trailing over the red marks, my arms and legs turning this way and that as I scan for anything that will give me a clue as to what is going on here. I need to calm down, think clearly. Hysteria and confusion have hijacked my thinking, swarming around my head, flapping and colliding; a flock of angry birds pecking at my brain.

The mattress groans under my weight as I slump onto it, the rational part of my mind willing the panic and confusion to dissipate. My eyes are drawn to the floor, to the trail of dirty footprints leading to the door. Out of the door. Onto the landing. I swallow. Listen to thrum of my own heartbeat that pulses in my ears, fierce waves crashing onto the shore, a lonely echo in the quiet of the room. A reminder that I am alone.

Beside me, slung over the chair, are yesterday's clothes – an old T-shirt, a pair of jeans and my underwear. I pull them on, step into the trainers I kicked off last night and head onto the landing, my throat thick with anticipation at what I might find there. I flick on the light. It highlights more muddy footprints scattered over the stair carpet. I continue down, following them like a trail of breadcrumbs, staring at the dirt and soil compressed into the grey fabric, until I reach the bottom step.

A cold breeze stops me in my tracks. I shiver, too afraid to look. Too afraid to move. Too afraid to do anything at all. Goosebumps prickle my skin. My breathing becomes noisy, ragged. I try to stifle it, to silence every movement I make.

A metallic clunk stills my blood. It's coming from somewhere in the house. The kitchen. I hear it again. A rhythmic thudding. Oh God. Somebody is in there, inside my house. Wandering about in my home.

Outside, the wind builds. It rustles through the trees, moans around the exterior of the house, a ghostly wail, demanding to be heard. Forcing its way into my thoughts. Making me think the unthinkable is about to happen. Because it could. I could stand here, timid and afraid, thinking, *why me?* But of course, *why not me?* Such things happen. All the time. And I should know.

I shuffle forwards, glancing around for something – anything that I can use to protect myself. I stop. Try to calm down, to go through all the possible answers, every conceivable scenario. Protect myself against what? An intruder? An overactive imagination? I need to think clearly here, not jump to irrational conclusions. This is a safe place to live. I know this area, grew up here. Nothing bad happens round these parts. I swallow, stare down at my feet and blink to clear my misted vision because I know that that is a complete lie.

Bad things did happen here, but not any more. The past is behind me. A long way behind me. A shiny new future beckons. I will do well to not dwell on what went before. Therein lies the inevitable route to misery. Forty years have passed, much has happened. It's as if it is part of a life that belonged to somebody else. I am no longer that bereft child. The girl who lost a sibling. I am me, a grown woman with children of her own.

I snap back to the present, shake off thoughts of my other life, those dark memories that plague me. Last night, I locked the door before going to bed. I have no doubts about this. None whatsoever. My fingers itch to grab at something. I need to feel safe. Beside me stands the old china vase given to me by my sister – a gift from our grandma that she didn't particularly like and I wouldn't allow her to throw away. I pick it up, my hand wrapped around it, its cool surface sticking to my clammy palm, its bright-yellow hue a dim shaft of colour in the murky half-light of the early morning.

As slowly as I can, as silently as I can, I edge forward, doing my utmost to stem my rising fear, to keep my breathing low and inaudible and not allow my emotions to overwhelm me even though terror is rising in my gut, creeping up my throat, shrieking into my head.

'This is my house, my safe place. Nothing and nobody can get to me here. This is my sanctuary.' I murmur the words over and over like a mantra as I creep through the hallway, my movements disconnected from my brain, my usual dexterity abandoning me, leaving me floppy limbed and feeble.

The thudding continues. Perhaps it's a window, slightly ajar and the wind has pushed at it, causing it to rattle. But that doesn't explain the blood. Or the muddy footsteps. My heartbeat quickens. I shuffle through to the kitchen, a spike of ice travelling up my spine, flooding my veins, spreading beneath my skin as I step onto the tiled flooring.

More thudding. A gust of cold air hits me. I suck in my breath. The back door is wide open. I close it, turning the key, then lean against the glass panel to steady myself, this unexpected find stripping me of all strength.

I look around the room, attempting to survey any differences, no matter how small or insignificant. Everything is the same. No changes. Nothing has been moved. No damage.

What if the intruder didn't leave? What if somebody is now locked in the house with me? I shut my eyes, swallow down a small amount of sour bile. I can't think about it. I won't. It's too terrifying a thought. I need to stop this. I have to get a grip. It's obvious I didn't lock the door properly and it blew open. That has to be the case. I was sure I locked it. I was wrong. That's all it is. As if to confirm my thinking, the wind gathers pace outside, tree limbs groaning and swaying wildly, their long, gnarled branches shifting like spindly, arthritic fingers, silhouetted against the backdrop of a burnt-orange sky as the sun appears, a watery orb lazily dragging itself upwards off the horizon.

I pace around the kitchen, switching on lights and lamps, then do the same in the living room and hallway to prove to myself that I am indeed, very much alone. Which I am. There is nobody here. I fling open cupboard doors, peek behind cabinets, turn on the radio, the background noise alleviating my fears. It's the voices. They fill the void of silence that is all around me. The house slowly comes to life, every second, every minute edging closer to the warmth and vibrancy of daytime. Outside, the dawn breaks.

None of the things that comfort me help me piece together what has happened. Once again, I inspect myself in the mirror, checking my face for cuts, scrutinising my arms and legs for damaged flesh, and find nothing. No pain, no dull aches, nothing to indicate I have a wound that caused this.

Another examination of the house before I head back upstairs for a shower. All clear. I sigh and allow myself a small smile. Relief unfurls itself in my chest, a warm, furry thing flooding my body, expanding in my veins. Any immediate danger has passed. I'm safe. Safe from an unseen, unknown menace. It doesn't explain the muddy footprints, however. I shut out that thought, tell myself to stop.

In the bedroom, the clock at my bedside tells me it is 5.30 a.m. Almost time to get up, to rouse myself, get showered, clean this mess off my skin and tidy the bedroom. Forget the open door. Forget my fears. Move on from it all. Try to pretend nothing bad or frightening took place.

An hour later I am dressed, the soiled bedsheets and my clothes thrown into the washing machine, my hair washed and dried, the house back to its usual calm and tranquil self.

Feeling braver than I did a short time ago, I unlock the back door and head outside, ready to confront whoever may be hiding out there, yet also knowing I won't find anything.

Not quite. I do find something. Not a person, but something that sends a deluge of disgust coursing through me. Something that raises more questions than it answers. Laid across the back lawn is a dead animal. It looks like a dog. Instinctively, I take a step back, my hand clasped over my mouth. Time ticks by – seconds, minutes perhaps before I can gather up enough courage to inspect the bloodied carcass.

Up close, I can see that it isn't a dog at all. It's a fox, its damaged form spreadeagled on the grass, its back legs partially concealed beneath the shrubbery. In its mouth is a small animal, the lumpiness of its body partially shredded and skewed. I stare down at my hands, recalling the blood on me, those sickening, red smears. It's too grim, too revolting to consider. There is no link. There can't be. I think of the open door and swallow hard. I think of the muddy footprints, recall the dirt on my feet as I showered, and try to stop my racing thoughts.

'Probably a badger what did it.'

A pain shoots up my neck as I swivel to see Mr Waters' head peeking over the top of the fence, his cloudy, pale eyes meeting mine before resting his gaze on the dead fox.

'A badger?' I don't know why I'm answering. I don't want to become embroiled in a conversation about this atrocity. I want to clear it away, dart back inside the house, double lock the doors and stay there for the remainder of the day.

'Aye. Vicious little buggers they are. Fox probably made off wi' his dinner or tried to steal one of its cubs and this is the net result.'

My eyes are suddenly heavy. I squeeze them shut, sigh, try to gulp down a nervous rush of saliva that has filled my mouth.

'Surprised you didn't hear it all last night. Right ruckus it was. I were stood at t' bedroom window watching it all 'appen. Could 'ave sworn I saw somebody down here afterwards. I thought it was you cleaning it all up. Mind you, my eyes aren't what they used to be. Bloody cataracts. Could have been the shadow of the trees. That wind blew everything around. I heard my bin topple over onto the patio at one point. What a clatter it made.'

The nervous rush of saliva turns into a tsunami, flooding the recesses of my gums, swilling around my mouth; a sour wash of liquid I am desperate to spit out. I try to smile, to appear at ease as he speaks, all the while wishing he would disappear. I need time to think. I need some space on my own.

'Anyway, if you need any help clearing it up, you know where I am, lovey.' His head disappears, sinking behind the fence.

I fear that he hasn't gone back inside his own little house but is squatting down on the other side, listening to me, working out whether or not I know how to dispose of this thing safely. Only when I hear the click of his door do I move, my head swimming, a cold sensation shifting around my belly, a coiled viper slithering around my guts.

Could have sworn I saw somebody down here afterwards. I thought it was you cleaning it all up.

I bat away the residual thoughts that linger in my brain, thoughts conjured up by his words. It's nonsense. Mr Waters is an old man. His eyesight is spectacularly poor. He is bored, has an overactive imagination. Likes to embellish on the facts, conjure up a story when there isn't one to be had. As he said, it was a stormy night. Bad weather, poor visibility, things strewn around the garden.

On and on I go, convincing myself of his many faults and delusions as I pull on a pair of latex gloves and wrap a towel around my face to mask the smell of the blood, to try to distance myself from this situation.

The fox is heavier than I expected, its body solid and still marginally warm. I retch. Despite my best intentions to stay calm and remain in control, I heave and gag. I stuff it into a black bin bag, tying it tightly before double bagging it and dropping it into the wheelie bin next to the back door. The weather isn't so warm. That's a good thing. No chance of insects swarming around. No danger of maggots eating their way through the bloodied corpse, wriggling their way around the bottom of the bin.

Only when I am back inside and the door is locked do I allow myself the luxury of crying, letting it all out – the worry, the fear, the terror of the unknown – it all comes spilling out of me, a river of anxiety.

My eyes burn, my throat is thick and glutinous as I make myself a coffee and sit at the table, a series of small, hiccupping sobs still constricting my breathing. It was always going to be difficult, living on my own. I knew this. None of it is my doing and yet as I sit here, trying to piece together what has just happened, I can't help feel that I am being punished. Recently widowed, frightened at the prospect of living by myself and, although it pains me to admit it, lonely. With one child living in Australia and the other living almost 250 miles away in Oxford, there are days when I feel totally isolated. The shiny new future I regularly speak of is still a far-off object, too distant to reach. I'll get to it one day. I'm just not quite there yet.

More tears fall. I wallow in self-pity until my chest aches and my throat is sore, my tear ducts desert dry. I force myself out of it, the abyss of misery I regularly stumble into. It's not healthy being overwhelmed like this. It's not who I am. Besides, I chose to live here, back at my childhood home. It felt comforting, the thought of being here. Still does most of the time. I could have continued living in York, in my lovely city home, grieving, expecting to see Warren every time I walked into a room, and compounded my unhappiness with unrealistic expectations. The move here made sense. Still does. Last night, this morning, the find in the garden, it's all a blip in my existence. Here had its losses as well but they are not as fresh, not as raw. Here is a compromise, not a new, unfamiliar home, someplace where I would struggle to adjust. My surroundings provide some comfort and God knows I could do with plenty of that.

I stand at the sink, splash my face with water, my flesh numb from the cold. Icy water laps at my skin, the gush from the tap dragging me out of my sullen musings. It feels good, the cold against my flesh – revitalising, blocking out any unwelcome thoughts. Thoughts that have been rekindled now I am living alone. I push them away, shove them back in that dark place in my head and get on with my day.

2

The words won't come. It's all such a mess, my ideas jumbled, my thoughts non-linear and chaotic. I should stop writing, not force it. Find something else to do, something that will distract me and free up my thinking. And yet I don't. I stay seated at my desk, deflated and desperate, my self-confidence shrinking by the second. Despite many cups of coffee, the plot and characters refuse to show themselves, staying half hidden in the shadows, dancing on the periphery of my thoughts.

A sandwich later and I am up at the kitchen window staring out into the garden, ruminating over last night. Thinking about the dead fox. Thinking about the blood. The muddy footprints. My dirty feet. Did I do it? Am I capable of such an act? Moreover, why would I be out there and why can't I remember anything?

Behind me, my phone pings, a shrill reminder of how empty this house feels today, how empty I feel inside.

It's Kim. She has sent me a text, checking how I am, monitoring my mood and making sure I'm up and functioning, getting on with my day.

I sigh, bite at my lip and think hard before sending my reply.

> I'm fine thanks. Sitting trying to write. Shall we meet for coffee sometime this week?

Communicating with her is never easy. In her mind, I am still her younger sister, the sibling who never grew up. She sees it as her duty to take care of me and whilst her interventions and actions are well-intentioned, she forgets that I'm now a grown woman with adult children of my own and therefore perfectly capable of taking care of myself. Warren's death heightened her need to protect me, to keep checking up on my every movement. It is kind and I'm lucky to have somebody watching out for me, I do know that, but there are times when her constant monitoring overwhelms me more than any bouts of loneliness ever could, her messages often reminding me of my current predicament. Of my bleak state of mind.

> That sounds perfect. Tomorrow at midday. Our usual haunt.

Her reply is immediate. I am being pushed into a corner. Her text reads as they usually do, worded as a fait accompli. I have no choice in the matter.

My head aches. I am being uncharitable. I am also at an all-time low. Kim knows this. I would do well to loosen up, allow her in, let her care for me a little. I should indulge her, let her feel as if she is helping. She too, has her foibles and needs. We all want to be wanted, including Kim.

I consume more coffee, dark and as strong as my taste buds will allow, while I sit at my computer in the small den next to the kitchen, hoping an influx of caffeine will stimulate my brain. Ideas begin to flow, a slow but steady stream. Not an earth-shattering amount but I manage to write over two thousand words. It's better than nothing and more than I expected after this mornings' rude and unwelcome introduction to the day. Words are words. They all help to build the story, to flesh out the bare bones of the plot. Words help me escape. They are a way of blocking out the darkness, a way of stepping back into the light.

Listen to me, wallowing in my own wretchedness. Anybody watching would think I enjoy living like this, suspended in a well of unhappiness. I don't. I need to stop it, start being more positive. My life has changed and it is what it is. Time to accept my lot and move on. Time to start again.

* * *

We have the café almost to ourselves. A young couple sit in the corner, their voices lowered as they sip at their coffee. They are locked into their own conversation, unaware of our presence. Outside, a large raven pecks at a pile of indistinguishable scraps in the gutter. People pass by the window next to where we are seated, their eyes fixed forward, their minds focused on other things. I sometimes forget that there is a world out there, a world full of people who have their own lives, their own thoughts and worries. All together and yet all very much alone.

'How are you settling in? I wish you'd let me come over and help you more often. I feel as if I'm neglecting you.'

I shake my head and smile. 'I'm fine, honestly.'

Kim is being polite, going through the motions. She doesn't particularly care for spending time in our childhood home. Never did, as I recall. She was utterly incredulous when I told her I wanted to buy it and move out of Lilac Crescent in York, convinced I did it just to infuriate and upset her. My sister forgets that not everything is about her.

'Put the past behind us. Put it behind you,' she had said when I told her of my plan.

She put every obstacle possible in my way when I tried to purchase it, claiming it had rising damp, that the 150-year-old roof was leaking and would need replacing. 'You'll live to regret it. That place is an ever-open mouth,' she had said, her eyes dark with smouldering fury.

I had ploughed ahead anyway, ignoring her words, blocking out her negative comments. Besides, I needed a project. Lilac Crescent was a bland box, each room resembling a show home with its magnolia walls and neat, modern furniture. I needed a change. I needed to challenge myself, try to take my mind off Warren, my circumstances, my fogged-up brain.

The purchase also put some cash into Kim's pocket. Mum signed the house over to us before her dementia accelerated, leaving her a husk of the woman she used to be. I bought Kim's half. She has no reason to be aggrieved. Apart from the memories, that is, those dark, harrowing remnants of our past. Yet, I'm the one living with them every day. If I can cope then why can't she do the same? Simon was a long time ago. And yet there are days when it feels as if it was only yesterday. I feel closer to him here. The thought of selling the house to strangers has always filled me with dread – an army of faceless people traipsing through the place, trampling the memory of our brother underfoot, ripping the very soul out of it – it makes me shiver. His memory is embedded deep within the house, imprinted into the walls, his voice, his face embroidered into the very fabric of the building. To leave him alone with strangers would be a sin. He may not be a tangible form but I have always felt that he is around, still here, his soul wandering free. Still the same boy he used to be.

That sounds ridiculous, I know, as if I am able to see into the future, which I am most definitely not. I do feel as if we would be abandoning him if we sold Woodburn Cottage. It is where Simon was born, where he lived as a child. Where he will always remain.

Warren died of natural causes, a heart attack taking him before his time and it was tragic, horrific actually, completely unexpected, but leaving Lilac Crescent wasn't a wrench. I wasn't leaving him behind. We had only lived there for five years, having moved from our previous home where we lived for much of our married lives. Lilac Crescent didn't define him, wasn't a part of him. As I couldn't go back to our other home, this place was the next best thing. It's comforting, living somewhere familiar when my world has been tipped upside down.

Warren was also a grown man. Simon was a child, still is. He will remain forever a child, his life stunted by the passing of time. He will always be my little older brother, the child who never grew old. The child who disappeared one day, never to return.

'I need to tell you something.' The words are out before I can stop them. Probably the best way. No overthinking or preamble. That would stop me and I don't want to be stopped. I want to talk about it, get it off my chest.

'Go ahead.' Kim lowers her cup, her eyes locked on mine.

I had forgotten how intense she can be, how powerful a presence she is. Most of the time, she is simply my older sister but then sometimes…

'I woke up yesterday morning covered in blood.' The sentence spills out of me. No more thinking or delaying. Just get on with it. Let it all out. 'It wasn't mine, the blood. At least, I don't think it was. I couldn't find any cuts or bruises. And when I went downstairs, I discovered the back door was wide open.'

I don't tell her about the dead fox. I can't. Something inside stops me, shame perhaps. Shame that I may have carried out such an atrocious act.

She clears her throat, glances away briefly, gives herself some thinking time. 'So, where do you think the blood came from? I mean, if as you say, it wasn't yours?'

She doesn't have to say, *I told you so. I told you that you should never have moved back in that house.* It's written all over her face: in her probing gaze, her sullen countenance, her hunched shoulders.

I lower my gaze, suddenly wishing I hadn't mentioned it. Kim doesn't know loneliness. She doesn't know me or how I feel. And as for the blood – well, I have no answers. I just wanted to talk about what happened, to have somebody listen to me. My words were impulsive, ill thought out. It's not easy having no sounding board, nobody around to listen to my woes. Having no Warren. And now I've said too much, made myself look foolish. My face burns, a rush of blood travelling up my neck, settling in my cheeks, my ears, making me slightly nauseous and dizzy.

I sip at my coffee. It tastes like nicotine, strong and bitter, coating my mouth, leaving a pungent aftertaste. 'Just forget about it. It was nothing. I made a mistake.' I sound bitter, my voice tinged with anger. Not a rough-edged sort of anger, more of a softer, resigned sort of anger. The type of anger that is tired of everything and everyone.

'Forget that you woke up covered in blood or that your back door was wide open while you were asleep upstairs?'

The heat in my face grows, my frustration at her lack of empathy gathering momentum. It builds in my chest, pulses through my veins. I do my utmost to appear calm, measured, sipping at my coffee and allowing myself time to formulate my answer. It's not easy being the younger sister, having an invisible barrier between us. I think of Mum and wish she were here now with her gentle ways and affable manner. The mum we once knew. Not mum as she is now. The large age gap between Kim and me has often set us apart, me feeling inferior in her presence and her forever wanting to control everything I do.

'Maybe you're doing it again. You did it when you were younger, Grace. Can't you remember?' Kim's brash tone has softened, her body supple and relaxed once more. I look into her hazel eyes, wishing I could see inside her head, work out her thinking. See who she really is beneath her tough exterior and steely resolve to never weaken.

'Doing what?' I won't want to remember once she reveals what it is she is about to say. Something about this conversation is making me uneasy.

My flesh prickles as she lets out a protracted sigh and drums her fingernails on the table. 'Sleepwalking. You did it when you were little. When...'

We both look away. No need to say it out loud. We rarely speak about Simon's disappearance these days. What is there to say? It's been over forty years. The case, although not entirely closed, has for the most part, been shelved and forgotten. Not by me, it hasn't. I will always remember even if Kim doesn't want to.

Something flits into my brain but is gone before I can pin it down, butterfly wings fluttering about on the periphery of my consciousness. Sleepwalking. Is that what it was I did yesterday? Sleepwalk into the garden and do God knows what to some poor, defenceless animal? It doesn't feel right, the words not fitting properly in my head. I know my own capabilities, my strengths and weaknesses and even in the grip of a deep sleep, am sure I could never do such a thing. And yet, it explains everything – the open door, the blood. Mr Waters thinking he possibly saw me out there...

I want to go home, now. I don't want to give any more thought to any of this. It helps cement the idea in Kim's head that I'm defenceless, weaker than her. Inferior. Which I'm not. I'm grieving, upset, lonely even but I can sort out my life without any judgemental input from anybody else. What I need right now is to be alone.

'I'm a bit tired,' I say, my voice feebler than I would like it to be. 'I need to get on with my writing.'

She nods and juts out her bottom lip. I know that look. I know it all too well. It is one of superiority. No matter how old we get, she will always be my older sister, the one who came first.

'See you next week? Same time, same place?'

I don't answer. There's no need. She knows me well enough to know that I will return. No matter how difficult life is, no matter how down I feel, no matter how domineering and annoying she is, I always come back for more.

3

I'm in the middle of the kitchen. It's dark. I'm cold. I shiver, hop about from foot to foot, squint and rub at my eyes, a veil of mistiness marring my vision. Once again, the door is open. Not wide open but ajar. A cool breeze laps around my bare legs, pricking the flesh on my calves, on my arms and face. I step forward, slam the door shut and turn the key, my fingers trembling, numb from the cold.

I look down at my feet. No slippers but at least I'm wearing a short nightgown. I'm not naked. I recall putting it on last night for fear of finding myself outside again and now here I am, standing barefoot, wondering if I am coming in or about to leave.

I lift up my left foot, inspect it for dirt and feel a small amount of relief when I see that it is clean. Small mercies and all that. I'm suddenly grateful for them. Grateful that I haven't been outside causing distress to helpless animals and rousing neighbours from their beds in the middle of the night.

Slightly less terrified, less hysterical than I was when this happened a few nights back, I grab a cup and make myself some tea. I need something to settle me, something normal and reassuring and comforting, and tea is just that.

The low hiss of the kettle fills the silence in the kitchen. As it boils, I inspect the rest of the house, peeking into the living room, the dining room, the downstairs shower room. All clear. All exactly as I left them before going to bed just over three hours ago. No need for any alarm or fear. No need for any hysteria. Not this time.

Adding a spoonful of honey to the tea makes me feel better. I sip at it, each consecutive mouthful soothing me. Why have I started sleepwalking? I don't try to think too hard about it, unwilling to stress myself and thus put sleep completely out of reach. I will give it more thought in the morning once I'm rested, once my mind is clearer, less prone to worry and anxiety, imagining scenarios that don't exist, coming up with explanations that don't quite fit.

Visions of me wandering out of the front door, heading down the road in my pyjamas or God forbid, nothing at all, fill me with horror. So far, I've kept my journeys to the back garden. What happens if that changes? What if I find myself outside the front of the house in the middle of the night? I push that thought out of my mind, finish my tea and rinse out the cup, the rattle as it lands on the draining board setting my teeth on edge. Enough with the overactive imaginings. Enough with it all.

I climb into bed and lie awake, fretting that I may get back up and wander some more, the thought of how to stop it niggling at me. When I do finally succumb, my dreams are littered with images of a naked me ambling down the road, my mind fogged up with sleep, people passing by, their eyes fixed ahead appearing to not see me. At the bottom of the street, I think that I see Simon, hear his voice calling to me. When I get there, I realise that it isn't Simon at all but Kim. She is standing next to a huge hole in the ground and she is crying.

He's in there, Grace. Can you see him? It's Simon.

I lean closer to look and feel her hand on my back as she pushes me in. I fall through the air, my stomach clenched, a scream caught in my throat.

* * *

I can see a narrow strip of daylight through the curtains when I wake up the following morning. My heart is thumping and a thin film of sweat coats my chest and neck, the dream still fresh in my mind.

My hands travel down to my torso, my legs. I feel the warmth, touch the creases in the bedsheets and almost laugh with relief. No nocturnal wanderings, thank God. I am here, safe in my bed. For now. Who knows what tonight will bring?

For the next few seconds, I lie and listen, tuning in to the silence, appreciative of the peace and quiet. Warren used to wake with a start, jumping up out of bed, banging about the bedroom, driving me insane with his relentless chatter. A tension of opposites tugs at me as I lie here, acutely aware of my solitude whilst savouring the stillness and calm of the morning.

I miss Warren. God, I miss him so much, it's a physical presence within me. Some of my days are so dark, I have to summon every ounce of strength to get out of bed. Then there are other days – like today – when everything doesn't seem so bad after all, when the sun is that little bit brighter, the grass that little bit greener, everything sweeter than it has been in a long time. Even that awful dream doesn't dampen my mood.

I get up, shower, force myself to forget about the sleepwalking. I refuse to ruin my day by researching it, by stumbling upon some rogue piece of information that will blacken my mood. Information that will fixate on a damaged mind borne out of a tragedy or a trauma. Instead, I set to with my latest book, surprised at how easily it all flows, such a change to the previous day when words got stuck, my mind clogged up with the clutter and detritus of my life.

The morning passes quickly, lunch consisting of a piece of toast and a soft-boiled egg. I don't spend the afternoon writing, deciding instead to rifle through some of Warren's things – things I should have sorted before I moved, things that made my stomach flip when I thought of looking at them. Before moving here to Woodburn Cottage, I put them all in a suitcase, refusing to glance at any of it, and placed the case at the bottom of the wardrobe in the spare bedroom. The time has come to finally look through them. Tomorrow may be a darker day. I need to do it while the sun is bright and the sky is blue, while things are less oppressive and I have the stomach for such a task. Kim wanted me to throw them away. She tried to take them from me, insisting they were no longer needed.

'It's just old work documents and stuff, Grace. Why would you want to hang onto them if it's a fresh start you're after?'

I held my ground, knowing that once the pain of losing Warren had passed, I might possibly find some solace from seeing his things again. I know she meant well but the idea of disposing of his belongings cut me in two. Getting rid of his clothes was one thing but throwing away his personal effects without first inspecting them felt completely immoral and cruel. Why would I ever consider doing such a thing? Warren was a person. He existed and to pretend otherwise just to preserve my sense of well-being is one of the most thoughtless things I could ever imagine doing.

The case is heavier than I remember as I drag it out onto the floor with a thump. The contents spill out when I open it, spreading around me in an untidy, papery mountain – envelopes of varying shapes and sizes, photo albums, notebooks – papers and documents that represent Warren's life. I fight back tears and set about putting them in order: envelopes in one heap, notebooks piled high in another. It takes longer than I expect and by the time I have assembled them into something I can confidently tackle, almost an hour has passed.

A small gathering of old business cards are the first things to be discarded. I doubt Warren would want me to hang onto the numbers of some of his colleagues and business contacts that he rarely spoke with when he was alive.

The photo albums I put in the bookcase – pictures of Warren with his siblings when he was a child, family gatherings, the picnics we went on after we first met – they all mist my vision, tears burning at my eyes as I leaf through them. Happy tears. No sadness or regret. Just buoyancy and optimism that I have found the courage to do this task. A month ago, it would have felt overwhelming.

I flick through the notebooks, stopping as one catches my eye. Most of them are lists of his contacts from work but one stands out from the rest. It's not an address book. It's a diary. My heart stutters about my chest as I flick it open and stare at his handwriting, at the words written there.

I saw her again. I shouldn't have. We talked, that's all. At some point, this all needs to come out in the open.

I can hardly breathe. It's an old diary from before we met. It has to be. That's the only explanation. It isn't. I know it isn't. It's new. No old papery scent about it, no frayed edges, no yellowing pages.

My fingers are made of stone, my palms clammy and slippery as I search through the pages for dates – anything that will tell me when this was written. The notebook slips out of my fingers, landing with a dull thud on the floor. I pick it up, the paper fluttering as I desperately skim through it looking for clues. There are other entries in it, dates for business meetings, a couple of vague sentences about new starters, a reminder for our wedding anniversary, a note about the kids moving away and how much he will miss them.

I take a deep breath, try to steady myself, to think clearly. I'm overreacting. Of course I am. This could be anything – a poem, song lyrics – anything at all. Warren was big on his music and often used to tell me about his latest discovery on the music circuit, regaling me with tales about concerts he attended. He would quote verses to me, asking me what I thought they meant, whether they were romantic or stomach churning in their vain attempts to be hip.

My insides loosen, the knots slowly becoming untangled as I think back. He did this so often, it would sometimes drive me half insane. This is what this is. It's from a piece of music or a poem that took his fancy. Warren wasn't an expert on poetry but always harboured a desire to do some writing of his own. He would often watch me at work, commenting on how I could sustain it for long periods of time, asking me how I had such patience for a slowly developing plot or characters that took time to emerge.

I'd go mad, sitting hour after hour like that, he would say as he shook his head and smiled at me. *I'll stick with writing emails and listening to my music. Or maybe a short story. I don't think I have a full book in me. I love words. I just don't love sitting still.*

A small bubble of laughter emerges out of nowhere, slipping out of me unbidden. Hysteria and relief, no doubt. I refuse to believe that Kim was right, that I should have binned these papers. This is something I have to do, to work through the documentation of Warren's life in order to move on with mine. These words written down here are meaningless. Meaningless to me and Warren for sure. They were possibly priceless to the author, but I feel sure that that person wasn't Warren. He was a romantic, a wannabe writer of modern poetry, a shameless plagiarist of the work of others. He wasn't a philanderer. We were happy. Just a normal couple who, like everybody else, had their ups and downs, their good times and bad times. That's how the world is, it's how people are and we were no different.

Were. That word still has the power to turn my blood to sand, my limbs to stone. I wonder how long it will be before I can truly say that I can accept what happened and press ahead with my life?

I am still ruminating this when I hear a knock at the door, a gentle tapping that takes some time to filter through my thoughts and rouse me, dragging me out of my reverie where I am mulling over the past, colouring it in pastel shades and ignoring the charred edges. It's easier that way, less painful. Less traumatic.

Mr Waters is standing there, his shoulders stooped, his hair a shock of white. It glints under the glare of the hovering sun, silver strands jutting out at divergent angles like lengths of invisible thread. I think back to when we were children, Simon and me, how we would go in his garden to pick apples from his tree, how he would chase us around the patch of lawn pretending to be an ogre. I still recall our screams, how being terrified gave us such a thrill, glee and excitement turning the pair of us into shrieking monsters. Kim was older. Too old and too reserved for such frivolity. So many years ago. So much has happened since then. It's as if my younger self was a different person. Sometimes, I think I've lived two lives – before Simon and after. Before Warren and after. Cut me in half, you may just find the real Grace Cooper somewhere in the middle.

'Just thought I'd call round. See 'ow you are after yer find t'other day.'

I angle my body and wave him inside. He shakes his head and turns his gaze away to face the back of his house. 'I'll not bother if it's all the same wi' you. Got my daughter calling around shortly. She's bringing her little grandson wi' her. He's a fine little thing, he is. Who'd have thought it eh? Me, a great-granddad.'

'Oh, that sounds lovely. And I'm fine, thank you. No more dead foxes so that's a positive, isn't it?'

The image of Mr Waters' daughter, Carrie, flashes into my brain, a brief picture of her as a child – quiet, withdrawn, the polar opposite of her father. Carrie was more like her mum. We rarely saw Mrs Waters. She was a homebody, always busy with housework, always scurrying around their kitchen, cooking, cleaning, her diminutive frame a shadowy form as we played in her garden and helped ourselves to the fruit from her tree.

Carrie moved away when she was in her early twenties and we lost touch. We played together as children but didn't form a lasting friendship. I think perhaps she moved to a little village somewhere in Scotland but can't be sure of that. Time and tragedy have blurred a lot of my memories, pushing them out of the way so grief could obliterate much of what happened. And now she is a grandmother. Time, that slippery, elusive thing, so much of it has passed in the blink of an eye.

'Right,' he says, his rheumy gaze catching mine before he steps away and moves off down the path. 'As long as you're okay, lass. We all need to watch out for one another, don't we? If you ask me, that's what neighbours are for.'

A lump is wedged in my throat. I blink away tears and nod, a sudden need to get back inside clawing at me. Such a kind man. I'm lucky in so many ways. I mustn't ever forget that.

I close the door and shut my eyes, squeezing away more memories, fighting them off. Rumours. That's all they were. Nasty, baseless rumours about Mr Waters and his family. I'd forgotten about them, my head too full of other things but now I'm back here, they have presented themselves, emerging out of the darkness, slithering my way, gathering speed and momentum as they hurtle towards me.

My chest rattles as I let out a long sigh and head back inside. I clear away the remainder of Warren's things, stuffing them back into the suitcase, all the while making a promise to myself that from now on, I will save the drama for my books. That's where it belongs. I've had enough of it in my life already, enough to see me through this life and another.

4

Kim sits, her coffee cup poised halfway to her mouth, eyes narrowed, glinting. Suspicion emanates from her, tiny, invisible tendrils that curl into the air around us. I hate it when she gets like this. It puts me on edge, frays my nerves. Makes me want to be somewhere else.

'I hope you didn't let him in the house. He's a creepy old bastard.' She drinks her coffee, a thin, foamy moustache of cream resting on her top lip. She licks it away, her tongue reminding me of a hungry lizard, stalking, waiting. Choosing its prey with the utmost care and precision.

'He didn't *want* to come in, but if he did, I would have let him.' I am tiring of this, the games my sister plays with me, the invisible power she tries to wield. Even now, after all these years, she cannot let it go, the older sibling act. My heart is a steady thump under my sweater as I stare at her. 'He was good to us when we were children. He was kind and funny. Still is.'

'Then you have a poor memory,' she murmurs from behind her cup. 'Or a selective one.'

She wants me to ask, to help perpetuate the story that Mr Waters was cruel to his family. It's an impossibility. How can somebody be one thing to friends and neighbours and another to his family, turning into a monster as soon as he walks back through his front door? We would have seen glimpses of it, caught snatches of his moods and temper, heard it from their house, and we didn't. They were a quiet, demure family. Always polite and helpful, always there when we needed them.

'And you have chosen to go with the narrative that he beat up his family because you listened to the village gossips.'

'Small villages have big eyes and ears. It wasn't just gossip. It was the truth.' Her mouth has curled up into a near snarl. She feels she knows everything there is to know about events that took place when she was young and inexperienced, lacking in enough wisdom to allow her to judge. Her view of the world was flawed. Youngsters see the world and those in it through different eyes. She was in no position to act as magistrate. Still isn't.

'That's your opinion. Mr Waters is now my neighbour and I intend to remain on good terms with him. He has done nothing to offend me.' I sniff and stare off into the distance to try to add some gravitas to my words. Beneath my skin, electric impulses prod at me, tiny, hot needles stabbing, reminding me of Kim's latent matronly ways, how easily she can turn, how quickly and without warning.

'Just be careful, Grace. That's all I'm saying. Just be careful.'

I drain my cup and offer to pay but she is there before me, placing her card against the machine.

'How's your writing coming on?' This is a lame attempt at re-establishing our connection. Kim doesn't know or understand my writing regime having not read any of my books. We are very different people, my sister and me. I sometimes wonder if we're actually related at all.

'It's fine. Slow but making progress.'

Already, her attention is elsewhere, her eyes darting about the café, her fingers carefully opening a compact mirror as she checks her make-up for minor flaws. She scrutinises her own features, her lips pursed in concentration. In just a few seconds, she has forgotten about me, her mind focused on her perfect face, her smooth complexion. Her fragile ego. Kim has remarkably thin skin for one apparently so self-assured. She is easily damaged, her nose quickly put out of joint. The immaculate appearance, the designer clothes are all a front, a veneer to mask the mass of writhing insecurities that burn and pulse just below the surface of her skin. I often wonder what it is she is desperately trying to hide.

'Good, good,' she murmurs, smacking her lips together, closing the mirror with a metallic snap.

'I need to get back,' I say, already wondering why we continue to meet like this. Habit, I guess. Habit and an invisible cord that will always bind us together. With Mum in the care home and Simon and our father long since gone, all we have is each other.

'I'm going to visit Mum in the morning.' She says lightly it as if it is a passing comment, something we say in everyday conversation, like *isn't the weather awful* or *how are things with you?*

Going to visit our mother is a major event. It is exhausting, traumatic and any other extreme emotion you care to add. Not a thing we do lightly.

'I'll go with you.' The words are out before I can stop them, an explosion of garbled syllables that have the power to make Kim freeze, to stop her from rummaging in her expansive handbag and to stare at me as if I have grown two heads. 'I haven't seen Mum for a few weeks. I'll tag along. If that's okay with you?'

She widens her eyes, nods at me warily, turns away but not before I see the tremble in her hands, the slight tremor of her head. The tic that takes hold in her jaw. I often need to protect Mum from Kim's sharp words, her unwillingness to soften her serrated manner. It may sound egotistical and I do not mean it to, but I am better at handling Mum. She is unpredictable, flighty. As her mind crumbles into dust, she has little or no control over what comes out of her mouth, saying things that simply aren't true, things that often rile her eldest daughter, causing her to defend herself against Mum's insults and accusations.

'Whatever you want to do. Completely up to you.' She shrugs and turns away, already slighted, already thinking that I have somehow usurped her. She shuffles through the door, her heels clicking on the stone flooring, making my scalp prickle with dread.

We arrange to meet at the care home at 10 a.m. Mum will be dressed by then, will have eaten and be at her best, rested after a good night's sleep and a decent breakfast. Her demeanour declines the closer it is to bedtime, her brainpower depleted by simply existing and trying to make it through an average day. Not that all of her days are average. Some are better than others. And some are particularly hideous – a protracted stream of vile words and allegations fired out at anybody who will listen – swear words, invectives, attempts to hit out and scratch at anybody unfortunate enough to be close at hand. It's as if the Devil himself has landed deep in her soul and is doing his damnedest to tear her apart and burst out of her chest, a writhing, spitting demon who will devour anybody within reach. We visit in the hope of catching her on a good day, but we never can tell.

'See you there,' I say as we part.

Kim gives me a cursory wave over her shoulder before sliding into the car and disappearing around the corner before I've even had chance to find my keys.

* * *

It's the howling wind that wakes me. That and the ground that feels unsteady under my feet. At least I think that's what it is. When I come to, I am acutely aware of the cold and the noise of the breeze passing through the treetops: the branches groaning, the leaves rattling and whispering. I was dreaming that somebody was calling out to me, murmuring my name, but the memory is too distant, too ethereal to define.

I stare down at my feet – bare, numb from the night air. I'm wearing pyjama bottoms and a vest top. I wrap my arms around myself, rubbing at the cool, prickled flesh with my fingers to try to warm myself up.

My eyes take some time to clear, my vision still blurry from sleep, my brain muddled and clogged up with dreams and weird visualisations. I blink, wait for things to come into focus and when they do, I begin to cry, shockwaves rippling through me. I am on the main road in the village, my house a good way behind me. Wandering into the back garden in my sleep was no longer good enough for me, not daring or brazen enough. My body and mind have now decided to steer me into a public area, half dressed and freezing cold while still asleep.

Gravel cuts at my feet. I stumble and right myself, aware that I am in the middle of the street. My toes curl, a response to the pain as I tiptoe onto the path, doing my best to dodge the sharp stones and loose grit and tarmac that roll around the ground.

The village is deserted. I thank God for that. Hempton is a small place. Nobody around, nobody out in the early hours who will see me. Or help me. What if something had happened? What if a car had come tearing around the corner at full speed in the dark?

I shiver, my feet burning and throbbing as I head down the path towards home. My home. The place where I grew up. The place where Simon went missing. My head is aching, my back rigid and sore, the cool breeze forcing me to tense up, my spine as taut as a bowstring.

The front door is wide open when I get there. Anybody could have wandered in. Any passing drunk. Any passing druggie or rapist. The chances of there being any in these parts is almost zero. I know this. It doesn't stop the fear from nipping at me, or halt the vulnerability I am experiencing at being so exposed and alone.

I peek my head inside and flick on all the lights before slamming the door behind me and locking it. Smears of blood cover the tiled floor. I grab at a scarf, place it next to my feet and stamp on it then turn the soles of my feet upwards to inspect the damage. They are red and sore, small lines of blood settling in the creases of my skin. I prod at a larger circle of scarlet, wincing as I check for any embedded pieces of grit.

One of the few upsides of living alone is that I can do whatever I want whenever I want. I turn on the radio, run a hot bath and sink down into the white bubbles, my toes and the undersides of my feet buzzing as the warm water laps over them. It will help me to sleep, to take my mind off the horror of what has just happened. How I managed to sleepwalk, leave the house and wander down the road in the dead of night. Even the hot water can't stop the chill that runs through me at the thought of what could have happened out there. Yet it didn't. I rest my head back, try to think of different ways to stop this happening again. Tomorrow, I will use the top bolt on both doors, perhaps even hide the key, putting it out of reach. My mind, clouded with sleep, surely won't locate it. There are ways to stop this weird occurrence, ways to make sure I don't end up out there again. It's a form of self-preservation. I have to do it. I need protecting from myself.

I lather myself down, gingerly dabbing at my feet with the bath sponge, relieved that the cuts and bruises will heal. No lasting damage. Part of me wishes there were. At least it might stop me from heading out again. Pain has got to be a sure-fire way of stopping any future sleepwalking, hasn't it?

Exhaustion envelops me. I stand up, wrap myself in a towel, empty the bath and switch off the radio. The sudden silence is like being plunged underwater. I'm meeting Kim later. I will have to be in the right frame of mind to deal her and my mother. What I need to do is to climb into bed and sleep soundly so I can wake rested and ready to face them both with a clear head.

The bed is cold as I slide in. I curl into a foetal position, shivering against the cool sheets, my brain still full of images – Simon's small face staring at me, my mother's wails as we searched for him the following morning, my father's arms pumping furiously at his sides as he ran from house to house knocking on doors, calling out to neighbours, asking if they had seen him.

His bed was empty this morning when we went to wake him up!

Those words will stay with me until the day I die. Those cold, terrifying words that left a lasting impression in my mind and a hollow carved deep in my heart that will never be filled.

Then Kim refusing to come out of the bedroom, her sullen face staring out at us from above as we searched the garden, pulling shrubbery out of the way, opening the door to the old coal shed. I stood and watched, my chest swelling with terror as she stared over into the garden next door where Mr Waters lived with his family before pointing an accusatory finger and stepping back out of sight.

5

I am greeted by a wall of heat as I step into Cherry Tree Home where Amanda, the deputy manager steps aside to let me through. 'Your sister's already here. She's in the lounge with your mum, who, incidentally, is having a really good day today.'

Relief blooms in my chest. I guess that Amanda, as skilled as she is, knows how much visitors long to hear this and is keen to pass it on to put everyone at ease. Going to visit Mum is always an unpredictable and sometimes frightening experience.

On a bad day, I can hear her shouts and protestations from the car park, am aware that behind closed doors, staff are working hard to calm her down and reassure her that they are not trying to kill her.

And then on a good day, she will sit peaceably, her hands folded in her lap, eyes twinkling with happiness as she reminisces about the past. Her own childhood past, not the near past, our childhood. Sometimes, she speaks of Dad and Simon, her words tearing at my heartstrings. I try to jolly her along, steer her away from the obvious, knowing she is in no fit state to cope with those sorts of memories, her mind too fragmented to handle them or make sense of them. I struggle with memories of that time in our lives. For her, it's almost an impossible task.

More often than not, she will speak of growing up with her siblings, how they all had to share a bed, how they would play out in the street from dawn till dusk with no fear of strangers or traffic. How they would hear the air raid sirens going off and make the terrifying dash to the shelter, covering their ears from the explosions, the crashing of buildings as bombs hit them, leaving nothing behind but piles of dust and rubble.

It's only when I hear this that I realise how brave she is, how much she had to endure; all that terror finally behind her after the war ended only for her to lose a child later on in her life: her boy, our brother who disappeared into thin air. Nobody deserves that. Nobody.

'Here she is,' Mum says, her face lighting up as I head towards them. 'It's the woman from next door. Have you brought us any cake?'

Kim is perched next to her on the tiny, velour sofa. She rolls her eyes and smiles at Mum's words. On my last visit I was her sister, Denise, and the time before that I was an intruder who was trying to steal all of her money. I'm a shapeshifter, transforming and morphing with every consecutive visit.

'Hi, Mum,' I say tenderly as I lean down to kiss her cheek. She smells of lavender and old talcum powder. Her skin is soft with a fine layer of downy hair that covers her sallow cheeks.

'Who's your mum? Is she here? I'd like to meet her. Don't mind if I do.' She narrows her eyes and stares at Kim. 'And who's this pretty young thing, eh?'

'It's me, Mum,' Kim sighs, her patience evidently wearing thin. She will have been here for all of ten minutes, and is already itching to leave. 'And I'm not exactly young.'

'Me mum? Who's she? Don't think I've ever met her. Nice, is she? Not like that Dorothy at number twenty-six. She was a right gadabout she was, always out and around town with different men who couldn't keep it in their trousers.'

I laugh. Kim joins in, her tense posture relaxing as I sit down and take Mum's hand in mine. It lessens the load, two of us here talking with her. My thumb strokes her fingers, straying over her parchment-like skin, tracing the deep grooves that line her palm.

'How are you doing, Mum? Everything okay with you?'

She turns away from me and I feel the air shift, sense the mood tilt, spiralling downwards, a barely discernible movement but it's there all the same. I have to suppress the usual anxiety that settles in the pit of my stomach. I want to be wrong. Perhaps I am. I hope so. She remains rigid, her back straight, the muscles in her neck twitching and jerking beneath her pale, papery skin as her mood and temper fluctuate. I've only just arrived. Please don't let this be happening. Not now. I wanted more time with her. More time with the gentle, happy lady she used to be. Not the unrecognisable, demonic creature she will become.

The face that turns back to stare at me tells me everything I need to know – that I'm right, she has changed, her affable self now absent, only to be replaced by her other self. The one that we struggle to contain. The one we struggle to control. It's in her eyes, that look, that flint-like stare. Probing, resentful. Full of malice. Dread coils within me, furling and unfurling. She had been doing so well, was happy, looked settled. It was short-lived. Now we're faced with this. In a matter of seconds, she has turned into someone I fear, an unrecognisable being whose anger and bitterness is endless.

'Who are you?' She leans forward. Her finger is almost touching Kim's nose. She waggles it about, sneering, bubbles of foamy saliva gathering at the corners of her mouth, her yellowing teeth bared in anger. 'I don't know you. I don't like you. Get away from me!' She is hissing. Her voice is low but her irritation is unmistakable. I know it as well as my own features, my own thoughts, and wish it away. Pray for her to stop, to calm down.

'Mum, please don't do that.' Kim sighs, her voice containing traces of near boredom. She moves away from Mum's bony finger, blinking, turning to me with an eyeroll and a curl of her lip.

My stomach clenches. I shake my head for her to stop, try to shuffle closer to keep the two of them apart. Kim's apathy will only rile Mum, turning that key in her back, setting her off like a clockwork doll. Mum isn't stupid. Demented, yes, stupid, no. She senses intolerance and takes an instant dislike to it, reacting badly like a spoilt child.

'Mum? Don't mum me, you little bitch. I've met the likes of you before: devils, all of you!'

I pluck a packet of sweets out of my bag, my emergency stash for occasions such as this. She stops with the insults, greedily eyes the packet, and before I have a chance to open them, snatches it out of my grasp and throws it across the room. It lands next to the feet of an elderly man who immediately snatches it up, rips open the packet, and starts shoving handfuls of pink candy in his mouth like a ravenous animal.

'Devil food for devil people. Leave me alone! Just leave me alone, all of you!' Her voice has risen a full octave to a shriek. She drools, globules of saliva hanging from her mouth, her chin, the flesh on her face the colour of candle wax as her anger drains every last bit of energy out of her frail body.

My heart pounds, my breathing quickens. Kim is up on her feet, looking around for assistance. In my peripheral vision, I see Amanda shuffle towards us, her movements showing no indication that she is concerned. This is her job. She is accustomed to it, accustomed to Mum's temper tantrums, her unpredictable ways, her sometimes violent behaviour and I don't think for one minute that my mother is the only resident who is prone to such outbursts.

'How about a cup of tea, Sylvie? Two sugars, just how you like it, eh?' She bends down and tries to catch Mum's eye.

'Bitch. Tart. Go back to your own country.' A pulse thuds in my neck, wincing at Mum's words and her newfound love of being racist. I wasn't aware she even knew of such insults but this is where we are at, here in this cloistered environment with my mother, the once kind and gentle soul who is now a foul-mouthed, bigoted, demented old lady who appears to hate everyone for reasons known only to herself.

I turn and mouth a heartfelt apology to Amanda who waves it away with a flap of her hand and a genuine smile. She touches my shoulder, squeezing it softly, and I find myself having to fight back tears of shame brought on by the individual before me, the lady that I once knew. The mother who is now back in her infant years with no decency, no barriers to her bubbling fury. Once the adult, twice the child.

'I'll do to you exactly what I did to him! Don't touch me. Don't you dare touch me!'

A huddle of bodies appears as if out of nowhere, surrounding Mum, trying to placate her, to soothe her. I have no idea how they do it, these people, how they can care for somebody who can change so suddenly and without warning, her moods permanently on a cliff edge. I have tried to work this out, to look for triggers, anything that can tell us why she randomly turns from a contented being to an intense whirlwind of anger in a matter of seconds, whether it be smells or sounds or the odd stray word, but it evades me, leaving us permanently bemused.

'They all died, you know. The men are all gone. He's better off dead. We're all better off without him.'

A silence descends. She has stopped with the screaming and is back to hissing at us, her spine arched as she bucks and fights before sliding down into the chair, spent. The bodies part, moving away from her. They recognise the signs, know her better than she knows herself.

'The boy and the man. All gone now.'

Her face softens, her lids drooping, her glassy eyes flickering before closing completely. Her head flops to one side, a small snore escapes from her pursed lips. I marvel at how quickly she can fall into a deep sleep, her energy levels depleted after an explosive outpouring of raw emotion.

'Well, that wasn't too bad, was it?' Amanda says triumphantly, a small smile forming at the corners of her mouth. 'We've had far worse, haven't we, ladies?' The assistants nod in agreement and amble off elsewhere, the moment forgotten as if it never even happened.

Except it did. And I haven't forgotten. Those words, her words – they stick in my mind, clinging onto my brain like glue. Even when Mum is rambling, barely coherent, downright furious, her words always have a grain of truth in them. She has dementia, has forgotten a lot of things but she isn't an idiot.

She doesn't wake. Kim and I sit for over half an hour, waiting, speaking about inane topics – the weather, my latest book, how her family are getting on – all the while avoiding the obvious. Guilt bites at me as I listen to Kim talk about her life, her children. I don't see enough of Luke and Olivia. Aside from the odd text or comment on Facebook, we barely communicate. That has to change. They are family, after all. For all Kim annoys me, her domineering manner overshadowing everything I say and do, she is still my sister. Her family is my family. We are all as one.

'How's Greg keeping?'

Kim shrugs, juts out her bottom lip. 'Same as always. Busy at work.'

Greg's job pays well. I would guess he earns more in a month than most people do in a year with his web design business that he set up many years ago when most of the population barely knew how to turn on a computer. He took a gamble, had vision and it paid off. Kim seems to have forgotten that. My sister seems to have forgotten a lot of things that should be remembered.

'Shall we go now? I think maybe we need to talk about what Mum said earlier.' I scrutinise Kim's reaction to my words.

We both know what Mum meant, what it was she was referring to. We *know* it. Whether or not my sister will choose to speak of it later is anybody's guess. Kim's responses are often unfathomable when it comes to discussing our past, preferring to stonewall me whenever I try to bring up the subject of Simon and Dad.

Mum's face is cool as I lean down to kiss her goodbye, her breath a thin trail of warm air that caresses my skin. Where has she gone, the woman that used to tuck me in at night, the lady who used to stand at the kitchen sink, singing softly as she prepared our food and washed the dishes? Is she still in there, clawing to be free, screaming out to be heard, for her story to be listened to? Or has she simply melted away, her other non-demented self, floating off into the ether, never to be seen again?

Before her mental decline, Mum used to speak about Simon, forever claiming she had somehow let him down. I have no idea why she thought that. She was a wonderful, loving mother, a selfless parent. She did the best she could.

'Bye, Mum.' Kim has already started to move away, as if the indignity of being associated with this scenario is too much for her. No kiss goodbye, no whispered reassurances into Mum's ear that everything is going to be okay. Just her heels clicking on the hard, white flooring as she brushes past me, her coat catching the back of my hand, its rough, tweed texture causing me to recoil as if burnt.

'I'll meet you in the car park,' I say, my tone sharper than I intend it to be. 'I need to ask you something.'

She doesn't reply. The sound of the door closing as she exits the large lounge, the warm rush of air she leaves behind are all that is left of her.

I pat Mum's hand, tell her we'll be back soon, give her another kiss goodbye and follow Kim downstairs.

6

'What did she mean by that – "I'll do to you what I did to him"? And, "He's better off dead"?'

We are standing opposite one another, our stance anachronistic in the sprawling car park, like a pair of duellers ready to do battle. Kim's expression is edgy, tension and annoyance apparent in her closed fists, the tic in her jaw, her darting eyes.

I try to keep my voice gentle. I don't want her to back off, to flee like she usually does whenever this subject is brought up, the subject of Simon and Dad, scarpering like a frightened rabbit as if the past catching up with her will somehow send her life toppling down around her, her carefully balanced Jenga stack collapsing and ruining everything she has worked hard to maintain.

'Grace, Mum has dementia. She says all sorts of things that are utter nonsense. What on earth are you getting at?' Her teeth are gritted, her jaw rigid as if it's too much of an effort to reply properly, the motion of her face wasted on me.

'You heard her, Kim. You heard what she said, and if there's one thing we know, it's that Mum's words always mean something. They may be disjointed and sometimes incoherent but if you look at them closely, analyse them in enough detail, it's apparent she is trying to tell us something.'

'What, so you're a psychologist now, are you? Or are you a consultant specialising in Alzheimer's?'

I blink away the hurt, ignoring the pinpricks of heat that cover my skin as she speaks to me in that way, as if I am an errant child, my opinions worthless. Everything I planned on saying melts away, my thoughts suddenly turning to liquid in my brain.

'Look, Grace.' Her words stop me as I start to walk away. 'All I'm trying to say is, don't let her get to you. She's in safe hands in there and she isn't the same person any more. Clinging onto the past and trying to link it with what Mum says is pointless. You'll tie yourself up in knots doing it. Once she wakes up, it will all be forgotten. The only thing on her mind will be what she wants for her lunch and how many puddings she can have afterwards.'

Part of me knows this is true, and yet another part of me can't forget what she said. Mum's past is also my past. It is also Kim's past but for some reason, she has chosen to shelve it, pretend it never happened and push ahead with her life. That is her choice. Trying to work out what Mum meant is mine. And if it means doing it on my own without her support, then so be it.

I tell her she is right and that I'm being over emotional. It's what she wants to hear so I'm not doing anything dishonest. I am simply pacifying her, letting her think I've forgotten about it, that I will move onto other more important things that don't involve Mum or Dad, or Simon and where he disappeared to, or how Dad met his untimely end. Kim is the only other person I can share my thoughts with about that period in our lives, the only other person who would understand and know how I feel, and her refusal to speak about it leaves me stuck in a moment, trapped and unable to move forward.

We don't hug as we part. Kim has never been particularly tactile. She loves me, I do know that, but am also aware of her ways: her abrupt manner; her need to be over protective towards me, and, dare I say it, her contempt for anybody who questions her methods. Instead, we wave goodbye, me watching from my driver's seat as she swings out of the car park with a screech, leaving the smell of burning rubber in her wake.

* * *

My God, she has changed. The pale, thin girl I remember from so long ago has transformed into an exquisitely graceful creature. No sagging skin, no midriff that hangs over the top of her waistband. I look down at my own middle and pinch a handful of loose flesh, then stare in the mirror at the jowls that cling to the lower half of my jaw and the crows' feet that appear as I smile. Carrie has none of those things. We are the same age, give or take a couple of years, and yet here she is, looking like somebody who has just stepped off the catwalk. She is a grandmother and yet looks half my age.

I refuse to go down the route of thinking that it isn't fair. Such thoughts are childish, maudlin. Instead, I console myself with the fact that despite having a tough few months since losing Warren, and despite spending many years as a child desperate to find out what happened to my brother whilst trying to get over the death of our father, I don't look too bad. I could look a whole lot worse, the years of worry, the sleepless nights and torment showing in my face. I am average even though I have led a less than average life.

I step out of the door and try to catch Carrie's eye as she lifts the toddler out of the car seat and heads up the path to her dad's house. Her attention is fully focused on the little one in her arms until I shout over, stopping her in her tracks.

'Hi, Carrie. Good to see you after so long.'

She falters, her mouth slack until her reflexes take over and she grins at me, revealing a row of pearly white, perfectly straight teeth. 'Grace! Lovely to see you. It's been such a long time, hasn't it?'

I move towards her, anxiety and excitement at seeing her after so long flushing around in my gut. Up close, I can see how the years haven't left her completely untouched. I can see that Carrie too, has succumbed to the ravages of time. A small amount of relief washes over me. She is dressed in expensive clothes, has a perfectly made-up face and is full of poise and confidence – no more that timid little child – but underneath it all, she, like me, is a middle-aged woman trying to delay the inevitable trek towards becoming a senior member of society.

Shame for thinking such thoughts grows in my chest. It is only my own lack of confidence that makes me think the way I do. Kim would never feel this way, constantly doubting herself and her abilities. She would sail through occasions like this one, thinking little of her own appearance, knowing that she is attractive enough, self-assured enough to carry it off.

'It really has! Too long. And I see you've got a little grandson. How did that happen? It was only yesterday we were playing together in your garden.'

She laughs, her eyes suddenly full of love as she turns and snuggles the little boy into her chest. His white bobble hat contrasts sharply against her red, woollen coat.

'Yes, scary, isn't it?' She attempts to turn his small body around to face me, twisting her arms as she holds his chunky little shape to her breast. 'This is Ted. He's eighteen months old and is visiting Granddad with me to give his mummy and daddy a break.' She takes a step closer to me. He wriggles in her arms and for one awful moment, I fear she is going to drop him. 'It's their wedding anniversary so I thought I'd bring him with me, let them have some time on their own.'

'What a lovely thing to do. So thoughtful.' My thoughts turn to my own two children and whether or not they will ever give me the gift of grandchildren, allowing me the luxury of babysitting, spending time on my own with them. With Lucy working at Oxford University and still single, and Gavin living on the other side of the word in Perth, Australia, it seems unlikely.

'Well, we have to do what we can for our families, don't we?' She stops speaking, her eyes suddenly dipping, the moment fractured as she considers her phrasing. This happens a lot, people who remember Simon and his disappearance, picking over their words, considering each sentence, every single thing they say, in order to preserve my feelings. I'm accustomed to it and although I would like to say it doesn't bother me, it really does. Nobody should have to overthink things to such a degree before speaking to me. It makes me embarrassed and awkward, as if Simon's absence, his sudden disappearance all those years ago is somehow their fault, which it isn't. This is the problem with being stuck in the past, trapped by my own family history – I attribute everything to Simon even when there is nothing there worth speaking of.

'We do indeed.' I am breathless, my anxiety levels rising, a flush taking hold in my face. 'You should call around for coffee while you're here. Or wine if that's your preference.' I manage a sly wink and she smiles.

'That would be fantastic. I could get this little wriggler to bed and we could maybe spend an hour or so chatting. And drinking.'

We both laugh. I realise that we have more in common than I first thought. She seems like easy company. Not at all the sullen, quiet child I remember from all those years ago, and a pleasant change from Kim's abrupt manner and curt ways. It will do me good to relax a little, chat about things that might help to take my mind off the obvious. Since Warren's death, I have lost touch with many of my friends, their contact well-intentioned but too exhausting for me to consider. I just wanted to be left alone, to grieve in the peace and quiet of my own home. And then even that became too much. The thought of moving back here to Woodburn Cottage became a smouldering flame in my mind, growing and burning until it became a furnace, white hot and demanding my full and undivided attention. I relented, unable to ignore it for any longer. We were about to sell Mum's home and it made sense for me to buy this place, to escape the claustrophobic confines of Lilac Crescent. It suddenly occurs to me that I haven't sent out any change of address notifications. I shrug away the thought. Plenty of time for that later. For now, I want to get settled, make a few changes and get on with my life.

'How about tonight? If you want to, that is?' My mouth is in gear before my brain. I hold my breath, wait for her reply, scrutinise her features for any signs of exasperation or disappointment and find none there.

'That sounds great! I'm sure Dad won't mind watching over this little one for a few hours while I get blind drunk with an old friend.' She returns the wink, giving me a lopsided grin, and I almost melt with relief. It feels good to smile, to talk about things that don't revolve around

Warren and Woodburn Cottage and how I should never have moved here. It feels good to be happy.

'You name the time and I'll be ready,' I say a little too animatedly. 'This little one needs settling first, don't you?' I lean closer and take Ted's hand, loving the warmth of his skin, the softness of his chubby little clenched fist. It is an age since I've felt this relaxed, this calm and languorous. 'I'm not going anywhere so just give me a knock and I'll be ready with a chilled bottle and a couple of glasses.'

The light in the cottage is brighter somehow as I say goodbye and step back inside. The air is less oppressive, cooler and lacking in humidity, making it easier to breathe. Even Mum's outburst earlier doesn't weigh so heavily on me, her words already relegated to the back of my mind.

The midday sun filters through the small windows, spreading in a pale-yellow beam across the windowsill, melting down the wall and onto the tiled flooring in a shimmering, triangular puddle. I pull back the curtains to allow more in, stopping to revel in its warmth, letting its heat-filled fingers massage my aching skin.

I close my eyes, happiness growing inside me. If I had known at that point what lay ahead, I would have been more prepared, not allowed myself to loosen and become too soft. Soft things break. They become damaged, scarred beyond recognition. Had I known, I would never have gone ahead with that drink.

7

The first glass of Chardonnay disappears in what feels like seconds. The talk flows freely, Carrie's company easy, the ambience in the room one of joviality as we reminisce about our shared childhood experiences. At no point has the conversation run dry nor has there been any awkward, protracted silences where we stare into space, scrabbling for something to fill the void. It has been easy, pleasant and we have laughed plenty.

'Whereabouts are you living now?' I pour out more wine, my face already flushed after only one drink. I am sitting opposite Carrie, who is dressed in casual clothes – jeans and a loose sweater. No more the glamourous woman. Before me is an ordinary, attractive lady who smiles effortlessly, talks softly and laughs tenderly, her voice carrying across the room like earlyomorning birdsong breaking through a storm, the sweet chirrups of swallows and blackbirds suddenly audible after a long, cold winter.

'In a village on the outskirts of Edinburgh. Innes, my husband, is Scottish and his job is in the city so it made sense to settle up there, really.' She catches my eye and takes a sip of her wine. 'And here you are, living back at Woodburn Cottage. I think it's terrific what you've done, buying your mum's home and keeping it in the family.' I don't have time to reply before she speaks again. 'I've thought of you a lot over the years, you know, Grace. You've never been far from my thoughts. I wished I'd bumped into you more when I visited Dad and your mum still lived here.' Her voice is a murmur, her expression wistful.

I swallow, try to suppress the butterflies that flutter about in my belly at the mention of Mum. I recall what she said earlier, those words, that cryptic message. 'Well, at least we managed it in the end. And look at us both now,' I say, my voice rising a full decibel. 'Two grown women with families of our own.'

She nods and persuades me to show her some photographs of Gavin and Lucy. I scroll through the full collection, suddenly overcome with a combination of longing and pride, swallowing down the feelings of loneliness and solitude. It feels like a hundred years since I've seen them even though it's only been months.

'They both look like you, especially Gavin. He's got your eyes.'

I place my phone down on the arm of the sofa, wondering what they are both currently doing, whether or not they give much thought to me. I shake it away, that shadowy, grey notion and take a long slug of my wine. Too much self-pity. It's not an attractive trait. I need to stop it. They are adults with lives of their own. I expect too much of them.

'What about your children?' I say, genuinely curious about Carrie's life and family. Her transition from wallflower to English rose has me intrigued. Such a stark contrast to the introverted child that she once was.

'One daughter – Beth. She's an only child and an only child is a lonely child as she was so fond of telling me when she was little.' She laughs, her teeth clinking against the crystal as she takes another long slug of wine. 'I had to have a hysterectomy after Beth was born. I suffered from a ruptured uterus during labour after having a myomectomy a few years before.' Her mouth twitches. I feel sad for her, want to reach over and touch her hand but we are not well enough acquainted for that level of intimacy. 'But I've got Beth and now we have Ted. We're lucky in so many ways. Some people don't have any children and then there are those poor souls who have them and—' She stops, claps a hand over her mouth, her eyes rapidly filling with tears. 'Oh, God. I am so sorry. That was horribly clumsy of me.' Her hands shake, her fingers trembling like small petals on a flower being torn asunder during a hurricane. She closes her eyes in a bid, I suspect, to stop the tears from falling. Or perhaps to avoid looking directly at me.

I follow my instincts and shuffle closer to her, placing my arm around her shoulder. I want to reassure her. I want to talk. About everything. 'Please don't be sorry. You have no idea how much I long to speak about my family. Even the bad times. It can build up inside, the memories and the trauma, and it feels good to let it all out, to hear their names being spoken. My children live away and didn't know Dad and Simon. Before Mum got dementia, she used to get too upset to speak about it, and Kim – well, Kim likes to pretend none of it ever happened. Warren was my only sounding board and now he's gone so their names never get mentioned apart from in my head.'

I stop, my breath coming out in small spurts, a tiny but solid pulse tapping away in my temple. 'Whatever you've got to say about it would actually be very welcome. I hadn't realised that moving back here would unlock so much stuff in my head. I bought the place because I couldn't bear the thought of strangers traipsing through here. It's Simon's home, was Dad's home, and I'd like to keep it that way for as long as I can.' I exhale loudly, unsure if Carrie can comprehend what it is I'm trying to say. It makes sense to me but I don't expect it to resonate with someone I haven't seen for many decades.

I can see the relief in her expression. 'And anyway,' I say smiling, 'it would be pretty difficult to sit here with me in this house and avoid the subject, wouldn't it? Let's invite this elephant in the room to join in with our conversation. He's far too big to ignore, don't you think?'

We giggle, a light tinkling sound at first that rapidly descends into full-blown hysteria, the effects of the wine kicking in, relief at being liberated from the shackles of the past fuelling our laughter.

'Oh God, Grace. Thank you so much for being you, for not letting me sit here getting myself into a complete pickle.'

I wipe at my eyes, noticing that our glasses are empty. Before she can refuse, I refill them to the brim, determined to go through both the bottles that I had chilling. I rarely drink alone. This is an opportunity to talk freely, forget about everything and simply get drunk without the usual solitude nudging its way in. I have a new friend and we are talking openly and laughing and reminiscing and it feels good. It's long overdue.

'You know,' she says, her composure returning as she tucks her feet up under her bottom and shuffles into a more comfortable position, 'I was always in awe of you and your family, how you just got on with everything after it happened. You came across as so strong, so determined to keep going despite what you had all been through.'

I try to think back to that time but my memories are dim. It happened such a long time ago. I was only six years old. Simon was eight. I want to remember more about it, to re-ignite that period of my life and put all the pieces together in my brain but it's so difficult, swathes of dark clouds obscuring everything.

'I suppose we just had to get on with it, really. No other option. What do you remember about Simon?' I also rearrange myself into a more comfortable spot, ready to hear Carrie's thoughts and recollections. Anything she says might help me to remember. Because I do want to. Unlike Kim, I'm not prepared to shut it all away. I'm here, living in the place where it all happened. I need to know.

'He was a cute kid. I loved it when you used to come and play in our garden. Not that I joined in that much. I was unbelievably shy and if I'm being honest, a bit jealous of you all.'

The wine almost chokes me, a cold trail of it landing in the base of my stomach. 'Jealous? Of what?'

Carrie laughs, a smudge of pink spreading over her face, down her neck, settling on her breastbone. 'The fact that you had each other. Like my own daughter, I was an only child, nobody to play with, nobody to share things with. I always swore that when I grew up, I would have a houseful of kids but of course, that never happened.'

This time, I do squeeze her hand, the barriers that only seconds ago kept us apart, now dissolving.

'And Simon, what do I remember about him? Oh, gosh. Some memories are more vivid than others, and of course he was in my class at school, wasn't he?'

It's my turn to feel a flush creep up my face. I wasn't aware they were in the same class as each other but of course that makes sense. Carrie is a year or so older than me, the same age as Simon. *The same age he would have been.* I can say that to myself now because it's obvious that he is dead. If not, then where has he been for the last forty-odd years? I repeat the phrase over and over in my head. *Simon is dead. Simon is dead.* If I allow myself to think that, then everything seems so much easier to handle. It's the unknown, the what ifs, the entire mystery that surrounds his disappearance that makes me ill at ease. Sometimes, it's as if I am waiting for him to walk back in the room, to smile and greet me as if nothing has happened. No passing of time.

'He was a sweet boy, very gentle. Withdrawn on occasions as I recall. Am I okay saying that?' She catches my eye, her head dipped slightly.

I nod and smile, willing her to go on. I want to know everything about him. Everything.

'It's weird, actually,' she says, her voice suddenly energetic, as if she has been waiting a long time to speak about it to somebody who will understand, 'because there was one particular memory that didn't come to me until quite a few years ago, a good while after he went missing. I never really believed in repressed memories but it happened when Beth was younger and suffered with night terrors. It sprang into my mind and has never left me since.'

I suck in my breath, waiting, hoping she will reveal something about Simon that will help me restore the full version of him in my head, the brother I am struggling to remember. I don't speak for fear of losing the moment. Instead, I sit and wait, my heartbeat a steady, solid metronome in my chest, my flesh prickling with anticipation.

'I'm not exactly sure of the timeline but I think it happened a few months or maybe a few weeks before he disappeared. We were in class writing about what we liked and didn't like, or something along those lines. I can't really remember the exact lesson obviously, but what I do remember was what Simon said as he read his out to the rest of the class.'

She takes a drink, unaware of how on edge I am, of how every muscle, every fibre and sinew in my body is tensed, stretched like cat gut while I wait for her to continue. This may be something, it may be nothing, but what I do know for sure is that I need to hear it.

'He said that he liked football and playing out with his friends, the usual stuff. But then he told everyone that he was frightened of somebody called The Midnight Child. He said he was terrified that The Midnight Child was going to come into his room and take him away.'

Perspiration breaks out on my top lip. I have no idea what this means but I can tell by Carrie's face that she thinks little or nothing of it, that it was simply the musings of a young child with a vivid imagination.

'Could it have been linked to him going missing, do you think?' I say, my breathing suddenly difficult and onerous, a large bubble of air trapped in my chest. I drain my glass, needing the effects the alcohol will bring, the blurring of the edges, the numbing of my thoughts. The switching off of the fear that has lain dormant in me for almost all of my life.

'Linked?' Her eyebrows shoot up, her mouth shaped into a small O. 'Oh my goodness, I shouldn't think so. In fact, I'm almost certain it wasn't. It was the awful coincidence of it that jarred in my mind. No,' she murmurs, smiling at me, her eyes twinkling with what – sympathy? Happiness? Relief at having finally spoken about it? 'It can't possibly have been linked, can it?'

'Really?' I say, aware that my voice is a squeak, like the cry of a startled animal. 'Why not?'

She puts down her glass and tips her head at me, a quizzical expression in her eyes. 'Why not? Don't you remember?' Her voice softens a fraction, as if she is speaking to a timid child, one who is confused, unable to understand the words being put to them. 'Because it was you, Grace. That was what they used to call you. It was your nickname. You were the one who scared him. You were The Midnight Child.'

8

I am lying in bed, the memory of Carrie and how her words left me winded as if all the air had been sucked out of the room, still in the forefront of my mind. And then her face when she realised my distress, her repeated apologies and then the memory of how she had to take my glass from me and place it to one side, like a carer with a patient who had become overtired and overwrought, unable to control their own emotions. It swallows everything, the image of her crestfallen expression, blocking out all logic and common sense in my head. I'm not sure I can bear to think about it, how upset I was, how embarrassing the entire situation became. My lack of control. My stricken expression. How I could hardly stand as I walked beside her to the door, my legs liquid, my guts churning like molten lava.

She left shortly afterwards, genuinely perplexed by my reaction, telling me it simply wasn't possible that Simon's fear of me was linked to his disappearance. I was a young child, she had said, a small, young child who was incapable of harming a boy who was older than me. It was all just a terrible coincidence, she had insisted before reiterating how awful she felt for mentioning it at all.

'It was a stupid, thoughtless thing for me to say,' she had said as we stood on the doorstep. Carrie red-faced, her manner jumpy and nervous, brought on by both the wine and the recollection of Simon. Of me. Me, The Midnight Child. And what I possibly did.

'Grace. I'm really sorry.' And she was. She was utterly ingenuous, convinced she had ruined a perfectly lovely evening. She didn't ruin it at all. I did that with my reaction, my inability to handle the conversation. I am an adult, still trapped in my childhood years, forever dragged to the past. I asked, *begged* her for her memories, her recollections and images from the past and then couldn't handle them when they surfaced.

I reassured her that it was perfectly fine and that I was over it even though my innards felt as if they were on fire, my bones as heavy as lead. Everything felt forced. Contrived. And it possibly would have been fine had the incident with the fox not taken place days earlier. The dead body in the garden. The blood. Me covered in it; crimson streaks smeared up my arms, over my legs and face. Her father seeing me outside in the early hours of the morning. The thought of that night had slammed into me as I listened to Carrie tell me that my own brother was frightened of me. That he was scared I would take him away. Perhaps I did? Perhaps something terrible happened and I've somehow blocked it all out?

I shiver, suppressing a sob. A shadow slinks around the back of my brain. How could I have not remembered such a thing? Was I even aware of it then? Am I aware of it now? There is a memory skulking about in the back of my mind but it is vague, elusive, refusing to reveal itself despite me trying to beckon it out of the shadows. Me, The Midnight Child. That title. That name. The bouts of sleepwalking. And now it's happening again. History is repeating itself now that I'm back living at Woodburn Cottage. I have stirred up something from the past, opened up a Pandora's Box of family secrets and I have no idea how to stuff everything back inside and lock it again.

The bed is cold as I turn over and curl up into a ball, my knees tucked up into my chest. I don't want to think about it any more. And yet I do. I can't just forget about this thing, allow it to fester in the recesses of my brain. It needs to be brought out into the open, teased and enticed out of its hiding place. Tomorrow, I will give Kim a call, speak to her about it. No matter how reluctant she is, I will demand she start being more open about our past. It was my childhood. Simon was – still *is* – my brother. Our brother. Whatever took place in this house, I have a right to know.

* * *

I'm standing in front of the garden shed, the cool breeze winding itself around my ankles, gliding against my bare calves, the flesh on my upper arms puckered in resistance to the cold. I blink, stare around. Everything is blurred, my vision marred by exhaustion and the darkness. An owl hoots in the distance, its call echoing through the night sky. Above, the inky blackness is punctuated with a smattering of stars, pinpricks of light that twinkle and glisten, forcing me to hang onto the fence for balance. My perspective is skewed, the darkness and the silence making me dizzy. I crane my neck, tilting my head upwards to stare at the sky, at the moon, the stars. I feel as if I can reach out and grab them, hold them tightly in my palm like diamonds, their weight and solidity anchoring me to this house, to this moment.

If I stand here for long enough, I am sure I can cast my mind back to all those years ago, force myself to remember my childlike nocturnal wanderings. They're in there somewhere, my memories of that time, tucked away in a dusty corner of my brain. Very little has changed in this house. Aside from my efforts at cleaning up the old place and giving it a lick of paint, the design of the building is still the same as it was when I was a child. No internal walls knocked through to allow for more space, no patio doors, no sweeping extension with skylights and an expansive view out onto the back garden. It's still the same ancient cottage with Georgian windows and uneven, flagstone flooring.

The only difference is that Woodburn Cottage, many, many years ago used to be two houses, built for local farm workers. Most properties nearby now resemble this one – two abodes knocked into one bigger house, making them more appealing to families. And the garden is almost the same. This shed, the old coalhouse, the shape of the lawn – it's as I remember it from when I was a child. It's being here that has triggered it, the sleepwalking. Of that I am certain. The familiarity of the place has unearthed something in my mind, the shifting sands of time calling me, making me cast my mind back to that time, to that night when Simon went missing from his bed, the one place where he should have been safe and yet wasn't.

The police at the time, after investigating and finding no evidence to the contrary, went with the theory that he took himself off for a late-night walk and got lost. What sort of child would do such a thing? It's silly. Unthinkable. Simon was a quiet boy, a gentle boy. Not the sort of lad to go off on adventures on his own in the dark. The police got it all wrong, of that I am certain. I don't remember the details of their investigation but I do recall it being over with in what felt like no time at all. Perhaps my woolly memory and the passing of the years have made me view things differently. Perhaps they did all they could to find Simon. Or perhaps they put it down to misadventure and closed the case due to lack of evidence with the notion that boys will be boys and he probably deserved everything he got, wandering off on his own like that.

The breeze picks up, the noise of it in the tree forcing me out of my thoughts. I blink, rub at my eyes and head back inside, locking the door behind me. I should have done what I promised I would do and hidden the key from myself. Tomorrow, I will do just that. I will tuck it away somewhere safe. Somewhere I won't think to look when I am confused and blinded by sleep.

My feet are freezing as I pad upstairs, longing for the warmth and comfort of my bed. After Warren died, I used to dread night-times, slipping in between the sheets knowing he wasn't there and that I would have to lie alone, cold and miserable, but as the months passed, I grew accustomed to it. Now I long for a night where I remain asleep. I long to wake and find my body still in the same position as when I climbed into bed; not find myself standing in the garden or – worse still – out in the middle of the main road in the early hours with no memory of how I got there.

The bed is still marginally warm as I climb back in. I'm glad I haven't been outside for too long and I am more than a little relieved that there were no dead animals laid at my feet.

Simon's face merges with Carrie's words as I slip into a fitful sleep, waking every hour or so before eventually falling into a deep and welcome slumber.

I finally wake up at 9 a.m., my body aching, my limbs heavy. Still, I am determined to plough ahead, to tackle some of the less appealing things that have been preying on my mind since last night. Somewhere amongst Mum's things are the details on the police reports about Simon's disappearance.

I am going to read them, if only to satisfy myself that they did everything they could to find my brother. I realise that policing methods back then weren't as advanced or as scrupulous as they are today but I want to be sure that every effort was put into finding Simon and that he wasn't written off as a wandering miscreant, somebody who became embroiled in an adventure that turned sour. I also want to find out whether or not our family is mentioned; whether or not my name comes up as a person of interest. I know this is highly unlikely but I won't settle until I see every single report, read every newspaper article I can find about when he disappeared.

Living at Woodburn Cottage has stirred up something in me, some latent force that has set me on the path to finding out what happened to Simon. And now I'm down that route, I won't turn back. Not until I discover what happened to him and where he is now.

9

'I got rid of them.' Kim's tone is sharp, unrelenting. She won't be backed into a corner on this. I have no idea why she thought it was in our best interests to dispose of them, but it would appear that that is exactly what she has done. She had no right to do such a thing without first speaking to me. I know this. She knows it too.

'All of them? Every single article and police report?' I am trying to keep my voice even, to disguise my growing frustration and anger, but it's not easy. My face is hot, my chest tight, every blood vessel in my body fit to burst. Frustration and anger swirl in my head, a dark, thick cloud leaden with unspent fury.

'All of them.'

I wait out the silence, breaking it only as my temper takes hold. 'You had no right, Kim. You should have consulted me first.' There is ice in my voice, fire in my veins, a fusion of the two fuelling me, pushing me on. 'I wanted to see them. You had no right!'

If she is shocked by my sudden outburst, she doesn't show it. I rarely lose my temper. I'm the quiet one in the family, the reserved one who tiptoes through life, smoothing troubled waters, building bridges. But not any more.

'I had no right? Grace, you were grieving. Mum's dementia had worsened. I did what I had to do. Keeping them was never going to bring Simon back, was it?'

I flinch, bruised by her callous manner, the way she can wound even from a distance, using words as weapons. This isn't Kim lashing out, defending her actions; this is Kim being vindictive, showing me that she is the one who is in charge in this family, that I am in no position to dedicate any time to finding out the truth about my brother. She thinks that it is none of my concern, that much is obvious. I was too young when it happened and therefore have been robbed of any liberties when it comes to enquiring about what took place that night all those years ago. Kim is in charge of our little family and decides who can rake through our past. That is her reasoning. It's not mine.

'And pretending he never existed is? I always knew you were a tough one, Kim. I just never realised that you're hard to the point of being cruel. You disposed of the last things we had of our brother. It wasn't your place to do that. And don't you *dare* use my grief as an excuse for trampling over my feelings, for making decisions on my behalf, pretending I was too cut up to be consulted.' I am breathless, my stomach roiling, my throat thick with unshed tears. I want to say more, years and years of unspoken words spilling out of me in a heady rush, but I don't. They stay inside my head, trapped by my lack of power, the inertia that often cripples me when it comes to dealing with my sister. Instead, I visualise myself marching into Kim's living room, snatching the phone out of her hand and slapping her hard across the face. It gives me enormous pleasure, sending a rush of blood to my cheeks, my neck and ears. I can practically feel the smart on my palm, the sting of pain as flesh meets flesh.

Her silence seems to go on for an age. I refuse to be browbeaten into speaking first, letting her wield her older sibling authority over me. I will wait this one out, stand my ground until the imbalance of power tips in my favour.

When she does answer, it's as if I haven't even spoken at all. She is calm, measured, and as always, brimming with self-confidence. 'Well, anyway, what's done is done, isn't it? Time to move on. Are you still up for coffee this week?' Her tone is brusque, efficient: the voice of somebody utterly unmoved by what we have just spoken about. Kim, the ice queen, impervious to the usual range of human emotions.

Once again, she has rendered me speechless. I stumble backwards, lowering myself onto the sofa in a clumsy heap. Lost for words. I am completely lost for words and do something I have never ever done. Not to Kim, not to anybody. I end the call without saying goodbye then throw the phone onto the floor, watching mesmerised as it spins around on its back, rocking back and forth like a tiny, upturned turtle.

Everything slows down, the world decelerating as my heart speeds up, pulsing angrily beneath my shirt. The floors swirls at my feet, tiny specks of dirt dancing around me. I rest my head in my hands, wait for everything to rebalance itself, for my blood pressure to lower itself. For my world to return to normal. Whatever normal is.

Only when I have calmed down do I stand and pick up the phone, replacing it on the table. I almost laugh at the idea of meeting her for coffee, picturing her sitting there, wondering where I am, why I haven't turned up, her mind genuinely perplexed at my absence. I wonder how Greg does it. Is he immune to her insults and overbearing manner? I don't see him as somebody who needs a strong partner in his life, the sort of man who likes being supported by a domineering person. Greg is a capable man. He has his own opinions, his own interests and a successful career.

That's when it comes to me – she isn't the same person when she is at home with her own family. Her absurd bossiness is reserved solely for me, her much younger sibling. Time has failed to diminish the roles of our family structure. If anything, it has strengthened them, fortifying Kim's belief that she can say or do anything she pleases when she is in my presence, strengthening her belief that I am still her little sister, that young, shy, scared little girl who admired her older sibling, following her around the house, begging to be in her company. It is a misplaced notion. Her ideas are out of kilter, anachronistic and skewed. I am her equal, somebody with the same rights as her, the same needs and wants. Somebody who is worthy of her respect.

I am thinking all of these things when I hear a tap at the door. Not the sharp rap of a delivery man, more of a gentle interruption into my day, an almost apologetic tapping.

Her smile is lopsided, her eyes half hidden behind the array of white, silken petals.

'Carrie?' My voice is hoarse, a low growl. I clear my throat and step aside to allow her to enter, my palm outstretched as I beckon her inside.

'These are for you. As an apology for having such a big, fat mouth.' There is a hint of laughter in her tone, not an abrasive sound, more of a soft quality that resonates with me, catching me in my solar plexus. I need this. I need this moment and I need Carrie to be standing there, smiling at me. She has broken the moment, severed the cord of anger that had me trapped in my own dark thoughts.

I reach out, touch her shoulder and smile. 'Absolutely no need. But thank you anyway. It's a really kind gesture.'

We walk into the living room, Carrie looking around for somewhere to place the flowers.

'Here, let me take those. I'll get them in some water. Coffee?' I take the flowers, surprised at the weight. There must be at least a dozen white roses here, interspersed with sprigs of fern and a sprinkling of pale, lilac flowers whose name escapes me. 'They are really beautiful. Thank you so much. But as I said, there really was no need, you know.'

'I didn't sleep last night, thinking about it. Every time I dozed off, the thought of what I said came back to me and woke me up. So stupid and crass. Innes often tells me to think before I speak.'

I think that perhaps Innes is wrong. Carrie certainly doesn't strike me as a particularly thoughtless or imperious woman. Quite the opposite. I cannot ever imagine Kim doing something like this, bringing me flowers by way of an apology. She would brush away my anxieties with a sweep of her hand and a rush of acerbic words telling me how pointless worry is, how it doesn't solve anything, blurring all logic and clarity of thought.

'Oh, poor you! Honestly, I am perfectly fine. It was a silly overreaction on my part.' I do my best to play it down. I probably did overreact. How could I possibly have done anything to harm my own brother and not remember? In the cold light of day, my near meltdown seems silly and embarrassing. An overplay of emotions on my part.

I place the bouquet in a large vase and make us both a hot drink, the blended aroma of flowers and coffee filling the kitchen.

Carrie is standing looking at a wedding photograph as I walk back into the living room. 'You look beautiful. And your husband was a handsome man.'

'Thank you.' I hand her the coffee, my legs suddenly weak at the thought of Warren and the shock of waking up next to him in bed, his body cold and rigid, his skin as pale as chalk.

'I'm heading back home in a couple of days.' She turns again to look at the photograph before catching my eye, our gazes locking, a moment of pure understanding passing between us. 'I was hoping maybe we could have another catch-up before I leave. And this time, I'll let you do the talking. I'll sit and listen instead of causing so much upset.'

We spend a pleasant ten minutes chatting amiably about our children, marriage, her life in Scotland until she looks at her watch and stands up, startled. 'God, sorry. Got to get back. I'm taking Ted to visit my aunt in Pickering. We're having a bite to eat then going for a wander around Rievaulx Abbey. I haven't been there since I was a little kid. Can't imagine it's changed much, though.' She smiles.

I laugh as she places her cup down on the coffee table, remembering the days as children when Kim, Simon and I used to clamber over the ruins, balancing on low walls and calling out to one another, our voices echoing into the emptiness of the crumbling remains.

'How about tomorrow evening?' I say, watching her face for any signs of reticence.

'That sounds perfect. I'll get Ted sorted then I can be here for about eight?'

Relief blooms in my chest. This is easy, effortless, this renewed friendship with a woman I've not seen for decades.

I almost reach out to hug her, stopping myself just in time. Too much, too soon. Perhaps this connection will prove to be nothing more than a fleeting thing. Or perhaps it is the beginning of a lasting friendship. Who knows? Life is unpredictable, special moments rare and transitory. We have to grab them while we can, hold them tight, cherish them. I know this now. Maybe I've always known it. It feels like a stronger emotion since losing Warren. I was a child when Simon disappeared and although I felt his loss, it was a different sensation, his vanishing shrouded in mystery. I was protected from a lot of it, my senses dulled to the real hurt and pain, seeing it as I did, through the eyes of a youngster. For years, I thought he would come back. Time held no true meaning for me. A day was a week, a week a month. Only now can I study it properly, scrutinise it with renewed purpose. I became too bogged down with my own family, my job. But now I have the space in my life to truly give it some thought, to allow myself the time to travel back to that night. The night he left our lives forever.

'Eight sounds great,' I say, snapping back to the present.

This house, meeting Carrie again after all these years – it has set off something in me, aroused a whole gamut of feelings that have lain dormant for most of my life. But now this concealed force within me is coming back to life, demanding to be heard. I can't ignore it. I do that at my peril. I don't care what Kim's feelings are on this matter; I am determined to put some real effort into finding out what happened to our brother all those years ago. He deserves it. He doesn't deserve to be shelved away, his memory forgotten, too difficult to speak about.

The sound of Carrie's feet on the concrete path echoes in my head, her retreating figure a reminder that soon, she will be gone again, travelling back up to Edinburgh. I need to make the most of our next get-together, ask her what she remembers, glean as much information out of her as I can regardless of my sensitivities and how upsetting it might be.

Simon was a person, *is* a person, and from hereon in, I plan on putting all my efforts into finding him.

10

I sit up, pain behind my eyes, around the back of my neck, the steady thump of blood into my head making me dizzy and nauseous. At least I'm still in bed, not outside in the garden, not in the middle of the main road in my nightclothes, or worse still, completely naked.

The quilt is cumbersome, heavy, heat billowing out from underneath it, my flesh burning beneath its weight. I place my cool hand across my forehead, the skin there hot and clammy. A furnace roars in my ears. Something has scared me, shocked me into wakefulness. I try to remember, pushing everything else out of my mind. It doesn't work. Fragments of thoughts, dreams, flit around my head. Fireflies dancing in the darkness of a mysterious land, an elusive place. Somewhere I know but cannot reach.

It's there, the memory. I can feel it but can't see it, am unable to catch it and contextualise it. And it means something. I just know it. One day soon, it will slip into the light unbidden, showing itself. And then I will know. I will start to piece together whatever is lurking there. Because there is something. I'm certain of it. And it is definitely about Simon and his disappearance. I need to be patient, wait for it to appear of its own volition. Forced thoughts rarely appear willingly.

I lie back on the pillow, knowing that sleep won't come easily to me. An hour later, I am still wide awake, my eyes glued ahead, my mind forming shapes out of the shadows cast across the ceiling, eerie, grey fingers that change and alter into ominous figures as my imagination runs riot and the darkness slowly ebbs away.

I sit up, the bed creaking beneath me. I turn on the lamp, dispelling the darkness, the silhouettes, blinking as the brightness in the room grows around me. My book sits on the bedside table along with a notepad and pen. I reach across and grab it, determined to do something with my time, not sit here, wasting precious seconds. I'm awake, alert, my brain itching to do something.

Ten minutes and I have made a list of what I plan to do this week. My writing can be put on hold. I need to do some research, sift through anything I can find on the internet about Simon's disappearance. Kim may have taken it upon herself to dispose of our records but there is still plenty of information out there. I could contact the police, ask to speak to someone regarding the case. Anybody connected to it will now either be retired or dead, I do know that; but I can ask to see the records, request that they take another look at the case, review it with fresh eyes. It's a cold case, not a closed one. Simon was never officially declared dead. With no property or financial records to take care of, we had no need to take such a step. Growing up, it was an unspoken presumption that Simon was never coming back. It fills me with shame at how quickly things got back to normal in our lives, as if his disappearance was something dirty, something that tainted our family name.

And then of course, there was the death of our father only months afterwards. Four months. That's all it was. In that space of time, our tiny family shrunk even further, Dad's death compounding our misery, fuelling our silence, pushing us further into ourselves. Further into that damp, dark corner.

We were never the sort of family who spoke openly about our feelings, brushing away sentimentality and soul-bearing conversations, and then things closed down even further after Dad passed away. By the time I was in my teens, I had learned to keep things tucked deep inside, never grieving properly or asking for help. Mum was a kind lady, always pleasant and helpful but rarely showing her true emotions. The fact they have all come spilling out in the last few months is a massive surprise and in complete contradiction to her usual self. Perhaps all those pent-up feelings and memories are now trying to work their way out of her system, her poor, addled brain unable to put up any resistance as every single secret and undisclosed thought wheedles its way out into the open. She would be horrified, that much I do know. Horrified and ashamed of her actions and words. I wonder what she would think of my mission to unearth what I can about the night Simon disappeared? Would she be relieved or would it be too much for her, having to relive that awful evening?

I shuffle down into the bed, the chill of the night air nipping at my exposed flesh. I stare down at my list of notes – scribbles, bullet points, random thoughts and questions that I want to ask – and put the notepad back on the bedside table. If I am to do this thing, take it upon myself to delve back into this painful case, then I need to do it with a clear head, not act on a whim after only minutes of snatched, fitful sleep. The police may have scaled back their enquiries but I plan on doing my own investigative work, with or without them. I owe it to Simon, I owe it to Mum, but most of all, after hearing about his fear of me as a child, I owe it to myself.

* * *

The internet is full of half-baked theories and inaccurate stories on hastily thrown together websites written by people with a morbid interest in the unfortunates who disappear into thin air. Apart from Wikipedia and the BBC, there are few sites that offer me any new information. Why would they? All we know is that one spring evening, Simon went to bed as usual and when we woke the next morning, he was gone. His covers were thrown aside, his slippers missing, but apart from that, nothing was awry. The rogue websites contain all sorts of ridiculous stories about our family – that Simon was bullied at school; that he had a difficult relationship with our mum; that he was a loner and found it hard to mix with other children. I close my eyes and sigh. Where do they get these ideas from? Or are they aware that they are lies and print them regardless, driven by a need to fill in the blanks and draw in more readers?

Whatever the reason, they have taken a liberty and it infuriates and depresses me in equal measure. I should have been prepared for this level of intrusion, for all these suppositions and lies, and yet it still hits me hard, making me feel as if I am dirty, contaminated by their dishonesty and fabricated stories. Simon was my brother. He was neither a victim of bullies in the playground, nor was he a loner. Simon was a little boy who went to bed one evening and simply vanished.

Except he didn't. That doesn't happen. People don't just disappear into the ether. They leave a trace. Everybody leaves something of themselves behind. Perhaps if it had happened now with all the advances in forensics and DNA, then maybe we would have stood a greater chance of finding him. But as it is, I am going to have to rely on Google searches, instinct and my memories. Memories that refuse to slot together in any semblance of order. Memories that dance around my brain, drunk, directionless.

And then I see it. A story dating back to a year ago. Another missing child from a nearby town. A boy slightly older than Simon. An eleven-year-old who went missing from his home. Just like Simon did. Is there a connection or is the forty-odd year gap too great to consider them aligned? I wonder if the police looked for similarities. I wonder if I am simply clutching at straws having drawn blanks in every other place I have looked.

I feel certain that a visit to the police will prove fruitless. Unless I can present them with new evidence, it is unlikely that they will take it any further. He is a cold case, a missing person with no new lines of enquiry worth investigating. I could mention the recent missing boy, see if they show any interest in the two cases. Part of me knows this is all pointless, that I am going round in circles, chasing my tail, hoping to find something that will spark an interest in Simon's disappearance. I don't want him to be forgotten. And what if the two cases are connected?

A lump rises in my throat. It's been years since I cried over Simon. All my recent tears have been reserved for Warren. I lean back, run my fingers through my hair, weariness gnawing at me, burrowing deep into my bones.

Warren. I think of his things that remain half sorted. I think of those words, the purported song lyrics. The lump in my throat grows, jammed in place by anxiety and self-pity. I should finish sorting through his things before I shift my attention onto Simon. It's the story of my life – starting one job before I've finished the first one. I smile at the thought of my editor's face if she were to trawl through my current manuscript. Ramblings and half-baked ideas flung together amidst a flurry of activity and two-dimensional characters is what it is. Eventually, it will take shape but for now, I have other things to do, more pressing matters that will eat away at me if I don't give them my full and undivided attention.

My body is heavier than usual, weighted to the ground as I lift the suitcase back out and place it on the floor. I vow to get these documents and papers sorted by the end of the day and then I can focus on Simon. *One tragedy at a time.* That's what I tell myself as I squat over the case and press both the locks, inhaling the swirling dust motes as the lid springs free and the contents spill out onto the floor at my feet.

11

It doesn't make any sense. This was meant to be a quick sort out, a rapid rifling of his stuff and yet here I am, perplexed and confused and once again upset by what I have found. Why are things never simple? They should be. This is a routine task, nothing too arduous, just a way of finalising Warren's affairs, working out what is important and needs to be filed away, and what should be disposed of.

This should have been easy and now here I am, sitting on the floor, another esoteric message crumpled up in my hand, the paper cool and sharp against my burning skin. I take a deep breath and close my eyes. My mouth is pursed, my breath sour; a mixture of metal and sand, bitter saliva swilling around the recesses of my gums. I swallow, stare down at the words before me.

> Please don't tell her Warren. Don't do it. We all have too much to lose.

It's a typed note folded in half and placed in an envelope. Why would anybody send a typed note? They are a thing of the past. People use texts or emails or communicate through social media. Unless they don't want to get caught, their identity made public should anybody discover said texts or emails. I often used Warren's phone and computer. The iPads and gadgets we both had were interchangeable, not solely reserved for one person. Whoever wrote this note knew that. Warren must have told them.

Keep it private, just between us.

I can hear his voice. Pleading. Insistent. Desperate to keep his secrets hidden, tucked away from me, his blindly faithful and clearly very stupid wife.

I shut my eyes, think back to the source of these documents. Most of them came from his desk at work. I recall Martin handing them over to me after Warren died once his colleagues had decided enough time has passed for them to clear out his desk without appearing cold or calculating. Martin's eyes were downcast, his voice low as he struggled to formulate a sentence, something that would encapsulate his feelings without making me too uncomfortable. In the end, he opted for, 'I'm so sorry. We all are. You might want these.' And that was it. That was the sum total of Warren's twenty-year career as marketing director for them. *I'm so sorry.* That was the best that they could do.

Ragged chunks of air bounce out of me, my chest wheezing as I struggle to breathe properly. We were happy, Warren and I. *Weren't we?* I thought so, but now I'm not so sure. I try to think back. Back to before that morning when I found him lying rigid and cold beside me in bed. The shock of that day seems to have blotted out everything else, leaving a lasting impression in my mind, nudging other memories aside, all the good stuff: the happier times, the warm, balmy days we spent down by the river, the days laid on beaches in sunnier climes, the walks we took up on the North Yorkshire moors. They have all been ground underfoot, turned to ash because of that morning, the finality of it. The abrupt end to his life and mine as I knew it. And now I have more to contend with. The discovery of these letters, attempting to work out who wrote them. Who the fuck was she? *Is she?* Because unless she died at the same time, then this woman is still out there, going about her daily activities.

The woman who had an affair with my husband.

It's the only explanation. Nothing else fits this stomach-churning find. My throat is thick with tears, my mind crawling with unpalatable images of the two of them together, two furtive people, secreted away in some seedy bar, snatching brief moments together, forever on their guard, keeping watch for fear of being spotted.

Does she know that Warren is dead, this femme fatale? Does she know that his heart gave out in his sleep, that he went to bed one evening and never woke up? Was she at the funeral, tucked away at the back, nestled between family and friends, clutching at her handkerchief as the pall bearers carried his body inside and placed it on the plinth at the front of the church?

I suddenly want to rage and scream and holler into the empty sky above. How dare she? How fucking *dare* she?

And then I think of Warren and my distressing discovery of this brief yet revealing missive that has helped cement my knowledge of his infidelity. I was wrong about the other note, so very, very wrong. My initial instincts that something was awry were correct. I tried to mask my hurt and surprise with a cock-and-bull story about song lyrics and poetry and how he would never do such a thing to me. And yet he has. He did. The husband I loved has once again turned my world upside down, tipping what little goodness and happiness I had left out of my life and scattering it to the four winds.

The betrayal and hurt I feel is overwhelming, so difficult to comprehend. It's patently obvious that I never really knew my husband at all. I think back to the weeks and months before his death. We were busy with our lives, busy working, keeping in touch with friends and family.

'I'll always be here for you. No matter what happens, we'll always be together, you and I. You do know that, don't you?'

The memory slams into me, knocking all the air out of my lungs. We had been sitting together on the sofa a month or so before he died. Warren was watching TV and I was busy tapping away on my laptop, making small changes to my novel. My mind was elsewhere as he spoke. I took his words as a reaffirmation of our relationship, something he said in passing rather than simply saying, *I love you*. We had been watching a film about a couple who had gone through a torrid time that had tested their love for one another. I presumed he had been referring to that. Perhaps he had but with this present finding, I am now doubting myself.

My head aches, a ribbon of anxiety wrapping itself around my skull.

He had worked late a few nights a week. I didn't enquire on his whereabouts. I had no need. We had a secure marriage. A happy one. Or perhaps my rose-tinted spectacles are distorting my vision. Our relationship had become like a comfortable old shoe, something I gave little thought to, taking it for granted day after day. Should I have tried a little harder? Injected some excitement into our lives to keep him by my side? Is that what people are expected to do? Constantly make that extra effort to keep their partners happy and satisfied? Are we never allowed to relax, to simply get on with our lives without needing to entertain and titillate them? It seems an absurd notion and yet if that is what other people do, then I have failed. I failed myself, my marriage and I failed Warren.

Everything mists over as I attempt to pick apart our lives before Warren's death, to scrutinise and analyse our movements, our conversations, everything we said and did. We paid less attention one another for sure but we had been married for over twenty-five years. Married bliss isn't getting up every single day and gazing into one another's eyes across the breakfast table. It isn't stating every five minutes how much you love your partner. Married bliss is functioning at an everyday level without any acrimony. Married bliss is knowing you can trust your other half implicitly when they leave the house or when they send messages on their phone or when they come home late from work a few evenings a week. Married bliss is never having to interrogate them about where they have been. It's about feeling contented and relaxed in the cloak of your relationship, not having to test its strength and durability every hour of every day with a stream of questions about who they have been with or whether or not they still love you.

God, I was stupid. Stupid and naïve. I sink down onto the floor, my limbs liquid, my innards twisting and aching with regret. I don't have the strength for this. I really don't.

* * *

I have no idea what time it is when I finally drag myself back up. The light around me is fading, dark clouds scudding across the sky, their bellies engorged with rain. Small splashes hit the window as I rise and lean against the sill, my arms outstretched, my head still heavy with sleep.

The droplets increase, growing in size and rapidity, turning into a downpour within seconds. Water runs across the road, bubbling down the gutters in a swirling eddy. The wind picks up, battering the window. The noise and intensity of it forces me to step away.

In the kitchen, I open a packet of painkillers and take two, swallowing them down with water. I can't decide whether to pursue this issue with Warren and the letters, delving further into his life, the life I thought I knew, or to leave things as they are. Why torture myself any further? Images of him wrapped in the arms of another woman, smiling and stroking her hair tenderly, gouge at me, scooping out large portions of who I am, leaving me empty.

I need to bring myself round, drag myself out this low mood. Carrie is calling here later. I have to be prepared, put on a brave face. Be who she expects me to be, not a browbeaten wreck of a woman whose world is continuing to fall apart months after the premature death of her husband.

After a quick tidy up of the downstairs, I head up for a bath. I am grimy after lying on the floor for so long, my hair smelling of dust and a petrichor type of odour that I cannot seem to shake.

The water is hot and I emerge refreshed, my skin squeaky clean, my mind still clogged up with my recent find. A chat with Carrie is what I need to clear it all away – all the seediness and misery that is doing its damnedest to engulf me and drag me away.

I put on some make-up, wincing at my reflection. Pale, wan, lined. A middle-aged woman with sad eyes and a downturned mouth. A deep groove between my eyes makes me look as if I have a permanent frown, like a disapproving Victorian school ma'am.

I used to enjoy wearing make-up, painting my nails, preening myself until I glowed. What happened to that positive-minded creature? Where did she go? Buried, I suspect, amidst the years of worry and anxiety along with a healthy helping of apprehension at what the future holds. A future without Warren. A future with no Simon, his body still out there somewhere, waiting to be found. Maybe what I see before me is what drove my husband away.

My stomach rumbles, a loud, insistent growl. I can't remember when I last ate anything. Breakfast perhaps. A slice of toast and a swig of coffee. Is it any wonder I look so washed out and am constantly lacking in energy? Warren was a good cook, always making sure we ate healthily. The thought of him, even the sound of his name as it rolls around my head, forces my stomach into a tight knot, the memory of earlier, that note, those words, continuing to bash into me, knocking me off balance.

I want to get on with things, get on with my life, my writing, settling into this house. I want to get into a routine, forge out a new path for myself. How can I do that when I have this hanging over me? How am I supposed to pretend it never happened and get up every day with a smile on my face? It doesn't feel possible. It was difficult before, dealing with Warren's death, my recent bouts of sleepwalking. Now it is intolerable. Beyond my capabilities. And yet, I have to cope. What are the options – curling into a ball and turning my back on everyone and everything? I have a life to live. There is a world out there I need to face, people I need to see, writing deadlines to meet.

And meet them I will. I will make sure of it. I've endured plenty in my life. A little more hurt isn't going to squash me. I won't let it.

12

Her smiling face is the tonic I need. Carrie pours us both a glass of wine and we relax on the sofa in the living room, the rain still lashing at the windows, small, liquid bullets hammering against the glass.

'I daren't drink too much,' she says mournfully, 'I'm driving back up to Edinburgh tomorrow morning.'

'Just a couple each,' I reply, my worries beginning to melt away in her presence. Having another person around is enough to take my mind off everything. My insular existence is a double-edged sword, allowing me time and space to write whilst also allowing my mind to ponder over worries that are often best left untouched. It's a less attractive trait of mine, treading over old ground until the furrow is a yawning abyss.

'Oh,' Carrie says suddenly, rummaging in her bag. 'I almost forgot. Dad says you might want to take a look at this.'

She hands me a small memory card, placing it on my upturned palm. I glance at her quizzically.

'He said it's from the wildlife camera in his back garden.' Her face flushes. She blinks and bats away a rogue eyelash, squinting and looking away. We both avoid the inevitable conversation, the reason she handed it over. That night. All that blood.

'Ah, okay. Tell him thank you. I'll take a look at it for sure.' Part of me wants to put it into my computer immediately and part of me is so full of dread at what I might find that I am overcome with a bout of dizziness. Would Mr Waters really hand me footage of me doing something dreadful to an innocent animal? I cannot believe he would ever do such a thing.

'He said you were probably worried so he wanted to put your mind at rest.' Carrie zips up her bag, her manner brightening.

I sigh, a softness taking hold deep in my abdomen. Good old Mr Waters. And good old Carrie. I slip the memory card into my pocket, take a sip of wine, rest my head back against the cushion. Sometimes, it's hard to remember how to relax, to feel normal and just be me, not Grace the grieving wife, not Grace the distant mother and isolated author working alone day after day, and not Grace the younger sister who needs to be kept in her place with sharp words and tight, unforgiving glances. I am going to have to learn how to just be me, to be comfortable in my own skin, not a jagged version of myself, all angular and ill fitting, limbs and bones protruding from stretched and badly fitting flesh slung around my frame.

We chat about anything and everything, promising to stay in touch as the evening draws to a close. Everything feels so easy with Carrie, so effortless and comfortable.

I find myself wishing it was this way with Kim. It is as if the age gap between us makes it more difficult for us to bond. Or perhaps it's because she refuses to get drawn into conversations about our past. There are always shadows there with Kim, things we cannot speak about. I often wonder if she is simply too fragile to open up about what happened, that her tough veneer is simply a mask concealing a frightened woman who finds it all too traumatic to confront.

We head into the hallway, our footsteps in sync with each other, our chatter drawing to a natural close.

'I'm hoping to visit Dad more often so hopefully we'll see a lot more of each other.' Carrie leans forward and gives me a hug, her breath misting into a tiny sphere as we stand on the doorstep.

'I'd like that. I really would.' Something moves inside me, a spark of hope exploding in my belly, giving me a warm glow.

'And anytime you feel like getting away from it all, you are more than welcome to come and visit us up in Scotland.'

We exchange numbers and she heads back into her Dad's cottage, giving me a brief wave before disappearing completely.

There is an unfamiliar lightness in my step as I close the door and lock it. Even Warren's philandering doesn't drag me down. Having a new friend has filled a gap in my life, renewed my sense of purpose.

I make a coffee, biding my time and preparing myself mentally before I view Mr Waters' footage on my laptop. I pull up a chair, flop down into it, my knuckles white as they grip the base of the cup. The boom of the clock in the background is an eerie echo as I sit, waiting for the computer to switch itself on, the black screen flickering to life.

It loads up. A picture fills the screen. It's a dark setting but I can see Mr Waters' back garden and a section of my lawn. I wait for two or three minutes, a thrumming sensation building in my temple and am just about to fast forward it when I see a sudden movement at the bottom end of my garden. Two small creatures scuffling, their shadowy outlines prominent against the pale grey of the grass that is silvered by the moonlight. A sudden jerking movement then a parting of the outlines as one of the shadows scurries away, disappearing into the shrubbery. The mound on the grass is still. No movement.

Another minute or so passes before I see it. I swallow, rub at my eyes, nerves tingling under my flesh, fluttering in my belly, exploding in my head. It's me, my outline, walking towards the amorphous lump laid on the lawn. All around me is still. A slight swaying of the trees but nothing else. I watch myself bend down and suppress a shriek as I pick it up, the limp body of the dead fox. I stand cradling it, rocking it like a baby, holding it close to me before sitting down and placing it on my lap. My head is rested against its body, my legs forming a shelf on which I lay it. On and on it goes, the same motion of rocking and cradling, cuddling and attempting to soothe a dead, bloodied animal.

I have no idea whether to be relieved or horrified. What in God's name did Mr Waters think when he watched this? Shame and revulsion pulse through me.

And yet I am also immensely relieved. I didn't kill it. I definitely did not kill that fox. As Mr Waters suggested, it was another animal, possibly a badger or maybe another fox. I couldn't quite make it out in the darkness but what I do know is that it wasn't me. I didn't do it. Why I decided to pick it up and curl it around my body will always be a mystery but at least I can rest easy knowing I am not the one who brought that poor animal's life to an end.

I pull out the memory card, having seen enough, with a promise to myself that I will go and see Mr Waters tomorrow after Carrie has left. I will thank him whilst also trying to explain why I was there in the garden in the early hours of the morning. He must think me unbalanced and that troubles me. I want to reassure him that I haven't taken leave of my senses and am not going down the same route as my mother. Having that conversation is important to me. My deep-rooted fear of developing dementia has bothered me a great deal since Mum took ill.

I am constantly having to prove to myself that my mind is as alert as ever. That's why the bouts of sleepwalking have caused me so much anxiety. Being out of control frightens me. It makes me feel vulnerable and exposed, like a small child left alone, frightened and dazed. Unable to cope.

The room is plunged into darkness as I flick off the lights and head upstairs, ready for my bed. I pray I stay put as I slip in between the sheets. On impulse, I get back up, pull on my dressing gown and head back downstairs. I check both the front and back door are locked, slide the bolts across and place the keys up on a shelf in the kitchen, covering them with a heavy, precariously placed vase. If I manage to move that in my sleep, it will surely slip and fall, waking me with a start. This is what I need to do to guard myself from my night-time wanderings. Nobody else is going to do it for me. I am the only person who can protect me from me.

I climb back into bed, tiredness washing over me, the wine, the conversation, Carrie's kind face and words taking me off to a place of warmth and safety where nothing and nobody matters.

* * *

I am in Simon's bedroom. His covers are pulled back, his sheets crumpled, the indent where his head has been, a small, dark hollow on the pillow. Where is he? I turn to look for him but the room is empty, everything washed out and tinged with shades of grey. The wardrobe seems enormous, towering over me like a skyscraper. Kneeling on the bed, I pull open the curtains and peer into the garden. It's dark out. I think I can see something, perhaps a flicker of a movement, but I can't be sure. It's night-time out there – the trees and flowers no more than shadowy masses, undefinable shapes in the silvery light. My eyes are heavy. I'm tired. I don't know how I got here and I don't know where Simon is. Everything feels different, as if something awful is about to happen.

A sound comes from behind me. I spin around, looking. It's not Simon and it's not Kim. Noises from the room next door. I hear the familiar creak of my parents' bed as somebody gets up, then the shuffle of feet as they head towards where I am kneeling. My back stiffens, my skin is cold with something that I can't put into words and don't quite understand. Fear? Why am I frightened?

I lean away from the window, my limbs hanging as I wait. What exactly am I waiting for?

The door opens a crack, a thin shaft of light sweeping across the carpet. Then a face peering around the jamb, eyes staring at me, a furrowed brow and a gruff voice that calls my name...

I am bent over, my body almost double, my arms hanging by my sides. I blink, straighten up and look around. I'm in the room I sometimes use as a study – Simon's old bedroom. The room Mum used to tidy regularly in anticipation of Simon's return. When it became clear he wasn't coming back, she removed the old wardrobe and replaced it with her sewing machine and a small stool.

My eyes are glued together, a viscous film blurring my vision. I rub at them with my fists, blinking repeatedly. I am standing next to the window, the blinds pulled roughly aside. Some of the plastic connectors that hold the pieces of fabric together have been snapped. Did I do this? Even as I'm thinking it, I know it to be true.

The memory flows back into my mind. The memory of being in here, unable to find Simon. Then my father coming in and sending me back to bed, his manner gruff, his eyes narrow with suspicion as he scanned the room after seeing Simon's bed empty.

I try to recall the events of that evening and the following morning.

Simon was there, sitting at the breakfast table. He didn't go missing that night. I am sure of it. So where was he? Why wasn't he in his bed? Maybe I'm getting it wrong, the chronology of that period in our lives skewed and out of sync. I was very young. It was a long time ago. I wish it was clearer in my mind, not a mish-mash of dates and faces and strange occurrences.

My skin is cold, chilled by the lack of heating in this room. I rub at my arms, shivering and staring at the wall clock. 2 a.m. I'm not outside. This is good. Did I try both doors and give up when I couldn't move the bolts or locate the keys? Part of me wants to go down there and take a look but the greater, fatigued part of me wants nothing more than to go back to bed and curl up in the warmth, to stay there until morning.

I pad along to my bedroom, the memory of Simon's empty bed refusing to leave my mind. I'm missing something here, something important. I just don't know what it is. I wish I had been older when he disappeared, older and with a clearer picture of what took place leading up to that evening but as it is, my memories are disjointed, the timeline not quite fitting together in my head. The images I have are fragmented and disconnected – a day is a week, a week a month. It's all too distant, too jumbled to decipher with any real accuracy.

The warmth of my bed is a welcome break from the cool air of the room. I pull the quilt tightly around my body and close my eyes, willing everything to go away, willing my relentless thoughts to just stop. Just a few nights of uninterrupted sleep. That's all I want. A couple of dream-free nights. Perhaps even a week. At this moment, I would give almost anything to put a stop to this sleepwalking and spend all night every night safe in my own bed.

I close my eyes, my hands gripping the covers, and drift off.

13

The vase slips out of my grasp, falls to the floor and bounces along the tiles, coming to rest against the far wall of the kitchen. I bend to retrieve it, amazed at its durability, thankful that it stayed put for the night and wasn't disturbed by my nightly rambles around the house as I searched for door keys.

I place it back in its usual position and remove the hidden keys, thinking how sad and desperate it is that I have to do such a thing. The two halves of me continually battling against one another, the sane, wakeful side doing what I can to keep the sleeping, unbalanced other half of me from carrying out something terrible, something dangerous while I am locked in another nocturnal world, unaware of my own movements and thoughts.

Perhaps I should see a doctor? I have no idea what they could they do other than dole out advice which would be to do what I am already doing – lock all doors and hide the keys from myself. Either that or they could refer me to a sleep clinic. I brush away that thought. I would rather work my way through this on my own without any interventions from specialists or therapists. After Warren's death, I saw a grief counsellor for a few sessions. It helped, but I don't want to revert to that time, to be reminded of it. I will simply push on through, solve it on my own without the assistance of any professionals.

I clear away the breakfast pots and sit at my computer, my mind telling me I should continue with my novel, my heart screaming that I should find out what I can about Simon's disappearance: print out every article I can find, start a new file and cram it full of evidence.

In preparation, I write Simon's name at the top of a folder, pick up the memory card and head next door to see Mr Waters. Once I have handed it back, I can focus all my energies on gleaning as much information as I can about Simon from the internet.

* * *

He looks old. Even older than he did last week. He is old, I know that, but I still have a picture in my head of Mr Waters as a middle-aged man with a young family. Up close, I can see that the years have taken their toll on him, as they do on all of us.

I hold out my hand, the memory card laid in my palm. 'Thank you for letting me see this. I'm glad I didn't do anything – well – anything to harm that animal. I was sleepwalking.' It rushes out of me, my disclosure, a slight wheeze screeching through my chest, bursting out into the open.

'I figured as much,' he says utterly unfazed by what I have just said, and at that moment, I want to hug him.

There is no awkwardness, no sense of being judged. And no look of shock at my revelation. Just two neighbours, two friends of old standing, chatting on the doorstep.

'Thought you'd want to see it, y'know, to put yer mind at rest.' He takes the card and slots it in his shirt pocket, the moment already forgotten.

'Thank you. And yes, it has.'

Behind him, I hear Carrie and Ted, the rustle of clothing and the unmistakable sounds of a toddler who is resisting any attempts to dress him. I smile and step away, keen to leave them alone. Family time is precious. That much I do know.

'Took me back it did, seeing you outside like that at night. I weren't sure it was you at first but then after seeing you on the camera, well, I knew then what had happened. Like I said, took me right back to when you were a bairn.'

I freeze, ice-cold water running through me, gravity trying to pull me downwards.

The Midnight Child. You were The Midnight Child, Grace.

And then within a matter of seconds, the easy moment is gone, turned brittle, just like that, our moment of understanding ready to snap in two with one rogue sentence. I have no idea what to say next, how to extricate myself from this conversation.

He remembers. Mr Waters remembers my bouts of sleepwalking from when I was little. What else does he remember from my past? Does he recall anything about Simon going missing, and if so, what? Everything suddenly feels so fragile, my life under a microscope, my movements monitored and measured. And if Mr Waters can remember, why can't I? It should be me who has ownership of my past, my childhood memories, not the elderly man who lives in the house next door to me.

I want to ask him, every fibre of me screaming to say those words out loud. And if I do, will he answer me? And what if the answer he gives me isn't something that I want to hear?

'Did I do it often, the sleepwalking?' I want to blink away the grit that has gathered behind my eyes, to rest awhile on his step and lean my head against the door jamb. Weariness gnaws at me. A dull ache has set in at the base of my skull.

'Can't say I recall. It was just what you did. Your parents hid the keys but you always managed to somehow find 'em, and then they put a bolt on both doors and that seemed to stop it.' He stares off over my shoulder, a nostalgic look in his eyes that reminds me of childhoods past and soft, summer days. And Simon. Oh God, I want *so* much to ask him about Simon, about what he can remember, whether or not he joined in the search for him, what he thinks actually happened that night. Does he believe Simon was taken or does he think that my brother wandered off on his own one evening, never to return, inadvertently stumbling into a catastrophic accident? I think of the river, the disused quarry a few miles away, the dizzying drop from a viewing point just off the main road through the village. And then something else pushes into my brain.

'The bolt,' I say suddenly, aware my question may sound slightly irrational, deranged even. 'Was it fitted before or after Simon went missing?' Warmth rises up my neck. I am uncomfortable and clammy, a wave of heat travelling up my body, coming to rest on my scalp. Tiny jolts of electricity needle their way through my hair follicles.

I'm not sure what sort of response I expect. It happened such a long time ago. Mr Waters is in his late eighties. We have both led full lives, other things that have happened since that night, life and its many associated memories taking up space in our heads. What I don't expect is for him to reply so quickly and with such alacrity.

'Oh, it was fitted before he went missing.' His eyes are firmly fixed on me now, a look of kindness shining through the rheumy film and the cataracts that impair his sight. I know that Kim is wrong about this man, about the rumours that he was cruel to his family. He cannot be the person she claims he is. It just isn't possible. 'I remember it 'cos of the police interviews, you see,' he says, cutting into my thoughts. 'They came round here, knocking on doors and the like, and I told 'em straight that your mum had told me about your sleepwalking and how they had had to get a bolt fitted to stop you straying outside.'

A weakness takes hold of me, a relief valve inside my body letting everything go, turning my limbs into putty, my bones suddenly liquid soft. I didn't take Simon. I couldn't have. There was a bolt locking us both inside. I was a small child. Dear God, the release I feel from a worry that has nagged at me since hearing Carrie's words is immense. Simon may have been frightened by my sleepwalking, but he wasn't actually frightened of *me*. I was his younger sister. I wasn't, am still not, a monster. My eyes fill up, a veil of tears obscuring my view of him, this wonderful man who has helped me so much. I have to stop myself from lunging forward and wrapping my arms around him.

Then more thoughts jostle for space in my mind – how did Simon get out if we had a bolt fitted on the door? None of it makes any sense. In fact, with this new piece of information, it makes even less sense than it did before. He can't have just wandered off, can he?

'Did the police give any indication of what they thought might have happened to my brother?' Once again, I find myself desperately wishing we were a more open-minded family, speaking about our tragedies. I tried. I really did, still do. But mine is the perpetual lone voice, whistling in the wind.

'They searched the entire village and beyond. They questioned everyone who lived here and even those who didn't, stopping tourists and visitors and the like, checking local hotels and guest houses and interviewing people who'd stayed there when he went missing but nowt came of it. The bolt was pushed back, you see. When your parents got up the next morning, the bolt was pushed back, the door unlocked and Simon was gone.' Mr Waters shakes his head wearily. 'It was as if he just vanished into thin air. And without a body, there's not much they could have done. No body, no evidence, you see.'

I wince, his last sentence slicing into me. He's right. Of course he is, but after years of not speaking about it, saying it only in my head, it feels alien to hear it spoken out loud.

'Aye, I'm sorry, lass. I spoke out of turn there. Got a big mouth on me, I have. Comes with living alone. Nobody to rein me in or tell me when to shut up.' He shakes his head sadly and I cannot reassure him fast enough, everything tumbling out of me, a flood of words to make him see that this is exactly what I want to hear. Need to hear, whether I want to or not. Sometimes, we have to face our demons in order to overpower them.

'No, please. Don't apologise. You're right. You are completely correct. Mum and Kim refuse to talk about this. It's refreshing to broach the subject and speak freely. Moving back here has pushed it all back into my mind, Simon going missing, and I can't seem to think about anything else. With that and the sleepwalking, it's like I've stepped back in time. There are days when it's like I've never been away.' The more I speak, the more I realise this is true. Despite having lived in London for over five years, then spending another five years living abroad, reluctantly relocating back to the UK once the children were born, it feels as if I have never been away. Woodburn Cottage has dragged me back to the person I was all those years ago. The Midnight Child. That's me. Nothing has changed. My life has come full circle and I'm not sure if that's a good thing or not.

'It were an awful time for you all for sure. And then there was the accident. Your poor old dad...'

I nod. It's no surprise that this episode of our lives has never left him, the memories still fresh in his mind. Negative events have a tendency to jar, leaving a deeper imprint than positive ones.

There was talk at the time of Dad planning his own death, neighbours and local gossips putting their own slant on it, making sure their warped version of events was being talked about, but the coroner recorded it as accidental. He had been upstairs painting the bedroom windows when he fell. Disturbed by heights, he had been leaning out, attempting to paint the outside rather than going up a ladder, when he leaned too far and fell to his death on the patio. Why would he go to the bother of painting and then suddenly throw himself out of the window? Why not just jump? And much like Simon's disappearance, we accepted it and moved on, rarely speaking of it, each of us going about our daily duties like little automatons, programmed to do our work and simply exist. They were joyless, silent years, speaking of anything other than our loss.

Is it any wonder I now need to unearth our family secrets? I have been forced into muteness for so many years now and refuse to endure it for any longer. All those decades of pent-up worry and concern. All those years of being denied the true facts by those closest to me. I am practically bursting at the seams, so many questions scratching at me, itching to be free.

'Anyway, it's good to have you living here, Grace.' Mr Waters' eyes crinkle at the corner as he smiles. He dips his head, slips his hand in his pockets. His skin is tanned, leathery and well-worn but his mind is as sharp as ever.

'It's good to be back here,' I reply. And it is. Despite my worries and the disquietude I harbour because of my sleepwalking, despite the need to know about Simon that has hijacked my life of late, I am glad to be back in Woodburn Cottage. And I'm glad that Mr Waters still lives next door. He is a part of my past and not the monster Kim painted. Her view of the world is crooked, her view of people often murky and lacking in compassion.

'I just wish I could 'ave helped more when the police questioned me but I had Jean to think of, you see.'

'Jean?' I bite at my lip, narrow my eyes, unsure where this is heading. Jean was a timid, mouse-like creature.

'Aye. It were her problems, you see. Mental health they call it nowadays. Back then, we just knew it as a funny turn or were told by doctors that she were just bad with her nerves. And she had plenty of 'em, those funny turns. I kept things running as smoothly as I could in the house but it weren't easy. The night Simon went missing, Jean and I had slept in the front bedroom. She were convinced that aliens would see us if we slept in our usual room out the back. The week before that, she had told me that the newsreaders were sending signals to her through the TV aerial and were planning on kidnapping her.' He shakes his head and sighs. 'As I said, it weren't always easy and I admit to losing my temper wi' her on more than one occasion but I did love her and always tried my best. I often think that if I hadn't been trying to console and quieten her down, then maybe I would 'ave heard something and could 'ave helped a bit more wi' police enquiries, but as it was, I were hunkered down wi' my wife, trying to calm her and reassure her that nobody was trying to hurt her or take her away.'

A sadness balloons inside me, the strands of Kim's words all weaving together, forming the fabric of Mr Water's life. All those gossipmongers and tittle-tattlers, standing in queues at the marketplace, dissecting this poor man's life, sprinkling it with untruths, embellishing it for the sake of entertainment and a need to feel superior about their own sad little existences. A tapestry of heartache and depression and grief. We weren't the only family suffering. Behind every closed door lies a combination of sweetness and sorrow. And yet, hearing of this makes me less burdened, as if a sharing of our problems makes us all the more human. We all have something to hide. Something to drag us down and make us wonder if life is always going to be this difficult.

We say our goodbyes and I make my way home, feeling lighter than I was just ten minutes ago. Things are easier to bear knowing Mr Waters is close by, knowing he had his own set of problems and is in a position to understand mine. He is like a comforter, a reminder of a past that, although not particularly pleasant, belongs to me. Simon has been hidden away for long enough. It's time to let him out into the light again, to hear his name spoken, to think of his lovely, smiling face without feeling riddled with fear and guilt.

And Kim can either come with me on this journey that I intend to travel, or she can step aside and watch. I don't care either way.

14

The phone is ringing as I step through the door, its shrill tone jangling at my nerves. I snatch it up and breathe a hurried *hello* into the handset, then stop dead as I hear Gavin speaking on the other end of the line.

'Hi Mum. You okay?' My son's voice will always have the power to stop me in my tracks. I hadn't realised how much he sounded like his father until his father passed away and I could no longer hear him. It is uncanny the similarity in tone and timbre, and it catches me off guard, my chest tightening, my scalp prickling.

But then I can't stop myself and I smile, a broad grin borne out of relief, something else that occurs whenever I speak to either of my children. A warmth spreads through me, heating up my blood, making me feel very much alive, the not half-dead creature I have become of late.

'Gavin! It's so lovely to hear from you. I'm absolutely fine but all the better for hearing your voice.'

I take a seat and lean my head against the small cushion of the high-backed chair. I want to savour every word that passes between us, to listen endlessly to my son's voice, be reminded of the boy he once was and the man he has become. The miles may have carved a distance between us, both of us separated by continents miles wide and by oceans and seas fathoms deep, but for me, he will always be close by. My son. My boy. Forever etched in my heart.

'Good, good. Glad to hear it. I've got something to tell you and I think it might please you.'

I place my free hand over my eyes, shielding it from the glow of the rising sun. My lungs feel solid, every breath suspended deep in my chest. Outside, a magpie pecks at the lawn, tugging at an unsuspecting worm, yanking at it relentlessly until its long, slim body slithers into the bird's beak and disappears down its throat. I close my eyes and wait, thinking of how cruel animals can be to one another just to survive. How cruel people can be to each other. How cruel Warren was, doing what he did to me. I stop, take a breath, block it from my mind, focusing instead on the moment. On my son.

'That's lovely. Pleasing news is always welcome.' My voice sounds disembodied, the words I speak coming from somewhere else. Somebody else. I think of this piece of news, visualise a wedding, a lavish affair in a country thousands of miles away, a country I don't recognise; Gavin and Gemma tying the knot and settling in to their lives half a world away. Then I think of a grandchild, seeing them only once every decade, our bond too difficult to forge, fractured and severed by time and distance. What I don't expect is what he says next.

'I'm coming home to live again. If you'll have me, that is? Or should I say, us.'

Blood rushes to my head. The room spins. My heart is a rapid beat in my chest, a small pulse of excitement throbbing beneath my skin. Coming home? To the UK? Or here, with me in Woodburn Cottage? Either is fine by me. More than fine. It's the best news I've heard in a long, long time. Dare I hope that this is true and not some kind of false, empty promise made on whim, Gavin completely unaware of how devastating it would be for me if it doesn't come to fruition. Dare I actually truly hope that after five long years, he is really coming back to England for good?

'Home? Here with me?' I swallow. A tic takes hold in my jaw, a small gavel thumping against my skin. 'I mean, of course it's okay. More than okay. It's amazing news. You are more than welcome.' Already, I am mentally planning how to redecorate the spare bedroom, the one that used to be mine when I was a child. I could buy some new bedroom furniture, a new bed perhaps. Maybe some new blinds, or even some of those modern shutters that everyone seems to be getting fitted. Their house in Perth is spacious, minimal. They won't want to be surrounded by any fancy frills or clutter. It will make them feel hemmed in, claustrophobic even after having all that space. I think all of these things as Gavin tells me about how he has been offered a new job, the one he has always dreamed of and how it is too good an opportunity to turn down even though he expected to spend the rest of his days in Australia and had no plans to return to England.

'Sales director for the whole of the UK, Mum. Double the salary, which we will really benefit from as it's more expensive living here in Australia than it is in England. We'll hopefully be quids in. So we won't be with you for too long. We'll have a deposit saved up for our own property in no time at all. As soon as we find the right house, we'll be out of your hair, I promise.'

'I don't mind, darling. Stay here as long as you like.' Already, I am grieving for them moving out, feeling an emptiness within before they have booked their tickets back to England. I have to stop this, getting ahead of myself. A hundred hoops have to be jumped through before any of that happens. I should simply enjoy the moment, hold onto the excitement and build-up to their arrival. This a positive memory in the making. I shall cling onto it, treasure it. Every good thing that happens here is a step towards banishing the bad stuff.

'We've got a month left on the lease for this place so the move should be easy and will hopefully work out really well for us. The board would like me to start as soon as possible so once we've got our tickets booked, it's all systems go.' I can hear the exhilaration in his voice, can almost feel the adrenaline as it surges through him at the thought of this next step in his life. He is on his way up that corporate ladder, my boy. His father would be proud.

After gaining his degree in engineering, Gavin decided to go backpacking with Gemma, take a year out before he settled down to the world of work. He got a work permit once he reached Australia and was offered a job in Perth a few months later. That felt like the end for me and I immediately resigned myself to having a long-distance relationship with my son and possible grandchildren. I didn't expect him to ever come back. They were so enamoured by the lifestyle over there, embracing the outdoors and their new social circle that I genuinely felt their future was sealed. And now here we are, coming full circle. Gavin returning to my childhood home in Hempton. North Yorkshire may not have the sweeping golden beaches of Perth or the year-round sunshine, but it has its own unique charm, a softer, gentler allure that once experienced, is hard to forget.

'This is marvellous, darling. I am so happy for you both. Give Gemma my love.'

We talk some more, Gavin promising to give me the dates for flights once they are booked, telling me not to do anything too fancy to the spare room. 'Honestly, Mum, we'll both be so busy working, you won't even know we're there.'

I pray he is wrong about that. I want to see him as often as possible, and Gemma too, to hear their voices, to have some life breathed back into this house again. They will bring it alive, the two of them, giving it the happiness and joy it so desperately needs. I am not enough, just me, a middle-aged, sad, old lady rattling around this place on my own day after day. It needs some vibrancy. Some youth and laughter and happiness. And if anybody can provide that, it is these two wonderful people.

I am bereft as we end the call, an emptiness settling around me, a tight veil of anticipation that refuses to loosen until my son sets foot in that door and I can hug him, to feel the strength of his arms around me as he reciprocates my affections. We have a lot of years to catch up on. His visit to England for his father's funeral was brief. Too brief. Here one minute, gone the next. Barely time to talk or grieve. He stayed for only two days. I was too wrapped up in my grief and shock to notice his presence, to truly appreciate the fact that he was here. But that is all about to change. Our lives are about to change. For the first time in a long time, things are looking up.

* * *

'That's good. It will help you to get over everything that's happened. You know my feelings about you living there on your own so we won't even go into it. I'm happy for you, Grace. I really am.' Kim is stirring her tea, her eyes downcast as she speaks. The biscuit makes a sharp snapping sound when she breaks it in half.

Even when we are out, purportedly having a good time, socialising, drinking coffee, eating cake, she cannot seem to help herself, taking every opportunity to reaffirm her superiority over me, making sure my family affairs gain her approval. I sip at my latte, regretting taking her up on her offer of coming here to our usual place, the small café on the corner of the high street. I should have gone with my gut instinct, stayed home and revelled in the happiness and warmth I felt after speaking to my son, but here I am, being put in my place again by somebody who is certain she knows my life better than I do, and feels it is her duty to control it and steer it in the right direction.

Again. I have no idea why I keep putting myself through this, apart that is, from loyalty. But of course, it's not always this bad. There are times when Kim is kind and thoughtful, when she is humorous and makes me laugh till my belly aches. She has helped me many times over the years. And then there are occasions, such as this one, when her manner, the command she has over me is all encompassing, stifling me to the point where I can't breathe properly.

'I'm loving being back in Woodburn Cottage and yes, I'm delighted that Gavin and Gemma are coming home. His promotion is well deserved. Warren would be proud of him.' I speak clearly, every word enunciated, spoken with true passion and pride. There are days when I am lonely. There are days when thoughts of Simon and his disappearance from our home continually prod at me but today is not one of those days. Today, I am blissfully happy and I refuse to let my sister spoil that feeling.

Kim's face flushes dark pink, shadows sitting beneath her eyes. She bites at her lip, takes a sip of her coffee, wincing at the hot liquid as it touches her lips. She recoils, slumps back in her chair and runs her fingers through her hair, weariness oozing out of her in bucketloads. What she has to feel weary about, I will never know. Life has always fallen in her lap, the easy routes that the rest of us have had to carefully navigate with precision to stay on track, presented to her on a golden platter.

'I know you think I'm bossy but I'm just trying to protect you, that's all.' Her words cut across the air between us, whip like. I shuffle in my seat, suddenly uncomfortable. A cold finger traces its way up my spine. 'It's all I've ever tried to do, Grace. I just want you to know that. I only ever wanted to protect you and look after you.'

When I do speak, my voice is shrill, like the scrape of metal against metal, loud and discordant. Heads turn to stare at me. I lower my tone, begin to whisper, moving closer to Kim, flickering flames simmering beneath my skin.

'Protect me?' I say heatedly, my voice low and hoarse. 'What on earth are you talking about, Kim? Protect me from what? I'm a grown woman, for Christ's sake. Who or what do I need protecting from?'

Her eyes are dark, something lurking there that I don't recognise as she lifts her gaze and stares at me. When she does speak, the room takes on different dimensions, the ground falling away beneath me, the walls leaning in drunkenly. My head throbs at her words, the intent behind them. She looks away, her shoulders hunched.

'Yourself, Grace. You need protecting from yourself. You always have, probably always will.'

15

I stand up. A noise escapes from my throat – a wheeze, like an animal in its death throes. Stars burst behind my eyes at my abrupt movement. I blink, steady myself, shake Kim's hand away from mine. The chair scrapes across the tiled floor as she stands up, tries again to place her arm around my shoulder. I shrug it off and turn to leave, concentrating on my feet, making sure I keep my balance and stay upright. Making sure I don't turn around and tell my only sister to fuck right off.

I haven't paid. It occurs to me that I don't actually care. Kim can sort it out, just like she sorts out and takes control of everything else in my life. I keep on walking, focusing on my feet, eyes downcast, body rigid. My spine feels like a steel rod has been inserted into it. Every step is an effort yet I stride ahead, refusing to stop, to turn around and look at Kim. I don't want to see her expression, to see the look of superiority on her face. I just want to go home. Back to Woodburn Cottage, the place where I belong, where I have always belonged.

The air outside is chilly, welcoming. I gasp, take in lungfuls of it, feel the cooling breeze as it passes over my skin, caressing me, calming me.

I stagger home, my gaze fixed ahead, back straight.

Keep on walking. Don't stop, just keep going. Don't look back. Ignore her words. Ignore her.

Kim has no idea why I reacted the way I did. Or maybe she does. She knew about my childhood episodes of sleepwalking. Did she know that Simon was scared of me back then? That my nocturnal wanderings frightened him? I'd be surprised if she didn't. She appears to know everything else about me and my life.

You need protecting from yourself. You always have.

I could have stayed, argued with her, asked her what she meant, but to what end? We would have gone around in circles, getting nowhere fast. Easier to conserve my energy, put it to better use elsewhere. Anger is exhausting. Putrefying and pointless.

What did I do back then? Is that what she meant? What the fuck did I do to make my own brother scared of me, for my own sister to tell me that I need and have always needed protecting from myself? What sort of a monster am I?

By the time I reach my front door, I have convinced myself that I did something terrible to Simon, that I was somehow responsible for him going missing. Trauma can wreak havoc with a person's mind, conceal memories, block out important, life-changing events. Is that what I have done? Harmed my own brother and suppressed the memory?

I am barely in the front door before vomit rises up my throat, burning my gullet. Dizzy and sick, I rush to the kitchen sink and lean my head over the porcelain, heaving repeatedly until my stomach is empty. I stand up, wipe my mouth with the back of my hand, try to clear my muddied thoughts, studying everything in greater detail.

Jesus Christ, what is happening to me? An hour ago, I was deliriously happy and now look at me, at what I have become. I'm a blubbering wreck, barely able to speak or think lucidly. This is the pendulum of my life, my emotions swinging wildly, oscillating between elation and despair in a matter of minutes with very little in between. I need to stop this, to get a hold of my emotions. I'm better than this. Better and stronger.

I gulp in more air – in through my nose, out through my mouth. I'm reading too much into Kim's words. They came at a bad time, that's all it is. I am being over-analytical, looking for flaws in my character, sifting through the sediment of her words and trying to connect the bits together regardless of how incongruous and clunky they may be. Gavin is coming home soon and I will hang onto that fact, use it as a focal point in my life, allowing myself the luxury of excitement and hope at his impending arrival.

What I need to do is avoid any future coffee dates with my older, overbearing sister. I head upstairs to freshen up, splashing my face with cold water, combing my hair and brushing my teeth. A minty zing bounces around my mouth as I sit down at my computer, rejuvenated and ready to do battle with my latest manuscript.

* * *

It's two hours later when I come up for air, my wrists and back sore from poor posture whilst hunched over a laptop, my eyes heavy from focusing on an unfiltered screen. I lean back in my chair, stretch, yawn and stare outside, observing the birds that flit around the garden foraging for food, their small bodies dipping in and out of the shrubbery and hedgerows that line the perimeter of the lawn.

How little it has changed out there. I'm relieved about that fact. There is a certain level of comfort to be gained from knowing that time has all but stood still in this house. The same rose bushes are dotted about, strung up against the fence, the same old shed in the far corner of the garden, half hidden by undergrowth and ivy that has snaked over the wooden slats, creeping over the exterior like some monstrous creature trying to swallow it whole. One day soon, I will go out there, cut it back. The same brick coalhouse that provides a perfect place for mice to nest. They're all there, standing the test of time.

It will be good to see that garden shed again. It holds such wonderful memories for me: days spent in there as a child playing; pretending to work in an office, sitting at an old desk that Dad had put in there simply because there was nowhere else for it to go. I remember shrieking at Simon that he was late and needed to clock in while I scribbled on large pieces of paper. I was the office manager and poor Simon was the junior clerk, forever at my mercy as I handed him lists of jobs, telling him I would dock his wages if he continued coming in late. We even had an old phone, a heavy, Bakelite model with a cupped mouthpiece that just about covered the lower half of my face. Glorious times they were, now forever stained with the murkiest of memories.

I make a coffee, sit back at my laptop and don't look up again until after three o'clock. My stomach howls at me, a loud, grating sensation that rumbles deep in my abdomen, reminding me that I haven't eaten anything after bringing up my breakfast earlier in the day.

On a whim, I decide to head out to the high street to pick up a snack. I do this rarely and view it as a treat.

Ignoring my flashing phone, knowing it will be Kim wanting to analyse our conversation, to question my abrupt exit, insisting she said nothing wrong, I head outside. The wind has built in strength, snatching the breath right out of me as I pull on my jacket and lock the door. The weather from this morning has lost its calm, morphing into an angry squall with the grey, bulbous clouds overhead threatening rain.

Despite the drab weather and plummeting temperatures, it feels good to be out in the open, to be out on my own, free from the pressure of writing and thoughts of Simon and coffee dates with Kim. To simply be me, doing whatever I damn well feel like doing.

My cheeks are numb, my hands icy by the time I reach the row of small shops at the end of the street. I curl my fingers up into tight fists, tuck them deep in my pockets, my hair strewn over my eyes in long, messy strands.

A smattering of shoppers scurry past me, bags slung over arms, faces set like stone as they battle against the freezing wind. It's hard to tell what season it actually is with the ever-changing and unpredictable conditions that flash hot and cold from day to day, hour to hour.

I smell of the cold as I step inside, the aroma of the outside air clinging to my clothes, an earthy odour that transports me back to being a child, playing out in the street, running free, blissfully unaware of what the future held in store for me; for all of us. If we had known what lay ahead, would we have continued to get up every day and go about our daily activities or would we have chosen to stay in the safety of our beds, curling into a ball, hiding from the outside world and all the terror and suffering it throws our way? Simon was taken from his home, the place where he should have been safe. For all we know, he may have been taken from his bed. When we are not safe in those places, then what hope is there for any of us?

I brush away those shadowy thoughts and head down the narrow aisle, my clothes catching against the rows of breakfast cereals and loaves of bread.

I don't hear it at first. My mind is focused on filling my basket, attempting to work out what I can cook with two tins of peas, a packet of dried pasta and a jar of mayonnaise as I throw in random items without any planning or thought behind it.

It comes again, first as a noise in the background, then louder as the person speaking steps in front of me, blocking my way, their face looming over me, ghoul-like. 'Grace Goodwill. How many years has it been?'

The use of my maiden name catches me on the backfoot. I haven't heard it said out loud for so many years now that it sounds peculiar and awkward. A frisson of annoyance darts through me. This person knows me. I don't know them, their features unfamiliar as they continue to block my way. I don't like it. It is a hostile move, threatening and menacing, as if they are trying to intimidate me.

I narrow my eyes, concentrate, cast my mind back as far as I can and come up with nothing. The woman standing next to me has a face I should remember. With protruding, slightly yellowed teeth and skin the texture of gravel, I'm sure any memories I have of her would stay with me. She has an expression and features that are hard to forget and yet no matter how much I try, I am unable put a name to her face.

My mouth opens but nothing comes out. Asking who she is and why she is blocking my route feels discourteous and that's not who I am so I opt for saying nothing at all. Easier and less confrontational. I don't have the energy for guessing games or arguments. I just want to buy my goods and leave.

'You don't remember me? How can you not remember who I am, eh?'

I want to tell her that I have led a full life with many occurrences, both good and bad, and I am almost certain none of them involved her. But I don't. Instead, I smile and grit my teeth, apologising for no other reason than to get her out of my way.

'Janine Francis? I went to school with your sister, used to go to your house for tea? Once played in your garden and fell into a patch of nettles? Course that was probably before you were born. You were much younger than me and Kim so I doubt you'll even remember me. And then Kim went away for a while, didn't she, with her illness?' She bites at her mouth and sighs, her tombstone teeth tugging at a loose piece of skin.

I am about to ask her what she means by Kim's illness when she speaks again. 'I used to come to your house when you were little. Me and Kim would be getting ready to go out to the pub and you would hang around the bedroom asking to come with us. We'd sometimes put a bit of make-up on you, make you look like a little doll. And then your mum would give us what for and make us wash it all off.' She sighs and shakes her head, her eyes twinkling, those large teeth resting against her bottom lip, graceless and inelegant.

The memory of her presence in our house gradually slides into my brain. An image of a loud teenage girl prone to temper tantrums when things didn't go her way muscles its way into my mind. I smile and nod, then hold out my hand for her to shake which feels silly and inappropriate. I am just about to snatch it back when she takes it and smiles, her other hand covering mine as she throws back her head and laughs, a hearty, loud guffaw that seems to rattle every shelf in the shop.

'I knew we'd get there in the end. Once met, never forgotten, eh?' She winks at me, nodding furiously, a glint in her eye that indicates she has lots more to talk about. I listen to her chatter incessantly about her family, how they never left Hempton. 'Love it here, we do. Wouldn't want to live anywhere else.'

She talks relentlessly, saying plenty, most of it inconsequential. Empty babble that goes on and on and on. She mentions old school friends of Kim's, tells me about her husband and children, the passing of her parents last year, how she gave them the best send-off ever. 'Dad always said he wanted to go out with a bang and that's exactly what he got.' She goes on to explain that after the service, they let off fireworks in their back yard. 'We must have spent £100 on a whole load of bangers and Catherine wheels. Still,' she says suddenly lowering her voice, 'it was worth it. We only get one set of parents, don't we? Speaking of which, how's your Mum getting on in the home? Sad to see her decline and end up in there but after recent events and what happened in the town square that time, I suppose it's for the best, isn't it?'

My muscles go into spasm, every ounce of blood turning to ice in my veins. I want to ask. I don't want to ask. I can see by the look on her face that she is desperate for me to query her statement. I won't. I refuse. Turns out, I don't have to.

Before I have a chance to move away, it spills out of her, the sordid story of how, her mind trapped in the cruel grip of dementia, my mother had begun to undress in the middle of the town while passers-by looked on, horrified. When they attempted to help, she swatted them away, screaming that she would kill them all just like she killed the others. Kim has made no mention of this. I had enough to contend with at the time with Warren passing away so unexpectedly. Something squirms and swells in my guts, an uncoiling of anger towards my sister. I realise that I have been shielded from the worst of what took place with Mum, my sensitivities spared while my attentions were focused elsewhere.

Regret unfolds inside me. I feel a slow spread of warmth towards Kim, the fact she kept this piece of news from me, allowing me to deal with my own heartache while she quietly and swiftly dealt with her own: getting Mum assessed, finding a suitable care home, sorting out Woodburn Cottage and getting rid of all the clutter that Mum had acquired over the years. And she did it all without complaint or requests for assistance. Perhaps I was too rash back at the café. Maybe I overplayed my hand, was too quick to judge and come to a hasty conclusion.

My face heats up. I need to leave, to get away from Janine's salacious gossip and her manic expression, a smile that borders on a sneer. What sort of a person would revel in talking about such an unsavoury business? Anybody with an ounce of integrity would show compassion, remain quiet about what happened, allow my mother and her family to keep their dignity intact, but not this woman. I haven't seen her for probably four decades and here she is, talking openly and with a little too much fervour and excitement about an illness that has taken our mother from us and caused us untold heartache.

I place the basket down at my feet and for the second time today, walk out of a public building without saying goodbye, leaving behind a bemused individual who may or may not be aware of how close they came to being slapped hard across the face.

It's as I reach the door that I hear it again, her grating voice that carries over the air like the shriek of a dying animal, an injured wolf howling from its lair. 'So, what do you think she meant by it then, your mum? Who did she kill?'

The shop door slams shut behind me as I pull it closed, my vision attenuating, my legs pumping furiously, not slowing down until I reach the safety of Woodburn Cottage. I yank open the door, all but fall inside and lock it with trembling fingers. I lean back onto the wooden panels, the solidity of it giving me some succour, safety from the outside world.

Blinking back tears, I bite at my lip and whimper like a small child. They can all go to hell, every single one of them. Every neighbour, every onlooker, every purported friend that listened to the ramblings of my distressed and mentally ill mother and then gossiped about it afterwards, and especially Janine fucking Francis, the woman whose face looks like it has been subjected to a rigorous scrubbing against a particularly sharp cheese grater. As far as I'm concerned, they can all rot in hell.

16

'Why didn't you tell me?' I keep my tone even, almost at a whisper. My words are met with a stony silence. 'I'm not cross, Kim. Quite the opposite, in fact. I feel guilty that you had to deal with this on your own. I could have helped. It must have been horrific for you, having to sort out all Mum's things without me there to help you and having to deal with that incident in the town.'

I can almost hear her sigh with relief, a low moan at the other end of the line. I picture her sitting down, running her fingers through her hair as she leans back and closes her eyes, her mood loosening and softening yet with an undercurrent of suspicion and trepidation. Always on edge, waiting for thinly veiled criticisms. Always waiting for me to snap. 'Who told you about it?'

'An old school friend of yours. Janine somebody or other. A brash woman with flabby arms and huge, yellowed teeth. She looked like a baby walrus. Had all the grace and elegance of one too.'

For the first time in a very long time, Kim laughs. A hearty, genuine chuckle that is infectious. I smile and eventually join in, laughter gripping me until tears stream down my face and I have to sit down to compose myself.

'Oh God, she was a real character,' Kim says, gasping and wheezing as she tries to catch her breath. 'I'd forgotten all about her.'

'She hasn't forgotten about you,' I reply, my mind raking over our conversation. 'She told me all about you, the stuff you used to get up to when you were teenagers.'

Even without her being in the same room, I can feel the change in Kim's demeanour, another shift in her mood, a stiffening of her inner core as she braces herself for some imagined slight, some insult that is about to be thrown her way. 'What stuff? What did she mean by that?' And it is back, the sharpness in her voice, the previous moment forgotten, the happiness of earlier quickly disintegrating.

I wonder what I've said, how such an innocuous comment can result in this swift and unexpected change of mood.

'She just told me about how you would put make-up on me while you were getting ready to go out, that's all. And how Mum would tell you both off and make you wash it off me.'

I remind myself that this is why I get exasperated by Kim, why her sullen ways and unpredictable manner always put me on edge. Sometimes, it isn't worth the effort continuing with our conversations, the stilted chats that make me feel as if I am treading on hot coals. 'Have I said something wrong?' I prepare myself for her answer, for the volley of abuse that I expect her to fire my way.

Instead, she turns it around, blindsiding me with her answer. 'Maybe I should ask you the very same thing after you stormed out of the café and refused to reply to my texts and the list of missed calls that must have come up on your phone.' She is breathless, as if those words have been stored up in her head, waiting for an appropriate moment to come hurtling out.

I take a couple of seconds before replying, trying to formulate my answer, to get it pitch perfect and not add any further fuel to the fire. 'I'm sorry about that. I misinterpreted what you said. With the sleepwalking, I think I'm just tired, that's all.' I am not about to elaborate any further. And I am not going to ask what she meant by it. Not now when things have once again hardened between us, the atmosphere thick with growing animosity. Another time, perhaps. Or maybe not. I doubt Kim would ever open up to me. When it comes to our past, her shutters are permanently down, fixed into position with rods of iron.

Instead, I lighten the mood, shift the focus away from our failings and foibles, keep the conversation light, superficial. Easier that way. Safer.

'I'm going to redecorate the bedroom for Gavin and Gemma coming home. Nothing major – just a lick of paint and some new furniture. I was thinking of going for grey, keep it neutral. What do you think?'

And within seconds, our anger has been squashed back into that dark, dusty corner, the place that absorbs and hides our family secrets: secrets that are too painful to examine. We talk about muted shades of paint and quilt covers and oak wardrobes and anything that stops us from speaking openly about things that should be discussed. We don't deviate, keeping on about inane, pointless subjects until I tire of it and say my goodbyes, promising, despite my inner objections, to meet for coffee in our usual place later in the week. It's easier to agree than turn her down. Routine is what keeps us going. Without that, what exactly do we have?

* * *

The person on the other end of the line couldn't sound wearier and more disinterested if they tried. I am a voice from the past, a nuisance, somebody who is making more work for an already understaffed force. I have to do it though, regardless of the lack of funds and the necessary number of experienced staff to help me. I have to do it for Simon, for Mum. I have to do it for me.

'And you haven't come across any new evidence?'

Already I know that I am beating my head against a brick wall. I knew this before I made the call, that it would remain a cold case unless anything new turns up. I have nothing to offer them except my anger and frustration, and a deep and growing need to find out what happened to my brother.

'No, not as such.' My heart speeds up. My top lip is damp with perspiration.

'Not as such? So, you have something new?'

I close my eyes, wishing I had thought this through, seen my point of view through calculating and precise eyes. The eyes of a young police officer who wasn't even alive when Simon went missing.

'No. I don't have anything new on my brother's case but could somebody not take another look at it? Just cast an eye over the witness statements? Maybe see if any forensic evidence can be found and sent off for analysis? Also, I noticed that last year another boy of a similar age went missing. Maybe there's a connection?' Even as I say it, I know it's unlikely. Four-and-a-bit decades. How could they possibly be connected? And yet I will be remiss in my duties as a sister if I don't mention it.

There is a short silence at the other end of the line. I can hear her breathing, this Sergeant Duffield who is probably young enough to be my daughter. Her exasperation at this strange woman who wants to talk about a case from forty-odd years ago seeps through the line, waves of resentment and irritation at being subjected to a time waster.

'Look, how about I take your number and get back to you? All I can say is, unless we have new witnesses or evidence then I doubt we'll be able to take it any further, but let's not close things off just yet, eh?'

All of a sudden, I like this young lady. Her tone has switched from jaded to warm and friendly and at this time, it is just what I need. I hope she has sensed my desperation. I will cling onto anything, any shred of hope or any glimmer of interest in this case. Simon may be, in fact is almost certainly, dead, but my hope of finding out what happened to him is very much alive.

'Thank you. Thank you so much.' Tears build. I fight them back. Somebody appears to care, to understand my dilemma and can empathise with me. Nothing may come of this but at least I can say I tried. At least Sergeant Duffield is going to make an attempt at doing something and for that I am and will always be eternally grateful. She is my life raft in a cold sea of uncertainty.

I give her my number and hang up, already wondering when I will hear from her again. Maybe tomorrow, maybe never. I can't allow myself to become consumed by this. I need to crack on with my usual routine, not clock watch, waiting to hear back. Every second will feel like a minute, every minute an hour. There are other things I can do to take my mind off it. I have a book to write, a brother to find, a room to decorate. My life has suddenly become very full indeed.

* * *

Another search on the internet proves fruitless. More supposition and guesswork by strangers who have nothing better to do than write vulgar, trashy articles about my family and pass them off as blogs. Details are thin on the ground, time blurring the facts and erasing anything of note.

It all seems so pointless, precious time disappearing as I spend hour after hour searching, every site a rabbit hole that sucks me in only to throw me out later, disappointed and no further on with my search than I was when I began looking earlier in the day.

The details of the other missing lad are sketchy with no follow up stories, just the barest of facts stating his age and height. Why is this so difficult? Nobody seems to care about missing children. If I don't make the effort then who will? If Sergeant Duffield doesn't come up with anything of value, then I have no idea what I will do, how I will shake this feeling that the answer is close by but always just out of my reach.

I am about to give up when I see it – a small article on a blog entitled *When Family Members Kill Each Other*.

Beneath the headline, I can see Simon's name and the details of the night he vanished. My eyes mist over. I blink, take a deep rattling breath and read.

> We all recall the disappearance of Simon Goodwill over forty years ago, but there are certain details that have never been investigated by the police – details that require closer scrutiny. Some would call them coincidental and circumstantial. I call them evidence of guilt.
>
> Police interviews reveal nothing of note. A child went to bed one night and when his family went to wake him the following morning, he was gone. All the stories given by the family match up. Neighbours saw and heard nothing. Without any forensic evidence or a body, at the time, nothing could be proved.
>
> But then something happened a few months later – John Goodwill,

the father of the boy, falls to his death from an upstairs window of the house where his son went missing.

Why was this event not investigated and a connection made? The coroner recorded it as an accidental death but we here at strangedeathsexplained are certain that coincidences such as this don't happen. Further investigations should have been carried out at the time and now, decades later, after much research and extensive interviews with people who lived close by, we can reveal one startling fact which is this – John Goodwill's death was no accident.

A quiet and often surly man, John had a reputation as being a stickler for discipline where his family was concerned. After the disappearance of his only son, Mr Goodwill became reclusive, rarely venturing out to the local pub. Many saw this as a sign of him avoiding questions rather than him taking time to come to terms with his loss.

'Dodging and weaving, he was,' one local told us. 'Too afraid to show his face around town.'

A neighbour who knew the man well said Goodwill once confided in him that he had had to discipline the boy harshly on more than one occasion, taking the belt to him and locking him in his room. Other neighbours said they had heard shouts and cries of children as they passed the house but it wasn't until after the boy disappeared that their suspicions about Goodwill's guilt became aroused.

'We told all this to the police but they didn't seem to show much interest,' one witness told us.

'It's clear that the guilt got to him. That's why he did what he did. He knew that the local community was onto him,' said another. 'Too proud and arrogant to do it properly, he made it look like an accident so nobody would think him guilty or weak, pretending to paint some windows and then falling like that. It screams guilt, doesn't it?'

I stop reading, find myself gasping for breath. Sensationalistic nonsense. I wait for the thrum of blood that is pulsing through my head to slow down and try again, scrolling to the bottom of the site, seeing plenty of spelling errors and realising that these websites are put there by bored voyeurs with no qualifications or credentials. Nobody mentions that perhaps Dad may have been depressed and that's why he jumped. Not that he did jump. They all automatically assumed it was guilt.

I shake my head, rub at my eyes. I have to stop this, getting sucked into other people's fabricated stories. They have nothing better to do with their time, these uneducated, wicked individuals who think they know all about my life and the lives of my family.

...he had had to discipline the boy harshly on more than one occasion, taking the belt to him and locking him in his room.

I bend over and rest my head in my hands. Everything feels heavy, my brain screaming out for a reprieve from all of this.

Do I have any recollections of Simon being beaten by our father? It occurs to me that memories of Dad are hazy. He was either at work or doing jobs in the garage or in the shed. I was young when he died. I have clearer memories of Simon. We walked to school together, walked home again. We talked, played. We were friends. Siblings and good friends.

Maybe Kim is right and I need to give up on this. As soon as that thought enters my head, I am awash with shame. Give up on it and leave Simon alone, wherever he is? I can't do that. I won't.

I stand up, my strength returning. It's easy to get knocked off balance by gossip and lies and toxicity. Because that's all it is. I know it. Deep in my gut, I know that I will unearth this mystery. It may take me a month or a year or even a lifetime but the one thing I do know is this – after seeing these measly little sites, I need to prove them all wrong. I'm not going anywhere and won't settle until I find out where Simon went that night. I'm in this for the long haul.

17

I can hear something. Whispering. It's coming from close by. I shiver. It's cold in here, a chill passing over my skin. Everywhere is dark. Everywhere is silent. No sounds that I can hear. Apart from the murmuring, that is. The ghostly voices of invisible people. Invisible people that are everywhere and nowhere. A low hiss, the talk of the invisibles concealed somewhere near but not here. Not in my room. But somewhere near here. Upstairs in the house.

A shadow slips past me, melting across the floor, a grey, vague shape that suddenly disappears as the moon slips behind a cloud. The large tree outside. That's what it is. I can see its big branches, craggy, long fingers that sway in the breeze. I pad over to Simon's bed. It's empty, his covers pulled back. My hands touch the sheets – still warm.

I spin around. Where is he? Where is Simon? More whispers. I turn again, my footfall a soft, shushing sound against the rug, my eyes wide as I scan the room, desperation tugging at me. I need to find him. I need to find my brother. Where has he gone?

Then it comes again, clearer this time, audible but only just – voices. Soft murmurs coming from beyond this room.

Exhaustion tugs at me, gravity pulling me down to the floor. My limbs are heavy as I turn and leave, following the noise, eager to discover where

Simon is. I have no idea what time it is but I am tired and it's dark and the noises are scaring me a little.

I shuffle along the landing to Kim's room, push open the door, wincing as the creaking grows louder, seeming to fill the house. The whispering stops as soon as I step inside. It's coming from in here. I know it is. I can sense it. It's still so dark. Too dark to see anything clearly. Too dark to work out what is happening.

The murmuring may have ceased but I can hear something else, a rustling, quiet yet sharp, like the crackle of a fire. We once had a campfire at Brownies. It reminds me of that time, the smell of burning, the slight fluttering in my belly as the flames grew higher and higher.

My knees crack as I step back from the bed and crouch down, my fingers clinging onto the edge of the mattress. There it is again – that sound of wood groaning and squeaking. The crackle of the fire. Except it's not a fire. It's somebody moving, wood bending and shifting. Flesh scraping against a carpet, the bristle of it instantly recognisable to me.

'What are you doing in here? You have to leave and go back to bed. Now!'

I try not to shriek but the shock of hearing Kim's voice cuts through me and I let out a short scream. Air passes next to my feet, a cold, swirling sensation that makes me shiver. A head peers out from under the bed, two bright eyes staring up at me, a shock of dark, tousled hair that touches my bare leg.

'Simon, get back under there. I told you to stay put!' Kim is hissing again, angry. Frantic.

The pair of eyes looks from me to Kim then back at me. I can hardly breathe. Kim's anger is intense, the room thick with it. I can't move. My feet are glued to the floor, my body refusing to follow the commands of my brain.

'Now, Simon!'

He gasps and disappears back under the bed and I am left standing there next to my older sister who is half sitting, half lying down, roughly propped up against the pillow, her long, curly hair falling over her shoulders in long, looping waves. She is almost a grown up, so much older than me. She knows lots of things, is cleverer than me. Far cleverer that I will ever be.

Kim makes to speak, a half sound escaping from her throat, then stops as a noise comes from behind us. From another room. The creak of floorboards, the slow shuffle of feet as they move along the landing, coming closer and closer.

Her head swings towards me, her voice like the buzz of an angry insect. 'Now look what you've done! Get back to bed, Grace. Get back to bed, now!'

Behind me, the door opens, a voice rings out in the darkness, low, inquisitive. I turn, see the outline of a figure I recognise and walk towards it, arms outstretched...

I'm choking. I bend over, grip my stomach and press hard as if the act will help to push more air into my lungs. The wheezing from my chest echoes around the bedroom – Kim's old bedroom. I am standing next to the place where her bed used to be, on the strip of floor next to the window that now contains a small, narrow bookcase. It's dark, still. Unnerving. Nothing moving inside or out. I am in my pyjamas, my feet bare, hair askew.

The air in the room is too thin. This is what it must feel like to drown, to be unable to get enough oxygen in your body. I take a couple of seconds, try to regulate my breathing, to right myself and start thinking clearly. To bat away the fear and confusion, see things rationally.

At least I'm still in the house, not outside. Not in the garden. Not in the middle of the street. That's got to be a positive. And yet I am disordered, muddled. Desperation wells up inside me. In the corner of the room is a chair. I drop down on it, lower my head to ease the tension, to try to think. My head throbs as I attempt to force myself back to that night.

I was here that evening, the evening Simon was skulking under the bed like a frightened rabbit. I remember it now. I had stumbled into Kim's room after finding his bed empty. He was here, shoved in a small space in the darkness. Put there by Kim. He looked scared. She was angry. Why? Was it the night he disappeared? I don't think so but can't be sure.

Myriad thoughts, most of them too awful to consider, crowd my mind. I squash them, refusing to think about them. Kim may be many things but she would never harm me, nor would she ever hurt Simon. Never. Would she? So why was he in her room, being forced to hide under the bed? He was clearly terrified. She was clearly angry. I disturbed them, stumbled in on whatever it was that was taking place there that night.

My face heats up. I touch my cheeks, feel the cooling sturdiness of my palms as they press against my face. Why had I forgotten that it had happened? Why does my brain conceal these memories? Memories that are important. Too important to forget. And yet I had done just that. I let this one slip from my mind.

I was young, that's why. A lot took place at that point in my life. I am allowed to let things slide. So much unhappiness from that time. So much unhappiness and misery. So much death.

I stand, turn on the light, look around, hoping more images from the past will filter in. Just a glimpse, a fleeting picture of the past. That's all I ask for.

The images don't come and I am not surprised. A boulder has filled my mind. A huge, jagged rock that blocks out the light, stops anything else from presenting itself. It remains there, the rock, a monstrous obstruction, refusing to budge.

My God, what is wrong with me? My past is controlling my future, often putting me in dangerous situations as I walk the streets at night, robbing me of all control. Sometimes in the house. Sometimes not.

I press the heel of my hands into my eyes, let out a trembling sigh. Maybe I'm going mad, having a delayed breakdown brought on by Warren's death. Do people who are having a mental collapse know they are falling into a void? Do they have that sort of insight? Or perhaps this is all a manifestation of grief. Everybody copes in different ways, their light escaping through the cracks without them even knowing. Maybe this is my light seeping out, leaving me groping about in the dark. I lost my husband and moved house – two of the most stressful things, according to psychologists, that a person can endure, barring living through a war.

What was Kim doing with Simon? Is this why she refuses to talk about it? The world tilts around me at the thought of her being somehow involved with his disappearance. She can't be. It's nonsense, terrible and disloyal to even consider such a thing. For all her faults, she is still my sister and even though she drives me half insane, I cannot entertain such thoughts. Ever.

My head aches. Sleep will help. Undisturbed sleep, not wandering around the house in a somnambulistic haze, half awake, half asleep, my body on the move, never resting, never properly replenishing itself, moving continually until I am so tired, I could curl into a ball where I stand and sleep for a hundred years. I need proper rest. Solid, unbroken time out from all my worries.

I rub at my arms, my flesh prickling as a chill sets in. This can't go on – this whole bloody mystery, the sleepwalking, my useless attempts at investigative work on a forty-year-old cold case. It's exhausting. I am exhausted. Totally consumed by it.

As I climb back into bed, I think that perhaps I should stop. But if I do that, it will always plague me, that need to know. That need to find out what Kim was doing with Simon. Why she forced him to hide away. Where he went after that.

I sit up. Pain shoots up my spine, stopping at the base of my skull, thudding away like a metronome. Was it because of me? Was she hiding Simon from me because I scared him? Surely, his fear of me wasn't that acute? And if so, why not take him in bed with her? Pushing him underneath the bed rather than soothing and reassuring him is downright cruel.

Dear God, I am tired of this. So very, very tired. I am going around in circles and getting nowhere. All I have to show for my efforts is a sick feeling in the pit of my stomach and the ache of sadness that I have carried around with me for as long as I can remember. It's always been there, even in better times, just varying degrees of it. Sometimes in lighter pastel shades that are tinged with grey, other times in great strokes of black, thick and glutinous like tar. A permanent stain on my soul.

I did not hurt Simon.

Kim did not hurt Simon.

The words roll around my head until fatigue wins and I fall into a deep and weightless slumber.

* * *

It's an instantaneous thing, a reflex, me reaching out and slapping at my phone. I just want to stop the noise. Did I set the alarm? I rarely do. It falls out of reach. I lean down, grapple with it, my fingers semi-dextrous, numbed by sleep. It slips out of my grasp, spins across the floor. The alarm continues, a shrill, piercing sound, rhythmic, pulsing. An assault on my ears.

My eyelids are glued together, still weighted with exhaustion. I haul myself out of bed, widen my eyes, grab at the phone, staring at the screen, a sudden realisation hitting me, a sinking sensation in my gut.

It's not the alarm. It's a call. 7 a.m. and somebody is ringing me. Not somebody. Mum's care home. The name flashes up on the screen – Cherry Tree Care Home.

A wave of dread hits me. This is an important call. It's early. It's serious. I need to focus, to shake off the shackles of sleep and rouse myself. Prepare myself.

'Hello?' Even the simple act of speaking makes me nauseous, my stomach clenching, my muscles locking as I brace myself, waiting for the inevitable. Mum has passed away in her sleep. That's what they will tell me. They tried to wake her this morning and found her unresponsive. It was peaceful, they will say. She looked happy. No signs that she struggled. *It's how we would all want to go,* they will murmur softly, a note of sympathy and regret in their tone. *Peacefully. No pain. For all of her troubles, in the end, she passed away quietly.*

'Grace, it's Amanda. Sorry to call you so early, but we're having a bit of a struggle here.'

'A struggle?' My head pounds. I wince, narrow my eyes against the solid slice of pain that travels up my neck, swirling around beneath my collarbone, streaking across the top of my skull.

'I'm afraid so. We've had a bit of a torrid time here with your mum during the night.'

I sigh, try to stifle it, my exasperation, to not appear cold, uncaring. She's not dead then. This isn't going to be easy. I should have known. Her condition is only going to worsen, more sorrow and distress due to come our way. Dementia is a bastard. A cruel, hard bastard. Pernicious and unrelenting. Have we not suffered enough?

'What's happened?' My voice is surprisingly light, deliberately so. I refuse to be dragged down by this, whatever *this* is. 'What can I do to help?'

'I called you as a last resort. We don't want to get her sectioned but we've not been able to get hold of the duty emergency team and unless we can get a family member to calm her down, then we might not have any choice...' Amanda's voice trails off.

I can visualise her as she speaks, her eyes flitting about the room nervously, readying herself for my complaints about her ineffectiveness and ineptitude and a general lack of care. It happens. If I were to do such a thing, I wouldn't be the first and I won't be the last. No amount of money could ever convince me to do Amanda's job.

'I'll come straight down,' I say, shoving my feet into my slippers, trying to work out how long it will take me to get there. No breakfast. No shower. I don't have time for those things. This sounds serious – *must* be serious to warrant such an early call.

'If you could. We'd really appreciate it.'

A stone drops from the base of my belly to my feet. Amanda is the consummate professional, always capable of managing Mum and her ever-changing moods. Amanda has dealt with it all – every high and low, every situation imaginable. What is so bad that she is now unable to cope?

I swallow and keep my voice smooth, even though my nerve endings are ablaze, my flesh crawling with trepidation. 'I'll be there within half an hour.'

'Thank you,' Amanda says, the relief in her tone evident. 'Half an hour sounds good. The sooner, the better, Grace. The sooner, the better.'

18

Amanda is standing at the door as I pull up and swivel my car into a space designed for a vehicle half the size of my large SUV. I manoeuvre it in and somehow squeeze out of the door then barrel across the car park to where she is standing, arms folded, her face creased with concern. The look she gives me turns my insides to water. Eyes narrowed, a groove in her brow, she looks every inch a troubled woman. Beyond the automatic doors, I can hear the wails and screams of a frenzied resident. I don't need to ask who it is. Nothing would please me more right now than to turn and walk away, to get in my car and just drive. To keep on driving with no destination in mind. Anywhere away from here. Anywhere away from what I am about to be faced with. Instead, I smile, do what I can to appear calm and controlled when I am anything but.

'I am so sorry, Grace. I wouldn't usually ring you, especially this early on a morning but our usual tried and tested methods don't appear to be working with her.' Amanda gives me a meek smile and I almost weep for her. She looks tired, her deep brown eyes full of shadows. I wonder if my mum did that to her – embedded the creases in her otherwise beautifully smooth skin. I suspect so but then remember that Mum isn't the only resident here with violent tendencies.

I also wonder how often they call on family members as a last resort because their usual procedures don't work. I pray I am not the only one, that my mother isn't alone in causing them these kinds of issues. The idea of being the daughter of the most aggressive person here fills me with a deep sickness. What happened to the sweet, caring lady she once was? The stoic woman who endured so much, complaining rarely, loving always?

I used to hear her, though, weeping at night for her losses, for the husband who fell, for the child who never came back, the sound of her crying escaping through the walls of her bedroom, filtering into my room, making me wish there was something I could do or say to right the many wrongs that had been thrown her way. I was a child, helpless, unable to do anything except be the best version of me that I could be to help make her life that little bit easier. The last thing I ever wanted to do was heap more misery onto our ever-shrinking family.

And now here she is, utterly helpless, often out of control, locked in a place she doesn't recognise with people she barely knows. I swallow down the lump that sticks in my throat at the thought of Mum's lot in life. I hope that deep in the part of her that still understands what is going on in the world around her, that she is happy, that she realises this is the best place for her and that neither Kim nor myself are trained to deal with her wants and needs, her unpredictable rages, her physical demands. She is fast becoming incontinent and her medication needs to be administered three times daily.

'It's not a problem,' I say, forcing myself to listen, bracing myself for whatever is happening on the other side of those doors. The yelling and shouting continues: the wail of a tortured woman, a desperate woman locked in a mysterious, strange world, robbed of everything she loves and once held dear. I wince, swallow hard and attempt a half smile.

Amanda bites at her lip and nods. 'Come on,' she says, our gazes locked in a second of mutual understanding. 'She may just stop once she sees you're here. I'll explain what happened once we're inside. We can talk on the way.'

* * *

'It started last night,' Amanda tells me as we head down the corridor to Mum's room. 'We decided to take a small group of our residents out into the garden. They love feeding the chickens. Your mum isn't so keen, but we thought she might appreciate a bit of fresh air before supper. She got a bit agitated when we first took her out but then seemed to calm down. Rochelle took her for a walk around the garden, showed her the roses coming into blossom. She was fine, quite perky actually, and then suddenly, she completely freaked out, started clawing at the chicken coop and screaming. It took three of us to drag her away and even then, she somehow wriggled free.' Amanda stops talking, sneaks a glance at me before continuing. 'She dropped to her knees and began pulling up huge clumps of soil with her bare hands. She tried to push herself underneath the coop, kicking out at anybody who was nearby. We had to get the other residents back inside before anybody got hurt.'

'I'm so sorry.' My words come out in a rush. I don't know what else to say.

'Don't be sorry, Grace. Your mum is ill. This isn't her. Always remember that. Dementia stole your mum a long time ago.' Amanda stops walking, turns to me and smiles. Every smile is gratefully received. Every kind word and gentle reassurance. I need them all, like a baby craving comfort from its main caregiver.

We are here, outside her room. The noise coming through the wall is an unearthly shriek. I shiver, swallow down my reticence and fears, wishing I had magical powers, any kind of ability to stop this horrid sound.

'Has she been like this all night?' I can't begin to imagine how she has found the energy to do this. Surely not all night?

'She's slept on and off. Half an hour here, an hour there but every time she wakes, it's with a scream. Usually, when she sleeps, she forgets what happened the day or even the hour before she nodded off, but it seems that whatever is bothering her now is still fresh in her mind. I must warn you,' Amanda says cautiously, her hand now resting on the door handle, 'that the room is in a bit of a mess. She overturned the cabinet and has tried to push the wardrobe over. I didn't want to get her sectioned, I really didn't. For the most part, your mum is settled here but last night, something set her off and no matter how much we tried, we just couldn't calm her down. We administered a sedative but it didn't work, which is when we decided to ring you.'

I nod, my heart beating fast as she turns the handle and we step inside. Even with Amanda's pre-emptive speech, I am nervous, unprepared, unsure of what I am supposed to do, how I will wield the few skills I have and use them to calm her down.

The room is as bad as I expect, the noise just as disruptive. Mum's wails bounce off the walls. In the corner sits Rochelle, her eyes as wide as saucers, her hands folded tightly in her lap. She is sitting near Mum on the bed, a safe distance between them as Mum's arms lash out, pushing and slapping at thin air.

I step forward. Amanda remains in the background, her figure framed in the doorway, watching me closely as I attempt to halt this terrifying tirade.

'Mum. It's me, Grace.'

A sudden silence. Heavy breathing. I'm not sure who it's coming from. There is so much tension and fear in the room, it's hard to distinguish who is doing what, what is coming from where. The hostility radiating from Mum is palpable.

'Am I okay sitting down?' I pick up an overturned chair and gently lower myself into it, making sure I keep my movements slow and non-threatening. My eyes follow Mum's as she scans the room, her anger and suspicion so thick, I can almost taste it.

'They're dead. They're all dead. But he's still here, you know. He's still here!' Her voice is hoarse from all the shouting, her words gravelly and rasping. Part of me thinks that sectioning her would have been the right thing to do. She would be cared for by people who are better qualified than I am to deal with this situation. What if she tries to attack somebody? What will I do then? What if I am the one on the receiving end of her fists? Something tells me she wouldn't do such a thing, but I don't know that for certain. Right now, I don't know anything.

'Hi Mum. It's me, Grace.' I hold out my hand and slowly place it over hers, keeping my touch as light as possible, as if her sensing me touching her will rupture this moment. I stroke the back of her hand with my thumb while leaning forward to get closer to her. It's paper thin, her skin. As dry as sand. A sour, stale odour is emanating from her body, the stench of frustration and fury wafting close to me. The stench of a woman locked in a world full of secrets and misery with no means of escape. 'What's happened, Mum? You can tell me what's upsetting you. I'm here to help.'

Silence punctuated with the growl of her heavy breathing. Then, 'You need to find him. He's still here.'

She begins to rock, a slow, deliberate movement that reaches a crescendo as she moans and lets out a high-pitched scream. I seize the opportunity and wrap my arms around her, pulling her into my chest. I'm taking a chance here. I have no idea whether it will calm or enrage her. I just know that it is the right thing to do. The only thing.

I take a breath, wait to see what her reaction is going to be and my whole body relaxes, crumpling with relief as she succumbs to my coaxing and begins moaning, a soft, rhythmic sound, the screams now melting away, replaced by a childlike whimper that tugs at my heartstrings with such fervour, I struggle to contain my tears.

Her body goes loose. She is weakening, her resistance waning. Then a sudden heaviness as exhaustion takes hold, her tiny frame leaning against me for support. The whimpering stops, is replaced by a stream of sentences, a tiny whisper like the murmuring of a small child but loud enough for me to hear every word. I push my body closer to hers, shush her and stroke her hair, resting my chin against her scalp, inhaling the scent of her, hoping, praying that Amanda and Rochelle don't get the gist of what it is she is trying to say.

'I did it. I killed him. I did it. I killed him. I did it. I killed him.' Over and over, her voice a murmur, sing-song like until she eventually stops and sinks into my solid embrace, sleep taking her to a place where she will be safe.

* * *

'This is the longest she has slept in the past twenty-four hours. I don't think she's going to wake now. Why don't you get yourself off home? We'll give you a call if anything else happens and we can't placate her.' Amanda is standing next to my chair, her body casting an elongated block of grey over the bed where Mum is slumbering silently.

I nod and stand up, afraid the slightest noise will wake her and we end up back into the same situation. That nightmare scenario where Mum's past came leaking out, our family secrets aired in public.

Leaning down, I kiss her forehead then step back, keen to let her rest. I hope she is resting properly, her body allowing itself time to heal and forget, not tortured by nightmares and images from the past that won't leave her be. Her words from earlier bang against my brain. Nausea sits in the pit of my stomach. I think about Amanda's reassurances, telling me that Mum has dementia and nothing she says or does is representative of the woman she used to be. This isn't my mother speaking. It's the disease, that's what it is.

And yet I cannot shake the feeling that something awful is going on here. Wasn't I the one who told Kim that Mum's words always contain a grain of truth? Why should this be any different? If that is the case, then I don't want to think about what she said only a few hours ago. I want to ignore everything that comes out of her mouth and shut off to any ideas about my own mother being involved in Simon's disappearance. It's nonsense. On this occasion, she is completely confused, her brain too scrambled to even begin to comprehend what she is thinking or saying. Words. That's all they are. Words tumbling around her head, coming out in the wrong order, senseless and anachronistic. They are meaningless, throwaway comments from a demented, old woman.

'Please ring me if she deteriorates again.' I almost mention calling Kim but decide against it. I cannot see my sister handling our mother with the care and compassion she deserves. There is too much fire in her, too little compassion to manage any of this with sensitivity. Despite Mum's temper and ongoing rages, she would be no match for Kim's cool and often ruthless manner. Kim affords her few cuddles, the very thing that brought Mum out of this latest rage.

'I hope we never have to, but it's good to know you're only a phone call away. And thank you. A secure unit isn't the right place for your mum. She's better off here. I'm just relieved she eventually calmed down.'

I nod my agreement and despite my warmth towards Amanda and her team, I am keen to go home, to leave this place and its memories behind me.

The drive back to Woodburn Cottage allows me enough time to unwind, to forget her words. I play my music loudly, think about my latest manuscript, about Gavin coming back to England, about anything but what has just taken place. Because thinking about it compounds my problems. I can't take the word of a demented woman and worse than that, even if I could, I can't do anything about it. So I do my best to forget.

19

The problem is, it won't go away, no matter how hard I try to squash it, that memory, her outburst. Mum's words are there, lodged in my brain, in bold print. A large headline that screams at me. There is already too much going on in my head. I don't have room for any more. Sleepwalking, family secrets, my philandering, dead husband – they are all more than enough for me to handle. Enough for me to dwell on. Any more will tip me over into a deep well of nothingness and swallow me whole.

After my third cup of coffee, I head out into the garden. It's overgrown, in dire need of care and attention. Getting in touch with nature may just help me to heal, gluing back together the fractured parts of my life. I have some old gardening tools spread between the garage and the shed. Enough for this job. All I need is some determination and a whole load of energy. It will give me something else to focus on instead of allowing the unthinkable to continue creeping into my thoughts. Keep active, keep busy, that's the key, the only way to get through this. Even the thought of Gavin coming home isn't enough to distract me, to lighten the mood that is weighing me down and pushing me closer to the ground.

Mum tried her best to keep things going after Dad died, even employing a gardener, letting him go only when she retired from her job as a dressmaker. Kim and I did what we could to help but with limited time and contact, the garden became tangled and overgrown. Occasionally, Greg and Warren would help out but a plot this size needs a pair of hands on it full time and we were all guilty of letting it slide, our time taken up with work and young families. Kim and Greg with their healthy bank balance, offered to pay for a gardener but Mum was too proud and too stubborn to agree. The jungle I am now faced with is the result of all those things.

I think of Mr Waters' immaculate cottage garden so close by and feel ashamed. The least I can do is keep this place tidy. I'm not a gardening expert by any stretch of the imagination but I can spruce it up, make it presentable, not leave it as the shambles it currently is.

An hour later and I have pulled away the ivy that had been clinging onto the fence at the bottom of the lawn, and dug out a mountain of weeds. I take the shears and cut at the hedge that runs around the perimeter of the first part of the rectangular lawn. My arms burn, my back aches but I refuse to give up. It takes another hour to even it up and as I take a step back, I feel a certain amount of pride. Already, the whole place is lighter, less oppressive. No towering privets or masses of overgrown foliage blocking out the natural light.

I step through the metal archway to the other end of the garden and heave a sigh. I had forgotten how huge this area is. It goes on and on. It was always too big a space, even for a family of five. Long before Dad died, he split it into two sections, segmenting it with a metal archway and a small hedge with the idea that the rear part would be used to grow vegetables. Like the rest of the garden, once time and finances got the better of us, it became overgrown, Neglected and forgotten. And now nature has done its thing, doing its damnedest to take over completely.

Deciding it is best left to another day, I head back into the main part of the garden, my mind now angled towards clearing the weeds surrounding the shed. Tucked in the corner, the small, wooden structure resembles a decrepit old shack. Gone is the place where Simon and I used to play. Leaning badly to one side, the window covered with grime and foliage wrapped around it as if trying to cover it entirely, it looks close to collapse. I can't allow that to happen. Too many memories of my early childhood live in that shed to allow it fall apart.

I set to pulling down the many climbing weeds and the dense undergrowth that have surrounded it, taking care to not pull down any of the rotten wooden planks. I want everything to remain as it was. My recollections pre-Simon are locked inside this place. I have to do all I can to preserve it, to keep it intact.

The door opens with a groan. I try to step over the threshold, but something stops me, coming at me unbidden. A shadow of the past, a fleeting thought or notion that I am somehow sullying Simon's memory. I have no idea what it is but going inside suddenly feels like the wrong thing to do, as if I am trampling over my brother's soul, walking on hallowed ground. I back out, a silent apology passing my lips.

I stare at the gap between the shed and the fence, a person-sized space that is now a jungle of shrubbery and brambles. Too much work for me. It can wait. Instead, I'll clear the rest of the exterior. Once the weeds have been pulled, I'll give the wood a coat of stain, clean the small window. I might even employ a joiner to replace the rotten planks. It will look as good as new once I'm finished.

An hour later, I have cut back the bushes and shrubbery, pulled away and dug up the tangle of brambles and ivy that have taken root. The structure before me transports me back to my childhood days, happier times before everything unspooled and fell apart.

I wish I had been older, my memories of that time sharper, clearer. They are fuzzy, disjointed, the passing of time and immaturity knocking them off kilter. Kim knows more but asking her is futile. She has tucked it away, refusing to bring it back out into the light for closer scrutiny, claiming nothing will be gained from it. Perhaps not for her, but it will allow me some closure on my past. Maybe she is right, and I shouldn't have bought this place. Maybe I should have allowed it be sold to the highest bidder then stood back and watch them rip the heart and soul out of the place. Strangers who knew nothing of Simon or my father, putting their own stamp on the cottage, obliterating Simon's existence.

No. Despite the sentiments and fears that swill about inside me, despite the bouts of sleepwalking, I don't regret moving here. This is my home. It's where I belong. And soon, Gavin will be here too. With that thought in mind, I finish tidying up and gather up the dead foliage, pushing it into the large wheelie bin next to the old coalhouse. Woodburn Cottage is where I was born and brought up and it is where I shall stay. There is more to keep me here than there is to drive me away.

* * *

I can hear them, whoever they are. Their voices are coming from outside the kitchen. I jump from foot to foot, hopping about like I do when me and my friends play leapfrog in the playground. The flagstone floor is cool and hard under my feet, the cold sensation travelling up my legs and into my spine. I shiver, shuffling forward, to find out what's going on. Because there is something happening. I can just tell. I'm not stupid and I'm not blind. When I woke up, I was standing here in the kitchen in the darkness, my eyes straining to see, my ears tuned in to every little sound. There is nothing happening here in the house. Here, it is silent.

But outside, something is taking place. It's not too loud. Not enough to wake people who are sleeping, but loud enough for those who are awake to hear it. And now I am awake. I wasn't a few minutes ago. A few minutes ago, I think I was asleep in my bed but now I am here, yet I don't remember getting up or even walking downstairs. It's just blackness in my head, a huge hole where my thoughts should be.

That's what Kim always says when I tell her that I can't remember getting up and wandering about at night. She says there is a hole in my memory and not to worry about it. So I won't. But I am a bit worried about the noises outside. It's a rustling sound, like somebody creeping through the hedgerows, twigs snapping and leaves crunching. It might be a fox or a wild animal. We get lots of them around here. That's because we live in a village in the countryside. It's not a big town or even a city like Sunderland or Middlesbrough or Durham. We're up on the North York Moors. We have lovely summers where the sun shines endlessly and then bleak winters that bring strong winds that turn the landscape cold and grey. That's what my mum and dad say anyway. Sometimes, it snows and we get cut off for weeks at a time, but I love it here. I wouldn't want to live anywhere else.

I have a lovely family and lots of friends. Sometimes, my dad is gruff, and he isn't one for giving out many cuddles but that's because he works hard and is always tired. My mum is gorgeous. I really love her. She is warm and snuggly and perfect. My older sister goes out sometimes and wears make-up and high heels and my brother Simon is one of my best friends.

I hear a whisper. Not a wild animal outside, then. It's a person. Or people. One person wouldn't talk to themselves, would they? Fear creeps under my skin. It feels like a snake slithering around my body, coiling itself into a knot, getting tighter and tighter in my tummy and chest. I feel as if I can't breathe. I should go back to bed, hide under the covers and wait until it all goes away. Except I don't. Instead, I open the kitchen door and step outside, my toes curling against the dampness underfoot.

The sound is louder out here, coming from the corner of the garden. Is it somebody crying? My knees shake, trembling and knocking together. It's cold. I'm frightened but I need to know what is going on.

As quietly as I can, I edge forwards, part of me wondering if I'm actually awake or still asleep. How would I know the difference? Dreams often seem very real. Too real. Mine are sometimes terrifying and sometimes really nice. I often wake up confused, wondering if they are true, if what I dreamed actually happened. Like the time I dreamt we were all going on holiday abroad, that we were going in an aeroplane like my friend Tamsin. I woke up convinced it was real and when I realised it was just a cruel dream, I began to cry. We didn't have a holiday that year, or the year after. We went to Whitby for the day, shivered against the cold breeze and then went home and that was that.

I keep on walking. Not a walk as such, more of a tiptoe. There is a crunching sound in my ears, like soldiers marching on gravel. I think it's the sound of my own blood as it rushes through my body really quickly because I'm frightened.

I stop. What am I frightened of? Maybe it's a burglar. I should really head back inside. This is dangerous. My mum would be so angry and upset if she knew I was out here on my own in the middle of the night. But then I hear it again. That sound. Somebody moving. Somebody crying. A quiet sob. So quiet, I can hardly hear it at all. Why are they crying? It's so low and soft and muffled I strain to hear it, but it's definitely there.

Without thinking, I continue walking, my feet taking me forwards when my brain is screaming at me to turn around and go back inside. It's like I have no control over my own body. It's instinct. I know what it means, have heard Kim talking about it before. She said that she always knows when something is wrong. It's her instinct that tells her, like a voice inside your head directing you to do the right thing, she once said to me. This is my instinct forcing me on. Something is happening out here. Something is wrong. I can just feel it and I want to know what it is.

I'm getting closer and closer. Almost there, to the place where I can hear the crying. I stop walking, the air in my throat thick, trapped in place. I feel as if I have swallowed a pebble and it's lodged there, stopping any air from getting in.

If I squint, I can see somebody, an outline of a figure. They have spotted me and have begun walking my way, getting nearer to where I am standing. I suck in my breath to try to stop the scream from coming out. Above, the clouds shift across the night sky, lighting up a small piece of the garden, allowing me to see who it is that is out here, their figure like a piece of silver, highlighted by the crescent moon. I can see them. I know who it is. But why are they crying?

20

My eyes snap open. I'm standing in the garden. Last night, I slid the bolts across on both doors, hid the keys and yet here I am, outside once again: cold, scared, shocked and bemused by the thoughts churning around inside my head, the images that present more questions than answers. Who was it that I saw that night all those years ago? Because I did see somebody. I know that now.

It's starting to come back to me, the memory of it, ebbing and flowing in and out of my mind like the drag of the tide, leaving pieces of debris behind for me to sift through. Not enough to immediately understand. Just enough to keep me wondering, keep me guessing as to what took place out here in the silence and the darkness with only the stars for company.

Was it Simon that I saw? I don't think so. I don't know how I know that, but my gut tells me it wasn't him. So who was it? It wasn't a dangerous criminal. I'm still here. I lived to tell the tale. Had I caught somebody doing something illegal, I'm almost certain they would have turned on me, done something heinous. Something unforgettable, possibly final. Yet they didn't. So, what did happen that night and was it connected to Simon's disappearance?

I bring my closed fists up to my temple, press hard, trying to manipulate the memories back into place, to fill the gaping hole in my brain where my childhood recollections should be. They are coming back, slowly. Sluggishly. Snapshots slowly filtering into my brain, fragments of thoughts falling through the sieve, but it's all so laborious, so painfully disconnected and listless. I don't know if I will ever piece it all together and the thought of possibly never knowing is driving me insane.

I am so damn weary, my body robbed of normal sleep, the sort of sleep other people take for granted, lying in the same position for hours at a time while their bodies become replenished and restored, their immune systems reset, ready for the following day. I am atilt, everything crooked and out of focus because of this sleepwalking palaver. I want it to stop. It needs to stop. I just don't know how that is ever going to happen. And if it does stop unexpectedly, will I ever remember what comes next? Do I really want to know what comes next? Maybe I will be better off staying in the dark. I have a horrible feeling that when or *if* everything does finally come together, I'll wish that I'd remained in blissful ignorance.

An owl hoots in the distance, its call a lonely reminder of where I am and how I got here. It echoes through the air, the sound, travelling across the darkness, searching for a mate. If I stay out here long enough, it will be replaced by the cooing of the wood pigeons, a comforting sound, reminding me of early spring mornings, summer slowly edging in.

I think back to those heady, halcyon days as a teenager and my early twenty-something years when I could forget everything, was able to bask in the sunshine and the warmth from dawn to dusk, doing little and thinking only of myself and my happiness. Occasionally, it would all come rolling back, Simon's disappearance, Dad's untimely death, but then I met Warren, bought a house, got married, had a family of my own and soon enough, my time was taken up with their wants and needs. Simon's disappearance took a backseat. I have a lot of lost time to make up for.

* * *

The next few weeks pass by in a blur of painting the spare room in anticipation of Gavin's arrival, writing, my usual meet-ups with Kim where we talk about the bland and not the blatantly obvious, and finishing the tidy-up in the garden. I stain the exterior of the shed and by the time I hear Gavin's voice over the phone telling me they will be arriving at the end of the week, I am too exhausted to think straight. I have sleepwalked as per but managed to remain inside the house and for that I am grateful.

My call to Sergeant Duffield just to touch base, to remind her that I'm still here, awaiting any more news of Simon's case, was amiable enough. I didn't want to push it too hard, paint myself in an unfavourable light, but I needed to hear something, even if that something was nothing at all. These things take time. I know that and I don't want to be viewed as a nuisance, somebody who is asking too much, but it had been weeks since we had spoken and I felt it was time to reconnect. A nudge to remind her I'm still here. Still here and still waiting.

It's a cold case. No new evidence. That's what she said. Unless something new crops up then the chances of getting it reopened are slim to non-existent.

'What about the other boy who disappeared last year?' I held my breath, prayed for a parallel to Simon's case to be mentioned, something that links them together no matter how tenuous.

'Mrs Cooper. Grace. I looked into that case and I can assure there is no connection whatsoever.'

'How do you know?'

I heard her sigh, knew that I was clutching at straws but ploughed ahead anyway, not wanting to be alone in this. I needed to hear that somebody else was going through the same thing, suffering the way I was. Desperate to find out the truth. Desperate to bring it all to an end. I used to think of the word *closure* as a twee description of such scenarios but now understand the need for it, how important it is to remaining family members. I crave it like a junkie needing their next fix.

'Look,' she said, her voice conveying her weariness, her willingness to bring the conversation to an end. 'I did some poking around in that case and although I can't say too much, I can assure you it isn't connected in any way.'

'How do you know that?' My voice was rising, my tolerance diminishing.

'Have you heard of county lines, Mrs Cooper?'

I told her what I knew in the briefest of details – my knowledge of it sketchy.

'The missing boy from last year was found. He had been groomed by local drug dealers. Nothing to do with your brother's case, I'm afraid. I'm really sorry.'

My stomach had dropped. Once again, I was alone. Nobody to turn to. Nobody else out there, waking in the night, pining after their loved one. Nobody else in the same position as me.

I was left despondent, knowing that unless I discovered something new, then things would grind to a halt. And God knows I have tried to find something new to go on, something that was missed out during the initial enquiry, and have got nowhere. I have read every blog, every news site, every crime site I can lay my hands on. I have tried relentlessly to wrack my brain, trying to work out what happened the evening that Simon disappeared, to scrutinise and examine in fine detail the days and nights leading up to it, to the point where I am utterly exhausted by the whole thing. And every time, without fail, I have come up with nothing. There is something there, lurking in the gloom of my mind, set back in the darkest recesses, but it refuses to show itself. Instead, it hides away, taunting me, dipping in and out of my consciousness, pushing me to the brink of madness with its elusiveness.

And now I have Gavin and Gemma's impending arrival to focus on. Something to throw myself into. I don't want to lose sight of Simon, however. I mustn't. It wouldn't be fair. I lost sight of him for most of my adult life, I'm not about to do that again but I need to think about my son, be there for him, not be half a mother, half a person, the other half of me locked into another world. A world where only Simon exists.

I am putting the final touches to the spare room, making it as welcoming as I can when I hear it – a rapping at the front door. Not the gentle tap of somebody announcing their arrival but the sort of hammering that is likely to make a person think something terrible is about to occur.

Fired by a need to stop the noise, I tear downstairs, my feet twisting beneath me, and pull at the door so hard, it swings open, hitting the wall. I let out a long breath and force a smile, suppressing an eyeroll.

Janine Francis is standing there, a broad grin on her face, her chest heaving, the sinews in her neck taut as she juts out her jaw in an effort to get a good look inside the cottage. 'Takes me right back to the old days, this does,' she says, her attempts to disguise her curiosity practically non-existent. 'I was just passing and thought I'd call round, see how you're settling in and everythin'. Was thinking about you after I saw you in the shop and thought to meself, why not call and see her, have a good old chat? You know, a proper catch-up.'

I squint at her bleached hair, a halo of yellow against the backdrop of the sunlight behind her. Wiry, blonde strands dance about in the breeze, like small, broken pieces of cotton that have snapped under the strain of too much hair dye. Etiquette determines I should step aside to let her in. Common sense tells me to block the doorway, stop her from entering. The thought of being forced to entertain Janine for the remainder of the day fills me with dread.

'Oh, you know,' I say idly, trying to inject a modicum of humour into my voice, not enough to give her the impression we have a bond and are becoming friends, but enough to put us both at ease, to dispel the tension that for my part, is definitely present, 'I'm muddling through. Who needs a man around the house when you can paint walls and stain fences with ten-year-old brushes?'

'You've been decorating? Which room?'

And before I can stop her, Janine has slid past me and is heading into the living room, her eyes scanning every corner, every surface, her head almost swivelling as she takes it all in. 'My word, how many years has it been since I've been in 'ere, eh?' She drops onto the sofa as if she has lived here all her life, like a prodigal family member returning to the fold.

A wishful image drops into my head – me pushing Janine towards the door as she begs to be allowed to stay, my palm pressed into the small of her back as I ignore her protests, before I force her out onto the street and slam the door in her face.

'Oh, well, I'm doing my best to decorate and modernise it while not ripping the heart and soul out of the old place. I like to think I've managed to get it just right, balancing the old against the new with a modern, eclectic twist.' I stop short of asking whether she endorses my efforts. It is none of her business and I have no need for her seal of approval. This is my home. She visited a couple of times when she was a teenager. That's where her connection with this house ends. 'So,' I say, trying to keep my tone neutral. Not too much enthusiasm but just enough ice to let her know that I am busy. That I don't want her here. I'm being unkind, I know that, but something about this woman makes my skin crawl, her over-familiar manner rankling with me. We're not friends and never will be despite what she thinks or hopes. 'I can't spend too long chatting. Lots of things to be getting on with.'

'Oh, don't mind me. White with two sugars if that's all right, that's all I ask, and I'll be more than happy to just sit here and reminisce. You get back to whatever you were doing. Please,' she says, her voice a loud rasp, 'don't let me stop you.'

A void fills my head where my common sense and linguistic abilities should be. I want to tell her to leave but the words won't come. I cannot seem to formulate the sentences required to ask this woman to leave my property. My home and sanctuary.

I don't attempt to make her the coffee she asks for but stand instead, hands curled into fists. A pulse thumps in my head, a dull, thudding sensation that beats away in my temple, solid and rhythmic. I want her to leave so badly, it is like a physical pain running through me, an ache lodged deep in the marrow of my bones. I have no idea why I feel this way. It's rare for me to take an instant dislike to somebody but this woman has needled me with her forthright manner and lack of decorum. I don't think I can stand her sitting here in my home, surveying it with her untrained, arrogant eye.

'Sorry to sound brusque, Janine, but like I said, I'm really, really busy and I need to get on so if you wouldn't mind...' I hold out my hand, my palm angled towards the door.

Our eyes lock, an understanding taking hold in her dull, bovine brain. The sparkle in her expression darkens, her eyes clouding over as she leans back and observes me with the sort of scrutiny usually reserved for bacteria under a microscope. I refuse to back down to this woman, to be belittled in my own living room by somebody who thinks they know me when they most definitely do not. Janine is a stranger to me, an invader in my personal space and right now, I want her to leave, to take her probing gaze and flabby arms and mottled skin and just go.

Relief blooms in my chest as she stands. I have neither the energy nor the inclination for any sort of confrontation.

'Right, well I s'pose I'd better be off then, eh? Not exactly the warm welcome I'd hoped for, but then I expect you won't want anybody traipsing through here, what with what happened to most of your family members. This place always did give me the creeps.'

A sudden pulse of blood explodes in my head. Star burst behind my eyes. My breathing is ragged, uneven. I want to run at her, push her out of my house. I want this dreadful woman to disappear into the crowds at the market and hopefully never see her again.

'Get out.' My voice is sharp. Clear. I surprise myself at how calm and authoritative I sound. No preamble or anxiety eroding the anger behind my words. Just a firm instruction for her to leave.

Janine's body language tells me everything I need to know. She stands, hands on hips, a furrow gouged between her eyes, flecks of spittle bouncing out of her mouth, erupting in the air around us as she replies. 'Well, aren't you the bloody charmer, eh? I call here tryin' to be all friendly like and this is what I get for my efforts. You and Kim are just the same – a pair of stuck-up bitches who think they're better than everybody else.' She takes a step towards me, her cheeks reddening, eyes bulging. 'I'll tell you this for nothin'. You and your sister ain't got nothing to be stuck up about, what with all your family secrets.' She hooks her fingers in the air to accentuate the last two words. 'And I'm not talking about your dead dad or brother. Ask your sister about her mystery illness.' She points her finger at me and laughs, her mouth twisted into an ugly grimace. 'Go on, I dare you. Ask her about it and then watch all those family skeletons come tumbling out.'

I don't have time to reply. Janine Francis pulls up the hood on her sweatshirt, stalks out of the living room, heads down the hallway and out of the front door, slamming it hard behind her.

21

Three times I pick up my phone with the intention of calling Kim and three times I put it back down again. Janine Francis is nothing but a lying, manipulative horror of a woman who derives pleasure from seeing others suffer. She is an irritant and a local gossip. Nothing more, nothing less.

And yet, I am driven by a need to know. Perhaps this is the indefinable memory that lurks in my subconscious, the one that could unlock our family mystery. I also know that her words were designed to wound, to drive in that knife and twist it hard. I was rude to her. She responded aggressively and to her mind, appropriately. I wonder if I was too hard on her, too quick to eject her from the cottage. And then I remember her refusal to take my cues, her determined stance when I informed her of how busy I was. No, I did the right thing and need to stop doubting myself. Janine Francis is not the injured party here. She came seeking information with the sole intention of spreading lies afterwards, smearing my good name and I will have none of it.

I grab at the phone again, tap in Kim's number and wait.

'Hi, everything okay?' She sounds relaxed and happy: free as a bird.

I wonder how she spends her days, what she does with herself as she rattles around in their large home. She no job to go to, no housework to be getting on with, no garden to tend. They have a team of cleaners and handymen helping out. I sigh and stop myself from thinking such thoughts. I am comfortably well off. My writing brings in an extra source of income that I can set to one side. I certainly don't need it to live off as many do. I'm fortunate in that respect. So why does Kim's light-hearted demeanour annoy me so much? For so long now I have willed her to be a happier person, to be upbeat and content with her lot in life. I should be glad she sounds chirpy, lighter than her normal self. And yet I'm not.

It occurs to me that it is possibly because Janine was Kim's friend. She is the one who is responsible for that dreadful woman's intrusion into my personal space. Had it not been for that connection, I wouldn't be making this call.

I sit down, aware that I am being unfair and judgemental. What just took place isn't Kim's fault yet here I am, the younger sister once again being subjected to the fallout of our family's dysfunctional history.

I stare out of the window at the clouds that are gathering, bubbling into an angry mass, turning the sky grey, working in perfect symmetry with my mood: an alignment of darkness both outside and within. 'I suppose so,' I say, trying to sound jovial, as if the weight of the world isn't pressing down on me. Then, 'Well actually, no. Everything isn't okay.'

Silence. No questions, no probing as to what has happened. Just a prolonged and painful stillness that causes me to squirm in my seat.

'Janine Francis called here today unexpectedly. I was finishing off the spare room when she hammered on my door and more or less forced her way in. I had to literally throw her out.' My voice is rising in pitch and volume. I am almost shouting, my skin suddenly burning up. I rest my head to one side, the phone trapped between my jaw and shoulder as I roll up my sleeves to release the waves of heat that are building beneath my layers of clothing.

'Right. Okay. I'm not sure where this is going, Grace, or what it's got to do with me?'

I have no idea how long it takes me to answer. I close my eyes, think about what I'm about to say, do my best to ensure it comes out coherently, not a furious stream of nonsense. Lose your temper and lose. I have to stay calm, not let my underlying resentment get the better of me.

'What was the mystery illness you had when you were younger?' I hadn't planned on asking but am glad that I have. It has niggled at me since Janine first mentioned it. The way she said it makes me think that there is something more to it and whatever that something is, I need to know about it. Yet another family secret. Another thing hidden from me. Even the local flabby-armed rent-a-mouth knows more about my family's past than I do.

I can hear Kim breathing down the phone. I don't speak, waiting instead for her answer, poised and ready for another argument. An argument that may not come. I won't buckle, however, no matter how long the silence lasts. I refuse to give in. This is a chance I'm taking here. I run the risk of having the phone slammed down on me. I run the risk of being told to piss off and mind my own business or being screamed at that it's all one huge lie and that Janine Francis has about as much truth and honesty in her as your average inmate at Frankland Prison. She doesn't do any of those things. What she does do next takes every little bit of breath out of me.

'Look, why don't we meet up for coffee, but not in our usual place? Let's go somewhere different, somewhere more remote and private. The weather's meant to be nice tomorrow. How about we meet up at Sutton Bank at eleven o'clock? We can get a takeaway coffee, sit at one of the picnic benches outside.'

I mumble my agreement, my words coming out in a flurry of confusion and surprise, every word echoing in my head, clanging against my skull like a rolling boulder. I'm relieved when the call ends. Sweat prickles my hairline, arcing around my head, running down the side of my face in tiny rivulets.

Something monumental has just happened. Something that I feel sure will shift my world, tilting it on its axis. Janine wasn't wrong. There is something in Kim's past that doesn't quite add up. Something mysterious that she didn't try to deny. And tomorrow, I will discover exactly what that something is.

* * *

I had forgotten how picturesque it is up here, how awe inspiring. And how wild and windy. High up and exposed to the elements with no barriers to lessen the impact of the weather, it is cold with a brisk breeze that takes my breath away.

After parking up, I decide to go for a stroll, follow the path to the lookout point. It claims to have best view in England and as I stare out over the landscape before me, I am hard pressed to disagree.

Invisible fingers of air push at my back, the gusts of wind so powerful, I find myself clinging onto the wooden rail to stay upright. In the distance, hang-gliders sail past, their bravery something I can never quite comprehend. Life is a path I have always found difficult to navigate; I could never add more danger and peril to it. I have enough in my life to keep me edgy and anxious. I don't feel the need to throw myself off a cliff with only a piece of fabric and a strong breeze to stop me from plummeting to my death in order to feel alive.

Finding Warren cold and lifeless next to me one morning, my search for Simon, for the truth behind his disappearance, coping with Mum's dementia and wondering who the fuck my husband was sleeping with prior to his death is all quite enough for me, pumping enough adrenaline through my system to keep me in a permanent state of unease. I fear a drop more would push me to the brink, tipping me over into that point of no return.

The wind slaps at my face, stinging my cheeks. I narrow my eyes, looking ahead at the sweeping vista, the rolling hills, the expanse of blue sky. Parts of my soul begin to restore themselves as I stare out at it all, insignificance washing over me when I compare myself to the vast, ancient slopes and peaks, the ground beneath my feet that has been here for as long as the earth itself. My problems slowly diminish. If I could just stay here for the longest time, perhaps everything would be less oppressive, less trying. I could walk away from here a different person. Lighter. Less troubled. Happier.

'I knew I'd find you here.' I spin around to see Kim standing behind me, a wry smile on her face. Her skin is flushed. She is holding out a large latte for me. 'Come on, let's find a bench and we'll talk, shall we?'

I walk behind her, Kim's surefootedness leading us to a sheltered area where we aren't battered by the prevailing winds. A secluded area where nobody will hear what she is about to tell me. That is my guess as we sit at a bench away from the crowds and she turns to face me, her eyes following my every move.

'So,' I say, needing to shift this thing along, to make sure she opens up and speaks to me before she has a chance to change her mind. 'I don't think you brought me here for the view. Or the weather.' I laugh and pull up my collar, turning my back against the sharp breeze that although less powerful now we are away from the edge, is still enough to make me shiver and wish I had worn a hat and gloves despite it being late spring. I place my hands around the large paper cup, glad of the heat it gives off.

Kim takes a long slurp of her coffee and lowers her gaze. I wait, I watch and I wait some more. When she looks up again, I am stricken to see her eyes are brimming with tears. My chest tightens, my ribs squashing everything as I stiffen. I brace myself for what she is about to say. I don't have to wait long. The words fall out of her, as if they have been stored there for the longest time, waiting to be spoken out loud.

'My mystery illness was a pregnancy, Grace. I had a baby when I was only thirteen years old. I was sent away to live with Gran in Northumberland for a while. And then after the baby was born, I came back home. Mum told everyone that I had gone to recuperate after a bout of chronic bronchitis.' She takes a shuddering breath, wipes away tears with the back of her hand. 'So now you know.'

My head buzzes. I am lost for words. I lift my coffee but quickly place it back on the floor beside my feet, the weight of it too much to bear. My limbs feel light and weightless, emptied of all strength. Air whistles through my veins, fills my head. I count my breathing, hear the words that come out of my mouth.

'A baby?' My voice is husky. I clear my throat, take a deep breath. 'But what happened to it? Did it...?'

'Live?' Kim says, her voice sounding disembodied, full of tears. Full of regret. 'Yes, it lived. It was taken from me. I was young. It was a traumatic time and I've tried hard to move on from it. So there you have it.' She stands up, pours out the remainder of her coffee onto a patch of grass then sits back down, a defeated look on her face. 'Janine had an idea that something had happened. She never really knew what had gone on but was always a prying little so-and-so, always had a nose for gossip. She possibly had an idea but didn't have any hard evidence. I hid it well.'

Instinctively, I lean into her, resting my head on her shoulder. We're not demonstrative, Kim and I, but this moment requires more than a simple sentence or smile to let her know how I feel. She reciprocates by resting her hand on my head and stroking my hair, her fingers soft as silk, light and reassuring.

We sit like that for what feels like the longest time although it is probably no more than a minute. Only when a family pass by do I move away, lifting my head off her shoulder and shuffling farther along the bench. Two young children skip past closely followed by their parents who nod at us and smile before continuing with their walk. The voices of the giggling youngsters trail behind them, disappearing altogether as they pass, leaving an emptiness that heightens our situation.

I don't try to fill the silence. Saying nothing is the best option when words are not enough. I stand up and Kim follows me. Linking arms, we head along the gravel path in mute companionship, the wind still doing its utmost to knock us off balance. I no longer feel cold. Nothing can touch me. I am impervious to everything. For now, all I can focus on is my sister and the years she has spent having to deal with this alone. Every time I feel as if I cannot contain my anger towards her, she unveils yet another layer of resilience stored deep within her that I didn't know existed. I'm not the only one who has suffered. We have more in common than I ever realised. More to keep us together than to drive us apart.

We reach the car park and I turn to speak to her, to ask just one question. I have no intention of going over this, forcing her to relive it, raking over unpleasant memories. What happened has happened. It is in the past, another page in our history. She has told me that barest of details and that is enough for me, but I want to know just one thing.

'Does Greg know?' I keep my voice soft, non-threatening.

Kim sighs, blinks back more tears and looks away briefly before catching my eye and giving me a half smile. 'I told him after we first met and made him promise to not mention it again.'

I take the hint and nod. She has said enough and looks exhausted by it all, her eyes dark, her face suddenly drained of all colour. Kim looks like a woman who has aged ten years in the last ten minutes. 'And do me a favour, will you?' she says, her voice gravelly. 'Next time you see Janine Francis, tell her from me that she can take her flabby belly and fat wobbly arms, and her yellow, plaque-covered teeth and take a running jump from the nearest fucking mountain.'

I laugh so hard that my sides ache. It's good to see Kim giggle, to see her relaxed, easy in her own skin. I reach out, our fingers almost touching before we break contact. She turns away, gives me a wave over her shoulder then winds her way through the cluster of parked cars. Her head disappears as she bends down and clambers into her own vehicle. I hear the slam of the door, the rev of the engine, the crunch of rubber on tarmac.

I am still standing there, mulling over what just took place when she drives past, her expression a combination of relief and sadness, her face still wet with tears. At that moment, I feel such a pull of love towards her, the likes of which I have never before experienced, the tug of emotions so strong, it overwhelms me. If only I had known that within the space of a week that would all change; that within just a few days, I would be so angry with her, hating her with such fervour that I would willingly place my fingers around her throat, squeezing as hard as I could until her eyes bulged and every last drop of life drained out of her.

22

The airport is busy – travellers coming and going, doors sweeping open, taxis pulling up outside the main entrance. The rumble of suitcases as they're dragged along behind tired, dishevelled people fills the air. I am surrounded by it all: a cacophony, a milieu of busyness and the raw show of emotion from bystanders as people depart, leaving loved ones behind while others arrive to a sea of smiling faces and outstretched arms.

A pulse taps at my neck; my palms are clammy. I make my way towards the arrivals area where a crowd of people stand, looking at their watches and checking the electronic board for arrival times. I insisted on picking Gavin and Gemma up. It's the least I can do after they have travelled thousands of miles to get here. They tried to resist my offer, insisting they would get a taxi to Hempton. I was having none of it. This is the beginning of their new lives and I want to be here to share it with them.

For some unfathomable reason, I am nervous. I keep reminding myself that this is my son, not a stranger. Time and distance have erased our familiarity. We will have to work at getting it back. And then there is Gemma to consider. What does she like to eat? What sort of hobbies does she have? It occurs to me that I don't really know her that well. They had only been together a few months when they left the country. That is something else I will have to work at – being attentive and friendly and polite, making sure she feels welcome and wanted. All of a sudden, this whole endeavour feels like a crushing task requiring more energy than I am able to muster up.

I check my watch and crane my neck, peering over the line of heads in front of me. I mustn't think like that, that their imminent arrival is onerous or overwhelming. It isn't. This is an exciting event, something to look forward to, to savour and relish. It's a positive memory and those kinds of memories are difficult to come by. I need to cherish it, hang onto it, not brush it aside as something that I find too difficult to manage.

Time drags as I wait, hopping from foot to foot, the base of my back aching from standing in the same position for too long, until eventually, a handful of people appear through the doors. They scan the crowd, searching for that familiar face, that welcoming smile, while others march past, heading out into the chilly evening air, shoulders hunched, expressions relieved yet weary.

Face after face after face – men, women, children, babies – they all pass by me until at last, I see him. My boy. My Gavin. I resist the urge to run to him, to wrap my arms around his broad shoulders and gaze up into his big, blue eyes. Instead, I remain dignified, reserved, giving them both a broad smile and a wave. I allow myself a small squeak of excitement as they approach, giving me a tight hug. They look tired. Healthy and tanned but definitely fatigued by their long-haul flight.

'Long journey?' I say, immediately chastising myself for stating the obvious. They've both travelled halfway around the world. Of course it was a long bloody journey. 'Here. Let me give you a hand.' I take a piece of luggage from Gemma, who smiles and lets it slip from her grasp with a grateful sigh.

'Thank you. It's really kind of you to come and pick us up.'

'My pleasure. I parked as close as I could to the building. Come on,' I say a little too loudly, my excitement inadvertently spilling over, 'let's get you both home.'

* * *

'I've left Gemma to sleep. I managed to get a few hours on the plane, so I don't feel too bad.' Gavin is standing next to me in the kitchen. I had forgotten how tall he is, how statuesque, his frame seeming to fill the entire room.

'Tea?' I fill the kettle, my back to him as I stare out into the garden.

'Please. I'm parched.'

'Air conditioning on the plane most probably,' I say, as if I am an expert on filtration systems and how they affect passengers' respiratory systems. I keep doing this – saying pointless, silly things. I'm nervous, fidgety. I shouldn't be.

I make the tea and we sit at the table, Gavin checking his phone while I stare out of the window. Tiny tendrils of steam curl up, misting my face. 'It's good to have you back,' I murmur. 'It's nice to have some life breathed back into this house.'

'Sorry? Oh yeah, it's great to be back.' He places his phone on the table and picks up his cup, smiling at me as he sips at his tea. 'We're both back at work tomorrow. Gemma got a transfer over to the UK division of the bank. She considered leaving, starting afresh once we got here but the offer was there so she took it.'

'I guess I'd better make the most of you both while you're still around then, eh?' I give him a wink and have to stop myself from throwing my arms around him and squeezing hard.

'Have you seen much of Lucy?'

I sigh and raise my eyebrows at him. 'No, not really. She always seems to be so busy. Have you been in touch with her at all?'

'The odd text here and there. We were thinking of travelling down to see her. No concrete plans as yet. Just have to wait and see how we get on with jobs and time.'

We move onto other subjects. Lucy's presence on the fringe of our lives is something that has always bothered me. I make a mental note to visit her sometime soon. Once Gavin and Gemma are settled, I could drive down there, or better still, get the train. Perhaps we could all go together. I don't want to be a burden but I'm sure she would appreciate a family visit from us.

Warren once said something unforgivable, not even realising the depth of hurt he caused me with his careless words. A throwaway comment after a glass of wine too many. 'Let's face it, Grace. Gavin has always been your favourite.' He alluded to the notion that Gavin was a substitute for Simon.

I hid my shock and upset with a flap of my hand, turning my back to hide my tears. What if Warren was right? I've had lots of time to think about what he said. Did I shut Lucy out of our lives unintentionally? Shames creeps up my spine, burning under my skin. I would never consciously do such a thing. Would I?

But then, this is the man who crept around behind my back sleeping with another woman, meeting up clandestine style, receiving mysterious notes and stashing them in his desk at work. Why should I take any notice of anything that passed through his lips? And yet, his words still needle me, making me uncomfortable, edgy. I love Lucy. I love Gavin equally. Don't I?

I decide that I will call her later, let her know that I think of her often, that she is as much a part of our lives as Gavin as. *My life.* I stop, correct myself. It's a hard habit to break. Warren is still there in my thoughts, will probably always be there, his presence too difficult to ignore. We had so many good years together, ruined only by the unearthing of those stupid bloody letters. Kim was right. I should have thrown them out, all those documents. She is right more often than I care to admit.

Gavin finishes his tea and heads upstairs while I sit contemplating everything – my family, Warren's death and how I can move on with my life without him in it. And Simon. He is always there, never forgotten, loved always. But now I have Gavin and Gemma to think about. Simon will have to wait. That thought pains me but once they have their own place, I can return my attention to him.

I hear Gavin coming back downstairs. It's not something I'm used to hearing – the footfall of other people around this place – but it's a sound I could get used to. It adds a touch of comfort to the cottage, taking away the sharp edges that the prolonged silences often bring.

'I was thinking about visiting Nana at the care home. I haven't seen her for ages. I was wondering if you fancy coming along? I don't know how busy I'm going to be at work once things get going so today seems like a good idea. What do you think?'

I'm not expecting this. It takes me by surprise, catching me in my solar plexus. It's a thoughtful thing to do. He could have chosen to unpack or do any manner of other more pressing tasks but has turned his thoughts to his ailing grandmother instead.

'I think it sounds like a wonderful idea. If you give me ten minutes, I'll be right with you.' It's good to have Gavin coming with me on this visit. Even if Mum has a meltdown, it won't feel as worrisome, not half as gruelling. I have back-up, some support. I have my son with me. Three generations of us together. It will be just perfect.

23

Mum is dozing in the chair when we arrive, her head lolling to one side, a thin line of saliva running down the side of her mouth, gathering in the recess of her chin. I touch her shoulder lightly. Her head snaps up, instant recognition in her eyes. It warms my heart to think she still knows me. That ability to know me within a matter of seconds will fade as the disease progresses, her recognition of her family a thing of the past as dementia leaves her locked in a world of fear and uncertainty where everyone is a stranger, every day a terrifying step into the unknown, but for now I will hold onto it, treasure it.

'And who's this young man before me, then?' She props herself up, levering her thin body upwards with her elbows on the wooden arms of the chair. 'Eeh, it isn't, is it? Well, well, well,' she says, her voice a thin squeak, her pale, watery eyes sparkling with excitement. 'If it isn't young Simon. Where have you been lately, little fella? Feels like years since I've seen you around.'

My knees buckle. I hang onto the back of the chair to steady myself. I want to look at Gavin's face but at the same time am too frightened to glance his way, to see that startled look in his eyes, the expression of confusion as he attempts to work out what to say or do next.

'It's Gavin, Nana. Not Simon. Anyway,' he murmurs softly, bending down on one knee to get at her level, 'how are you? You're looking wonderful. Still as glamorous as ever, I see. A Greta Garbo lookalike.'

And the moment is forgotten. Just like that. Mum chuckles, places her hands on his face and tells him how wonderful he is, stroking and cooing at him. Within seconds, she is captivated by his charms, smiling and giggling like a small child as he showers her with compliments and affection. Her laughter fills the small room, bouncing off the walls and ceiling. My heart swells, pride blossoming in my chest. Why can't every visit be like this? Gentle, happy. Easy.

Amanda's smiling face appears around the door. She nods, winks and disappears into her office opposite Mum's room. Everything feels just right. Perfect. Whether the planets have aligned or there is something in the air, I cannot say but I am reluctant to move for fear of breaking the spell.

'I'll pop along to the machine and get us all a coffee, shall I?' I don't wait for a reply. I leave them together. They have many years to catch up on although how lucid Mum will be after ten minutes of conversation is anyone's guess. Her reserves will be used up, her conversational skills as dry as sand.

I linger at the machine, loving the fact that Gavin has taken the time to speak to his nana. They need time to catch up. It's been a few years. Gavin will have noticed the difference, be shocked perhaps by her general decline as dementia takes hold of her poor exhausted brain and wrings it out until it is desiccated and devoid of anything that resembles the wonderful person she once was.

Mum was too ill, too frail to attend Warren's funeral. Truth be told, I'm not even sure she knows he is dead. I remember telling her and also remember her staring out of the window, eyes glassy, a look of non-comprehension etched into her tiny features. I chose to not mention it again after that.

Why sit and talk about death to a person who doesn't understand the concept of death, its finality, what it actually involves, especially somebody whose end could be nearer than we all realise? It's cruel and unnecessary, so instead we talk about flowers and butterflies and the weather and the war. That's her favourite. A time when everything was so fragile and terrifying and yet at the same time so comforting, her young life filled with a community spirit that now seems sadly lacking. I sigh, shake my head. That isn't entirely true. For every Janine Francis, there is a Mr Waters and his family, always ready to help. I banish the maudlin thoughts, focusing on the good, decent people. Gavin, Carrie. They are all out there. Even Kim.

I step away from the machine, my arms loaded up with coffee and biscuits and am almost back at mum's room when I hear the scream that curdles my blood, turning my insides to water. In an attempt to put down the coffee cups, I accidentally drop them on the floor, the brown liquid spilling and spreading like rivers of mud at my feet. The biscuits drop in a broken heap as I loosen my grip and race to Mum's room.

My heart throbs with dread at the sight before me. Mum is leaning over Gavin, her hands locked around his throat. As tiny as she is, her rage is all encompassing, a substantial force that fills the room.

Gavin's leans back away from her, his hands resting on the arms of the chair, his lips parted in shock. He could knock her away with one movement, one slap of his hand, his strong arms catching her off guard, her body taking flight and hitting the nearest wall. But he doesn't.

He speaks softly, coaxing her, his muffled, strangulated voice a plea. I suck in my breath, chew at the inside of my mouth, helplessness piercing my gut.

'I'm not him, Nana, I promise. I'm Gavin, remember?'

I turn to shout for assistance but they are already there, Amanda and Rochelle, standing next to me. They bustle through the doorway before I can utter a word: a team of experts at hand, ready to extricate my mother from my son, to prise her hands away from his throat.

'It's you! Don't lie to me. I know it's you. He's gone and it's your fault, you bastard!' she is shrieking, setting my nerves on edge, each word tearing at me, cutting into my flesh, drawing blood.

'Mum, it's Gavin, your grandson. Remember? The boy who used to play in your garden. He's grown up now. It's Gavin.'

My words are drowned out by rustling and murmuring and shouting as Rochelle and Amanda restrain Mum and lay her on the bed. She fights back, refusing to acquiesce, her stick thin limbs thrashing about, her voice a scratch in the small room.

'It's him. I know it's him! It's John, my Johnny. He did it. It's his fault!'

Gavin sidles over to me, places his arms around me, seemingly unperturbed. I wish I had a tenth of his bravery and gumption. My innards are squirming and coiling, my heart hammering away beneath my sternum, a dull thudding that leaves me wobbly and nauseous.

'It's fine, Mum. They've got it under control now.'

'Your neck?'

He stretches his head towards me. 'See, nothing there. No marks. I could barely feel anything.' He is smiling as if nothing happened, as if my mother, his dear old nana, didn't just try to strangle him.

I fight back tears. This is not how I planned our visit. I had visions of us chatting, of Mum patting Gavin's hand while he regaled her with tales of his life in Australia, telling her how surfed and visited beaches and hung out with cool people who lived life to the full but here we are, watching her being restrained after she tried to kill her own grandson.

Her shrieking becomes more muffled, the distant cry of an angry, frightened woman. Gavin and I are gently ushered out of the door, Amanda's hand at my elbow, the other one in the small of my back as she propels me forwards. 'Let us calm her down, Grace. It's upsetting for family members to witness such a display but we're used to it. Why don't you go and have a coffee in the lounge while we sort your mum out?'

'Oh God. I spilt some on the floor outside and I—'

Amanda shakes her head and smiles and I couldn't think more of her than I do already. 'It's getting cleaned up as we speak. You just go and sit and have a drink. Sarah will bring you one from the office but don't eat all the shortbread biscuits or I might just cry.' She winks and before either of us can reply, the door is closed and we are standing outside Mum's room, the aroma of spilt coffee wafting up from the tiled floor. I still hear it, however: the last thing Mum says before she is sedated and drifts off into a drug-induced slumber.

'It was John. He did it. He hurt the boy. Him! It was always him.'

* * *

We're settled in the living room, glass of wine in hand. Gemma is curled up on the sofa, feet tucked under her legs. Gavin is beside her, his body leaning into hers. They cut a fine pair: two handsome, young people with their lives ahead of them. Both employed, both healthy. So why am I so on edge, fragile and out of sorts as if the world is spinning out of control? My little world hurtling towards the unknown.

Mum's voice reverberates around my head, her words, saying my father had hurt Simon. That was what she meant. It's obvious. She's ill, I know that. Last week, she was screaming that she had killed people. I shouldn't hold so much store by her words. She's confused, doesn't always know what she is saying. Words come out of her mouth unchecked, events that have become jumbled in her poor old brain coming out as fact. And yet, they always manage to worm their way into my mind, mounting up into a huge, ugly pile that is ready to come crashing down at any moment.

'Top up, Mum?' Gavin sits up, picks up the bottle and pours some into Gemma's glass. The glugging sound cuts into my thoughts.

'I'm fine for now, thanks.' My face is warm, the alcohol heating up my flesh as I take another sip.

The subdued lighting, the conversation, the company in my living room all add to the ambience of the evening. I should be happy, elated. So why do I feel as if everything is falling away from me, my delicately constructed existence going into freefall?

'We haven't really had time to ask you how you're settling in here? It's looking so cosy, Grace. Woodburn Cottage is utterly gorgeous.'

I smile at Gemma, her words moving me, dragging me out of my reverie. I grew up here, have good memories of this place, battled demonic ones along the way and haven't ever really given any thought to it being pretty or homely. It's just my childhood home. The place where Simon grew up. Then I think of Janine Francis and her toxic presence in my living room. I shut her out, stamp all over her presence. She doesn't deserve any space in my head. She deserves to be forgotten, her words and insinuations and filthy tittle-tattle trampled underfoot and ground into dust.

'I'm settling in really well, thank you. My neighbour, Mr Waters, lived next door when I was a kid and he's still living there now. He's a lovely old chap: so kind and helpful. I met his daughter, Carrie. She was visiting and we had a drink together.'

Gemma and Gavin nod and smile. This is what they want to hear: that everything is ticking along perfectly. Why burden them with my issues and drag them into my sordid pit of secrets?

'I guess you've been seeing Aunt Kim as well, have you? It's good that you have each other,' Gavin says as he drains his glass and refills it. 'By the way, did she sort out that thing with Dad? He said he'd had to meet up with her a few times for a chat about something or other. Some family issues, apparently. He said they'd seen quite a bit of each other and that you would get to know about it soon enough that it was time to "bring it all out into the open".' He hooks his fingers in the air as he speaks and widens his eyes, giving me lopsided smile. 'It all sounded very mysterious and intriguing.' Gavin sighs, dips his head then drops his hands and runs his fingers through his hair. 'I never did get to hear what it was about, but I don't suppose it matters now and I guess it's all sorted, is it?'

Bells clang in my ears, a deep, metallic thrumming. The temperature in my face ratchets up a couple of notches. I can hardly breathe. That letter, that diary entry.

Please don't tell her, Warren. Don't do it. We all have too much to lose.

Not Kim. Surely not my own sister?

I saw her again. I shouldn't have. We talked, that's all. At some point, this all needs to come out in the open.

I want to speak, to say something to fill the interminable silence that seems to have suddenly filled the room, but nothing comes out. Cotton wool fills my mouth, sticks in my throat, clinging to the sides, stopping the words from escaping. I need to say something, anything to fill the void of silence that has descended. I am empty, a blank canvas. There's nothing left of me. Nothing of any substance. I am a cardboard version of Grace Cooper, a person running on empty.

I find myself nodding, my head rattling and buzzing with each movement. I watch, disconnected from reality as Gavin and Gemma finish their drinks and stand up, their voices echoing around my head as they bid their goodnights and go upstairs. Their footfall is muffled against the rush of my own blood, the thrashing of my heart, the screaming in my head.

My instinct is telling me to go around to Kim's house this minute, to drag her from her bed, put my face close to hers, let her see my anger, let her feel it, smell it, taste it. To tell her what a worthless piece of shit she is before cutting her out of my life altogether.

But I don't. I have another drink to help still my beating heart and stem my growing fury. I run through various scenarios, make plans, rehearse speeches, choosing my words with care and precision. I have to get it right. No second chances, only one opportunity to tell Kim what I think of her and her devious, cruel ways. Her attempts at ending my marriage.

I can wait, time tempering my rage and adding fuel to the words I plan on saying. Words that will bring our relationship to an end. When I do see her, I want to do it with a clear head and a sharp tongue. I want my well-rehearsed speech to flow, for the ice in my veins to cut her to the quick. I want her to know that this is the end of us.

24

I must have slept even though I feel as if I've been awake for a hundred years or more. I recall dozing off into a dark dream full of secrets and lies and shook myself out of it. I ache everywhere, as if my bones have been compressed into a tiny, metal box. I unfurl myself, clamber out of bed, my joints flaring with pain. I shower, grateful for the heat and strength of the water as it massages my bones, pummelling my skin, injecting some life back into my weary body, and dress, throwing on the first things at hand. Clothes feel inconsequential, trivial.

Downstairs, Gemma and Gavin are dressed and finishing their breakfast. Gemma stands at the sink, staring out into the garden.

'Busy day ahead?' My voice is different: low and husky, in need of sustenance and sleep. I shuffle past her and pour myself a coffee.

'Not sure what's in store, to be honest. I think I'll just be introduced to the rest of the staff and get shown around. I'll probably take some time to get used to the new systems. You?'

She turns to face me and my flesh vibrates, the contents of my head visible, all my dirty secrets there for her to see. This poor girl, only one day in our family and already things are falling apart, our grimy past and many misdemeanours spilling out for her to observe in stupefied horror.

Does she have any idea what she is getting herself into? Does she know how damaged we really are?

'I think I'm going to pop over to see my sister, Kim. I'll be back by lunchtime at the latest. I'll probably write another chapter after that. Or maybe not. I'll have to wait and see how I get on.' I'm rambling now. I have no idea what I'm going to do once I have spoken to Kim, no idea what sort of a state I'll be in, whether I can focus and write something worthy of publication or whether I will be close to collapse after hearing her admit to what she has done, shattering my life with her duplicitous ways.

'That sounds lovely. You're so lucky to have her. I'm an only child. I would have loved siblings, especially a sister.' She smiles at me and I find myself turning away to hide the wave of misery that threatens to engulf me. Such innocence and acceptance. All of a sudden, I feel envious of her carefree life, her blemish-free existence. Does she know how lucky she is?

'I hope your first day goes well. They're lucky to have you. And by the way,' I say, fighting back tears, 'I haven't said it yet, but it's wonderful having you both here. Please treat this place as your own.'

They both leave the house looking every inch the professionals with their slick suits and briefcases, Gemma with her phone tucked under her chin, talking animatedly and Gavin strutting along beside her. They hop into their taxi and head towards the train station, then I slump down into the nearest chair, the exhaustion of my playacting – pretending that everything is going swimmingly when in reality, I am close to collapse from lack of sleep and the fear that my life is about to fall apart – almost too much to tolerate.

A strong cup of coffee later and I have summoned up enough energy and courage to do what needs to be done. No more prevaricating. It's time to face it head on.

* * *

I don't knock, entering instead unannounced. They wouldn't hear me anyway through the huge rooms of this house, my tapping disappearing into the ether, absorbed by the sheer vastness of the place. So I walk in instead, using the element of surprise.

'Grace? Everything okay?' Greg appears in front of me, a plate of toast in one hand and a laptop in the other. He frowns, glances around like a startled creature ready to take flight.

I should explain, tell him why I'm here. None of this is Greg's fault. He is a victim in all of this, just like me, but I am too angry, too hyped up to go into the minutiae of my visit. 'It will be once I've spoken to Kim,' I say with a smile that belies my true intentions. 'Is she about?'

He points through to the kitchen, a frown engraved into his brow, carved by confusion and anxiety. Greg isn't an idiot. He senses my anger. I haven't tried to disguise it but neither have I stormed in here shouting, tearing from room to room searching for her. Controlled. That's what I am. Controlled and precise. But not for much longer.

I spot Kim in the distance, standing at the sink, her hands lowered into the water, her hips swaying as she rinses pots and places them on the drainer. She looks relaxed, easy in her own skin. That's because she has no idea what is coming, what sort of havoc I am about wreak. How I am about to rip her carefully planned life into tiny little pieces.

My legs are rubber, my heart a trapped bird beneath my ribs, fluttering wildly as I stride towards her, a trail of sentences stacked up in my head, words that will tear her in two, expose her tawdry secret. Possibly even end her marriage.

'We need to talk.' My fingers push at her shoulder, knocking her off balance.

She spins around, soap suds dripping from her fingers onto the polished floor. Her eyes are wide. She has seen my face, the exhaustion, the ferocity there. Now she will know. Now she will understand.

'Grace? What on earth...?'

I cut her off before she can say any more, grabbing her by her arm and dragging her over to the table where I press her down into a chair with force. She doesn't resist, shock rendering her weak. Defenceless.

'I know now why you wanted me to dispose of all Warren's documents. It's all so clear to me. God, I've been blind. Stupid and so fucking blind but not any more.' I sit opposite her, my face close to hers, our noses almost touching. 'When were you going to tell me about you and Warren, Kim?

Or were you just hoping that now he's dead, it can all be conveniently forgotten about?'

She narrows her eyes, her defences awakening. I sense Greg's presence behind me, hear him shuffling about. Kim glances at him briefly, shaking her head for him to retreat and leave us alone.

There is a barely discernible shift in air pressure at my back as Greg moves away and closes the door with a muted click.

I am panting now, my nostrils flaring, beads of sweat covering my top lip. I have to stay cool, calm, not lose myself in my anger. I need to be surefooted. Precise. Ready to do battle.

'Grace, with the greatest respect, I have no idea what you are talking about.' She sighs and closes her eyes for a second, biting at her lip feverishly. Good. She is starting to buckle under the pressure. I'm not the only one feeling the strain. 'Or maybe I do, but it definitely isn't what you think.' Her voice has lowered, is almost a whisper. She sounds resigned to this, as if it's been a long time coming.

'So, tell me then, what exactly *is* it you think that I am thinking? Because as far as I can tell, before my husband died, he had been having an affair with you. My husband and my sister, my only remaining sibling, sleeping together, sending one another secret notes thinking I would never find them. But the thing is, Kim, I did find them. I opened them, read them, wondered the fuck was going on, gave Warren the benefit of the doubt, but then heard from my son that you and Warren had been meeting up and realised what an idiot I had been, not seeing the obvious. You must have both had a real laugh at my expense, knowing you could carry on behind my back and I wouldn't suspect a thing. Stupid, pathetic Grace, eh? So wrapped up in her writing, so caught up with her own dull little existence that she is too stupid, too dim witted to see what is going on right in front of her nose.'

I bring my fist down onto the table with a thump. She jumps then straightens her posture and lets out a trembling sigh, hoping to appear unmoved by my words. She is shaking her head repeatedly, rubbing her curled fists into her eye sockets and moaning softly.

I prepare myself for a stream of denials, for her apologies and repeated requests for forgiveness. I am not prepared for what she says next.

'I was definitely not having an affair with Warren. Yes, we met up, but it was to discuss something that affects you, something *about* you. Something that Warren felt you should know.' She stops, stares off over my shoulder, glances back at me, then continues, her voice a whisper, hoarse and full of resignation. 'Grace, the pregnancy, the baby I had – it was you. I'm your mother, Grace. I'm not your sister. I'm your mum.'

The room sways, the floor turning to liquid as I try to stand, to back away from her. I slump down onto the chair, my head swimming, the steady thump at the base of my skull making me nauseous.

'Warren went out for a drink with Greg a few months before he died and Greg got drunk, told Warren what I had told him about the baby. So Warren got in touch with me, told me you should be informed, that it was wrong for you to not know. And he was right. He was so right.' She leans towards me, her eyes shiny, wet with tears, her chin trembling violently. 'Please say something, Grace. I am so sorry. So very sorry. We never meant to hurt you. It's just that the lie went on for so long, there seemed to be no way back from it, no easy way to break it to you after all these years.'

Her voice is distorted, my thoughts askew. I cannot make any sense of this. I have no idea what to say or do next. I am too heavy, too solid and dizzy to stay upright as I attempt to stand, everything leaden, my body a dead weight. I cling to the rim of the table for balance. It slips from my grasp, my fingers, my arms, flailing, grasping. I reach out for purchase on something – anything to stop me from falling. There is nothing. Nothing at all. Only a head full of angry insects, buzzing and flapping, battering against my skull. Skin that burns like a furnace. All my senses heightened. A thick veil of darkness descending. Then nothing.

***

Faces hovering over me. Blurred, indistinguishable faces. Voices in the background. Low, disembodied. I try to sit up. No strength. A headache. My cheeks hurt, my chin, my forehead filled with pain. A dull thump hammering in my head. Fingers stroking my hair. A soft voice calling my name. I try to remember. Am I at home?

'Grace?'

That voice. I know it. So familiar. A soft voice calling out to me, offering platitudes.

And then it comes flooding back.

Layer upon layer of deception and hurt. Years of it. Decades. My entire life. One big lie. I am nothing more than one fucking awful, fat lie.

I try to sit up, slapping away the hands that press down on me, the voices coaxing me to lie still, to remain calm and gather my strength. A cup is held to my lips. Warm tea. I gag, spit it out, fluid leaking out of my mouth, drool running down my chin. Moisture settling on my face.

My eyes snap open. I blink, focus, blink again then grab the cup, throw it as far as I can. A smash close by. Crockery breaking. A cry. A pleading insistence for me to listen. Then tears. From me and Kim and possibly Greg as well. A river of tears that threaten to drown us all.

I want to go home. I don't want to hear anything else. No more lies. No more of anything. Just a reprieve from this whole damn mess. A reprieve from my life.

'Leave me alone! I want to go home. Just let me go home. Please...'

25

Torturous and endless, that's what this is: a journey fraught with acrimony and hurt and resentment. It goes on for forever: trees, shrubbery, pedestrians, fast-moving vehicles all a blur as we move past them at speed, my face turned away from Kim, my refusal to look at or speak to her the only power I have to show her how angry and upset I am. How I despise her for this, for how she has upended my life. Everything about me is a huge fabrication. I am nobody, nobody at all. I no longer know who I am. The invisible person, the ghost of Grace, that's me. The unseen. The unspeakable. The mistake.

Behind us, Greg follows in my car. Even my ability to get myself home was snatched away from me, the pair of them insisting I was in no fit state to drive. So here I am, being ferried about like an errant child. At this moment in time, I hate them both. I hate Warren for not being brave enough to tell me himself and I hate Kim and Greg for conspiring with him; all of them knowing this terrible fact and omitting to disclose any of it to the person at the centre of it. Me. My life. One big lie. Everything I thought I knew has been turned upside down, inside out, shaken about like a snow globe, the tiny fragments of my existence falling about me like confetti.

'I need to know everything,' I say as we pull up outside Woodburn Cottage. 'Every single thing.'

Kim is shaking her head, tears rolling down her face. 'Not now, Grace. I know you're angry with me and I totally understand that, but this is painful for me too. Talking about it brings it all back.'

Another fire rekindles itself beneath my breastbone, flames flickering, scorching me. How dare she? How fucking *dare* she deny me what I need to know? Deserve to know. Painful for her? How the hell does she think I feel about it? Does she even care?

As if sensing my rising fury, she sighs and taps her fingers on the steering wheel, a soft hammering that booms in my ears. 'Look, what I'm trying to say here is that what I tell you might not be what you want to hear.' Her words are a desperate attempt to deflect the blame elsewhere, to sneak under the radar of my anger. Even at this moment, this pivotal moment in our lives, she portrays herself as the victim. I am the aggressor for daring to question my own identity. She is shameless, her arrogance breath-taking.

'I'm a grown woman, for fuck's sake, Kim, not a petulant ten-year-old. I have two adult children of my own. Don't tell me what I am and am not capable of handling.'

I hear her sigh, swallow hard, can almost hear the cogs whirring in her brain as she tries to placate me. To tell me yet more lies. It's an easy task for her. She is a past master at it now, an expert. She has had over forty years of practise. Nothing she can say will evoke any sympathy from me. This misery is mine and mine alone.

'Please, Grace. I'm begging you. Not now. Let's meet up tomorrow when things have settled down a bit, when we've both had time to come to terms with this.'

The slowly burning fire in the base of my belly suddenly combusts, flaring through my veins. 'Come to terms with this? Christ almighty, Kim, you've had all your life to come to terms with it! Why does everything always have to be about you? For once in our miserable little lives, just this once, let's not dance around your sensitivities, eh? Just for once, let's consider me and how this makes *me* feel!'

I grab her shoulder, swing her round to look at me. She loosens her grip on the steering wheel, drops her gaze and sobs. 'I was raped, Grace. I never ever wanted you to find out about it. And this is why. I knew the misery and hurt it would cause. My only aim in life was to protect you. That's all I've ever wanted to do.'

My hands drop. I let out a groan, dip my head to stop more tears from falling. I am freezing. My teeth begin to chatter, my flesh prickles with dread. I envisioned some teenage romance, a spotty, callow youth or an older man from the village, somebody who wooed Kim, taking advantage of her stunning looks and maturity. I didn't expect this nasty little scenario, a grubby, savage situation that resulted in my entry into the world.

'No. No, no, no!' A thousand thoughts crowd my brain, questions jumping around, legions of them, too many to utter. Only one escapes. 'Who?'

She shakes her head, brings her hands up to cover her face, Tears leak through her fingers, running down her arms, soaking the fabric of her cotton jacket.

'They were never prosecuted.' Her sobs fill the car, sliding off the interior, bouncing off the leather upholstery.

And here we are once more, Kim, my sister, my mother, exposing another layer of herself that I didn't know existed. I have lived in ignorance for so long. Another tough coating of Kim being torn away to reveal a damaged, frail woman underneath. Seconds ago, I had no pity for her, only deep hatred. Hatred at being betrayed and once again, she has turned it around, shown me that people are multi-faceted, the depths to their character immeasurable.

My parents were not my parents at all. My father is a rapist. My mother is my sister.

'I had to keep you. There was never any other option. I want you to know that. I loved you more than anything else in the world. Still do.'

And now it is my turn to cry, to let it all out – the torment and hurt and despair I have tucked away in the last hour, the last year, the last decade – it all comes pouring out.

I need more time to come to terms with this. More time to rebalance my life, my relationships with Kim and Mum. My poor old mum who is currently attempting to work her way through her own set of problems, her damaged brain too diseased to ever understand. But not my mum. She is my grandmother. Kim is my mother.

'I can't call you Mum. It doesn't feel right.' I try to sound casual, not cruel or insensitive but I'm tired and everything is so hard to control. I don't have the energy to temper my reactions. Everything is still so raw, my emotions a bloody, open wound.

She pats my hand and smiles and I feel more of my anger begin to ebb away, anger I thought would eventually consume me. It's subsiding. I suddenly feel lighter, everything easier.

I open the car door and take my keys from Greg, who looks like a man who would like nothing better than to be spirited away from this situation. I bat away Kim's requests to accompany me inside. I tell her that I'm fine, that I need some space, a couple of minutes alone. She nods, smiles. Understands. We have recalibrated, Kim and I, our lives meeting and merging once more. For every divergence, there is convergence.

The air inside is thick, warm, carrying undertones of Gavin's aftershave, Gemma's perfume, the aroma of toast and coffee. I lock the door and lie on the sofa, closing my eyes against the headache that clamps itself around my skull, a combination of relief and shock meeting and fusing, exploding in my brain. My eyes are heavy, weighted. I close them, and everything slips away.

* * *

It's cold out here. I'm cold, my arms and legs rucked with goosebumps. I shouldn't be out here. Not like this. Not in my nightdress when it's dark. I rub at my eyes, unsure how I got here. Did something or somebody wake me? I thought I heard somebody crying but I'm not so sure. I do remember the bolts on the doors were slid back and the door was unlocked. I don't think we should go to sleep with our doors unlocked. It's dangerous. Anybody could get inside and that frightens me. I don't want strangers coming into our cottage while we're all asleep. It's not right. What if somebody who wants to hurt us gets inside, or worse still, a murderer breaks in? I shrug away that thought. We don't know any bad people. Our neighbours and friends are all nice people. Nobody is going to hurt us. At least I hope not.

I stare down at my bare feet and wiggle my toes, trying to dislodge the bits of dirt and grit wedged in between them. I look around, squinting to see properly in the darkness. Why am I here? There's a reason, I just can't remember what it is. And then it comes to me, the memory, rushing at me like a rocket. I definitely heard somebody crying and I saw them too. They sent me back inside, told me to get back into bed. I did get back in but now I'm here again. I don't know how I got here. I just know that I am outside once more and it's cold and something is going on at the bottom of the garden. Something scary. It has to be scary if it's happening in the middle of the night and it made Kim cry. She didn't like me being out here, seeing her upset. She wiped her eyes and sent me back to bed, wouldn't tell me what was happening.

I walk towards the shed. That's where I saw her last time. I wonder if she is still here? Why is she outside? I want to call her name but then everyone might hear me and I'll get into trouble. Mum and Dad don't like it when I do this, wander about in the middle of the night, half awake, half asleep. I don't do it on purpose. It just seems to happen without me knowing about it. I go to bed as normal and wake up in a different place. It doesn't frighten me but I am often cold and tired when I wake up.

Sometimes, Kim takes my hand and leads me back to bed, telling me to stay there as she tucks the covers under my chin. But then at other times, she has Simon in her room when he is meant to be asleep. I saw them once. He was hiding under her bed. She wouldn't tell me what he was doing there. It wasn't a game. He looked scared. His eyes were all big and glassy, like huge marbles staring out at me. So why is he allowed to be out of bed and I'm not? Maybe it's because I'm the youngest and they still think I'm the baby of the family. I'm not. I'm sensible, quiet. Everybody says so.

All of a sudden, I am a bit frightened. I want to go back inside and see Mummy, to climb in bed next to her and feel her lovely, soft arms around me as she cuddles me in. But I can't. I can't do that because as I stare down to the bottom of the garden, my eyes slowly allowing me to look at things properly, I can see who is standing there. And it isn't a burglar or a bad man or somebody trying to break into our garden shed; it's my mummy who is down there, her back to me, her nightgown wet and dirty as she bends over, drops to her knees and starts to cry.

* * *

I wake up. My eyes snap open. Heat floods my body, circling around my head, dampening my hairline. My throat is dry, coarse like sandpaper. I cough, clamber off the sofa where I have been lying, curled up foetus-like, and grab at a glass, filling it with cold water. I glug it back. An icy trickle trails down my throat, landing in my stomach with a punch, cooling me.

My palm is clammy as I place it across my forehead and press hard to alleviate the pressure and pain building there. I was dreaming. Something about Woodburn Cottage and my childhood. Fragments of it float in and out of my brain, disconnected, jagged, like lost pieces of a puzzle that don't slot into place as they should.

I sit down, my limbs leaden. I try to think back to the dream, to what it meant. Was it a dream or was it a memory, a childhood recollection? Another fleeting thought that I can't pin down.

Gavin and Gemma will be back later. I need to get myself together, be the welcoming, capable mother they expect me to be, not some hollowed-out shell of a woman who can't cope and is unable to carry her own emotional baggage. I can carry it with ease. I can and I will. It's who I am, who I will always be.

The words, *Kim is my mother, Kim is my mother* rattle around my head as I rinse my face with cold water, open the fridge door and get ready to prepare our evening meal.

26

The next few days see me going through the motions, being the genial host to Gemma, the perfect mother to Gavin. I smile and chat and cook and clean, making sure the house stays tidy and they are given a warm welcome when they come home every evening. I don't call Kim even though she leaves half a dozen voicemail messages for me to contact her. I need more time. Time to assimilate my thoughts, to think about and come to terms with who I really am. She doesn't call around uninvited. She understands my need for space and for that I am grateful.

By the Friday of the following week, I'm ready to face her. We arrange to meet at a layby on the moor road. I take a flask of coffee to appear civilised. We can meet, sit in my car and talk, something we should have done a long time ago. Why is it those closest to us are always the farthest away? We spend a lifetime of keeping each other at arm's length, batting away questions, shielding our insecurities, widening the gap until it is a yawning chasm. I have always felt like the mistake of the family, the error that needed correcting. And now I know why. Not an error. An accident. Unexpected. But loved all the same. It's now time to bridge that gap, to heal our self-inflicted wounds, to tend to the cuts and bruises we have given one another.

The journey is smooth, the roads quiet. I can see Kim's car parked up ahead. I pull in behind her, kill the engine and step out into the brisk wind that blows freely over the moorland. A carpet of lilac sways back and forth, a sea of coarse heather caught in the breeze.

Kim's car is warm, sweet smelling as I slide into the passenger seat. She squeezes my hand and I let her. No more pulling away, no more acrimony or anger. I am tired of it. Exhausted by my own perpetual fury. It's time to put an end to it, to extinguish my burning anger and direct my energies elsewhere. Somewhere more positive, more rewarding.

I pour out the coffee, the aroma adding to the easy atmosphere between us, our previous feelings melting away. It's time to start again. I've had time to think, time to come to terms with what happened, with who I am. Griping won't change anything. I am who I am and no amount of complaining and crying will alter that.

'Everything okay? You sleeping any better?' Her voice is soft, encouraging.

I want to tell her that yes, I am, but that would a lie. Twice this week, I have woken after vivid dreams, threads of a forgotten childhood that ties me in knots, broken images flashing before me, splintered snapshots of a missing brother. I don't tell her that she is in there as well. I don't tell her that I have suspicions about the part she played in Simon's disappearance because I am not sure. I can't trust my own instincts and I can't rely on my dreams. Twice I have woken up downstairs, standing at the kitchen window, staring out into the garden squinting into the darkness convinced I can see him, the shadow of a boy who vanished into thin air.

So I say nothing, changing the subject, assuring her that everything is ticking along nicely and that yes, Gavin and Gemma are settling in perfectly and that yes, I am rested and well. And that yes, I forgive her. That part is true. I do. Time to move on. No energy left for any more hatred but plenty of room for love and clemency and compassion.

We talk about our families, agreeing that a get-together is long overdue.

'Maybe next time Lucy comes up from Oxford, we can all go out, have a meal, some drinks, make an evening of it?' Kim squeezes my hand.

The thought of seeing Lucy gives me a warm glow. Maybe my daughter and I have more in common than we could ever know, both of us floundering, struggling to fit into our designated familial roles, pushed aside for other siblings, confident siblings that shine. Like Lucy, I've always been the dull star of the family, never flickering as brightly as Kim. I think of Gavin, his poise and confidence, and feel a stab of regret. Maybe I did favour him. Maybe I inadvertently and unknowingly pushed Lucy aside, seeing too many of my own flaws in her character. Quiet, introvert, always lacking in the one thing that I could have given her – self-confidence and a steadfast faith in her own abilities, she was only too glad to loiter backstage, to let her brother bask in the limelight.

I try to stop the tears but they find a way out. Once I let them roll, I can't stop them. I could cry for a hundred years and my well of tears will never run dry. I cry for Warren and for Lucy. I cry for my mother and for Kim and Simon. I cry for a father I can barely remember but most of all, I cry for myself, for all the faults and insecurities and fears that ruled me for so many years, the fact I allowed it to happen, letting them control me. A life half lived, that's what it feels like.

We finish the coffee in companionable silence, conversation unnecessary. Birds flit over the moorland, swooping and diving, a scimitar of swallows visible in the distance, their return a sign that spring is here, summer nudging ever closer.

'I'll be in touch,' I say as I pull at the handle, the car door swinging open.

Kim kisses me on the cheek, an uncharacteristic act but a welcome one all the same. This is the catalyst for us, the turning point of our lives. Everything is different now. Different and better. An improved version of us.

'Speak soon,' she says softly.

I close the door, the wind buffeting me, stinging my face, reminding me that I'm alive.

27

It's the right thing to do. It is empowering disposing of Warren's documents and papers. Kim was correct all along about getting rid of them, her judgement bang on the money. I stop, take a breath, remind myself of how often she was right and how many times I resisted her comments and suggestions. Always wise, always ready to help out, I rejected her assistance and sage ways, her words bouncing off my tough veneer. Maybe our asymmetric relationship was always an indicator as to who we really were and I just couldn't see it. Another thing I missed, blinded by resentment and a constant burning ball of anger that I couldn't dampen or quell. Kim's protective ways, her superior manner – she was never quite able to shake off those maternal bonds and yet I didn't pick up on it. I wonder what else has slipped under my radar?

I take the pile of documents and empty them into the bin. They are no longer needed, surplus to requirements. Warren would understand. Guilt pricks at me for thinking the worst of him, for suspecting him of infidelity. I was blind to how wonderful he was, only too ready to point the finger and accuse him of the worst kind of marital crime long after he was dead and unable to defend himself. He was trying to help me, to protect me. I hope if he's looking down, he can also find it in heart to forgive me.

Gavin was another one who was right. Both he and Gemma work long hours, their time here limited to late evenings and mornings where they snatch a quick breakfast before darting out for the early train. We have fallen into an easy routine, each of us rubbing along together effortlessly. I'll miss them when they leave. Which they will. Perhaps not now or even next month but at some point, they will want their own place, driven by a need for privacy and space. I can't get too attached to their company. I have to remember to keep my own routine going, not depend on them for solace.

The clear-out doesn't take too long. Many of the papers are no more than old bills and invoices. I keep the diary entry and letter for posterity. One day, I may need reminding of how close I came to losing my sister, cutting her out of my life completely. I need to remember how wrong I was, that my instincts aren't always correct, that there is often another story lurking, another point of view that hasn't been given the light of day and scrutinised closely enough.

The last two visits to see Mum have been peaceful. I suspect the staff have changed her medication, sedating her before we arrive. I don't question their methods, glad of the easy atmosphere and gentle rapport, and they don't offer any information as to why Mum is so placid and docile. We all just accept the situation and carry on with our lives. Why rock a steady boat that is sailing on calm waters?

My visits to the market have been few and far between. I'm not actively avoiding bumping into Janine Francis but my life is far easier, far simpler without her in it. I don't think I would be able to hold my tongue should I meet her in the aisle of the local supermarket. Or my fists. I'm not a violent person and have never struck anybody in my entire life but in her case, I am prepared to make an exception.

I don't hear anything from Sergeant Duffield and that doesn't surprise me. A cold case, that's what Simon is and what he will remain unless some unsuspecting rambler or dog walker stumbles across an old shoe or a piece of fabric or, God forbid, a pile of bones hidden beneath the undergrowth in a remote area of the woods. I tell myself that no news is good news. Sometimes, it's easier to live in ignorance. The truth is a painful cross to bear and part of me is relieved that nothing has emerged regarding Simon's disappearance. My life has become settled of late, easier. Do I really want everything tipped upside again? Am I strong enough to stomach it? I think I actually am; the problem is, do I really want to put myself through it?

I finish clearing everything away and slip on my jacket, ready for the next part of my plan, a journey of self-healing I have promised I will make, regardless of Kim's advice to stay clear.

It came to me yesterday, the idea to do it, hitting me side on. Dad has never played on my mind the way Simon has, his existence, his death largely forgotten. Simon's disappearance is an obstruction in my life, blocking out everything else. Everyone else.

When I called Kim and told her of my idea to visit Dad's grave, I didn't expect her response to be so robust, so strong. So visceral. Her condemnation of my idea was evident from the very beginning.

'You're going where?'

I froze, detecting her anger immediately. 'To visit Dad's grave – Granddad's grave,' I said, suddenly breathless and wheezy.

'Why? I mean, why now after all these years?'

'Why not? He's our dad, after all. Well, your dad. My granddad. What I mean is...' I stumble over my words like a child lost, unsure which direction to take. I didn't know what else to say, her reaction leaving me dumbfounded.

'You don't remember him, Grace. Not like I do. Don't put him on a pedestal is all I'm saying.'

I had held the phone away from my face, a creeping heat flushing beneath my skin. 'I'm just going to put some flowers on his grave, that's all. Surely there's nothing wrong with that?'

I heard her sigh, could picture her rolling her eyes, chewing at her lip, biting down on it until she drew blood. 'Okay, just bear in mind, he wasn't a saint, Grace. Far from it. And don't expect me to go with you. Ever.'

We had never really discussed our father before that point. I had dim memories of him and never felt the need to probe. It had just seemed like the right time to visit, to open my mind to the idea of him. I told her as much and we both agreed to disagree. I didn't have the energy to question her reasons, her need to sully his memory. We said our goodbyes with a tacit agreement that I wouldn't speak of it again.

* * *

The graveyard is empty. I am alone, standing at Dad's graveside, shocked at how overgrown it is, disappointed at the state of the stone. Moss has grown over the base, a spread of green felt covering the wording. Next to me lies a shattered, old vase, the flowers broken and snapped, the petals strewn about the grass, small curling ovals of colour slowly rotting into the soil.

I look around for a groundsman, someone who takes care of the place, but can see nobody. I am completely alone. An eerie silence descends. No passing traffic, no birdsong. All signs of life absent. I shiver, pull up my collar then squat by Dad's grave and begin picking up the pieces of broken glass, gathering up the dead flowers, their petals brittle and crisp, flaking to dust between my fingers.

It doesn't take long to clear a space, to tidy up, make Dad's resting place look almost presentable. I should have done it before now. It's embarrassing, my father having the worst-tended grave, the oldest flowers, the dirtiest headstone. I'll come here every month from now on, keep on top of it, give him somewhere decent to rest. He may or may not have been the best dad or husband but he was a human being and deserves to be cared about, to have his final resting place kept neat and tidy. It's the least I can do.

I stand, brush the dirt off my clothes and head back to my car, buoyant about having done this thing, questioning why it has taken me so long to come here. A few minutes out of my day. That's all it has taken and already, I feel a bond with a man I barely remember. A bond with somebody who left this life well before his time.

Sadness blooms within me. Sadness for a dad I cannot remember, sadness at Kim's words regarding his character and integrity. Sadness for a family who never got to grow old together, all of us fragmented and torn apart, our memories, our potential happiness scattered far and wide.

I spend the remainder of the afternoon cooking, cleaning, doing what I can to settle the growing disquiet stirring deep within me. Kim's words, as hard as I try, won't leave me. I tried to distance myself from her dislike of our dad – the only father I had – to form my own opinion of a man I hardly knew and remembered, but words once said, cannot be unsaid. They leave a lasting impression, gouging out a dirty, great hole that is filled with doubt and uncertainty.

By the time Gavin and Gemma arrive home, I am determined to find out more about the man, to work out where Kim's dislike of him comes from. It's just another portion of the jigsaw of our lives, a missing piece that can help me work out what went wrong, why we ended up as we did. Something doesn't fit. What was it about him that Kim disliked? And why don't we have any photographs of us together as a family? Why is that? Where are our holiday snaps? The photos of us frolicking on the beach? Our family picnics, Christmas Day, birthdays, pictures profiling our childhood – where are they all? There is a chasm in our lives, a gaping crevasse. I am missing something important here. I don't know what it is but I intend to find out.

28

He had few friends, if any, preferring to keep his own company. That's as much as I can work out from the scant photos we did keep. On each of them, Dad is sitting alone, a newspaper planted in front of him, his face expressionless as he stares at the camera. I located the pictures in an old album that was here when I moved in, something that had slipped Kim's scrupulous eye and evaded being thrown in the skip. Perhaps their blandness is the reason for their survival. There are no photos of him drinking with friends, playing with his family. Nothing to suggest he even had any loved ones: no wife, no children present on any of the snaps. Just a solitary man with a newspaper, a cigarette and a scowl.

I place the album back on the shelf and sigh. Perhaps I should resign myself to the fact that I will never know anything about him, that he was simply a working-class man with working-class ethics and behaviours: a man who laboured hard and smiled rarely, giving little or nothing of himself away. That was how it was back then; hands-on parenting for men wasn't something that went on in towns and villages like ours. Things were different, the roles of parenting more clearly defined. Men worked, women took care of the house and the children. It's just how it was. So why did Kim say those less than favourable things about him? Yet more family skeletons stuffed away in a cupboard. If we have nothing to hide then why not bring them all out into the open? No more whispers and frown and veiled insults. It's time to come clean.

The knocking at the door pulls me back into focus, sending a sharp blade of disquietude down my spine. Please God, don't let it be Janine Francis. Not that awful woman trying to force her way into here again, elbowing past me, desperate to glean as much information out of me as she can, her nose for other people's dirty linen like that of a bloodhound following the scent of its prey.

It's Mr Waters standing there, his smile broad, his eyes warm and welcoming.

'Come in,' I say beckoning him inside, relief coursing through me.

'Aye, I'll not bother if it's all the same wi' you.' He passes me something, his big old hands rough and leathery. 'I've got t' kettle boiling. I just wanted to give you this. Carrie sent it to me, said she wanted you to 'ave it. Thought it might bring back some memories for you.'

I stare down at a grainy photograph, the colours faded to a pale ochre, the edges yellowed with age. It's a picture of three children dancing around a small paddling pool. My eyes fill up with tears, the image catching me unawares. A fist punches at my chest, hindering my breathing.

Me, Carrie and Simon. Three children playing in the garden on a summer's day many decades ago, ignorant of what the future held for us, blind to the dangers of the world. Blind to the lifetime of misery that lay ahead.

I swallow, blink back my unhappiness, the misty memories of a yesterday that vanished into the ether. 'Thank you,' I manage to say, my words a stutter as I struggle to contain my emotions. 'This is wonderful. Please say thank you to Carrie as well. This means such a lot to me.'

He smiles, turns to head away. I speak before he leaves, keen to ask him, to get him to fill in the blanks of my life. 'Mr Waters, what was my dad like? As a person, I mean. What sort of a man was he?'

He stops, casts a glance at his feet then looks at me, his rheumy gaze searching for something I cannot give. An answer perhaps, as to why I am asking. Why after all these years, I have suddenly taken an interest in a man who has been dead for most of my life.

'Well, he were a quiet sort, you know? Kept himself to himself. A hard-working man. Not the type to stand and chat in the street, if you know what I mean. Some thought him a bit morose but I'm not one to judge. Everyone has their own problems. Why do you ask, lass?'

I shrug, try to answer as honestly as I can without coming across as self-pitying or excessively emotional. Why *do* I want to know? Perhaps it's to prove Kim wrong. Perhaps it's because I don't want my father to have been a rude, callous individual. Perhaps it's because I want to think of him as a loving, demonstrative man even though I know that this was clearly not the case.

'Not sure really. My memories of him are dim. I see snatches of him in my head but I'm not sure if they're real or imagined. I guess moving back here has shaken up a lot of old thoughts and I'm just trying to put everything together, to conjure up as many memories as I can and put them in the right order.'

I want to ask if he was the ogre Kim has made him out to be, but it's a step too far. I wouldn't want to embarrass Mr Waters, to expose him to our crude family affairs. He had his own sets of problems and more than enough to contend with back then with his wife's issues. Why force him to relive it all, to drag him back to a time when everything was full of shadows and fraught with difficulties?

'Well, all I can say is, it were a real shame what happened to 'im. A terrible tragedy, but your family accepted it with good grace, never complaining or asking for pity. You just got on wi' your lives like the good people that you are.'

He heads away and I am envious of Carrie, wishing I had had a father like Mr Waters. Any father would have done. I realise that I have missed having a dad. That's what is driving me. There is hole in my life. A Simon and a father-sized hole, a gaping fissure where the wind blows through. I need to stitch it up, to put an end to this longing, this need to know. I just don't know how to do it, whether I will ever bring it all to a close.

I spend the remainder of the day wandering around aimlessly, a rudderless being with no idea of what to do next. Nothing appeals to me, my writing a dry and unattractive idea. I cook our evening meal, run a bath and have an early night, telling Gavin and Gemma that I'm exhausted and no, I have no idea why I'm so tired and no, I don't think I'm coming down with something, and that yes, I'll call them if I suddenly feel unwell or need anything.

My book fails to hold my attention and I eventually turn off the light and curl up on my side shortly after 9 p.m., quickly falling into a deep and welcome sleep.

* * *

My legs are wobbly. I feel quite sick, butterflies dancing about in my belly, fluttering and flying, making me wish I had turned around and gone back inside. But I didn't. I kept on walking because I wanted to know what was going on out here in the garden. And now I'm out here, still walking, I don't know what to do.

I can see her, my mummy, and she is still on her hands and knees, crouched down in the small space next to the shed. Something is wrong. Very, very wrong. I can feel it. I'm not a grown-up but I know when something bad or nasty is happening and that's what is going on out here. Something bad. Something very bad indeed.

One foot in front of the other. I keep on going, moving closer and closer. Until I stop. Am forced to stop. A large shadow blocks my way. Strong arms spin me around, pushing me back into the house. I wait until they loosen then turn back and run towards my mummy, towards the shed where she is still kneeling. I want to see her, to hug her. I want her to stop crying, to ask why she is out here in the dark. I hear his gruff voice whispering my name, pleading for me to go back inside, but I ignore him. Instead, I keep on running, stopping only when I stumble over something that sends me crashing to the ground. I land on my hands and knees, my chest wheezing as I try to catch my breath.

I sit up, my bottom wet from the grass, dirty and soggy from the squelchy mud after all the rain of the last few days. My hand lands upon something. Something solid. Something heavy, wet, velvety. Shoe shaped. I pick it up, spin it in my hands, staring at it, confusion biting at me. It's a slipper. It's Simon's slipper. Why is it outside? Is Simon out here with Mum and Dad?

My hands land in a puddle as I scramble to my feet, cold air catching in my throat. It's hard to breathe. I'm dizzy, a bit sick. It burns at my throat, the vomit, bouncing around in my tummy as I slip and slide in the mud. I'm tired, confused. I want to go back inside. I want to stay here. I want my mum. I want my mummy...

29

I sit bolt upright in bed. My throat is sore, dry as toast. I'm gasping, retching almost. I clap a hand over my mouth to silence the noise. It was a dream, wasn't it? Or a recollection of the past, a memory resurfacing, clambering into the spotlight, crying out to be noticed? No, it can't have been. It had to be a dream. And yet it strikes a chord with me somewhere in the back of my mind, like a memory I have stored there from my childhood, those shadowy, elusive images that present themselves rarely.

I take a shaky breath, sour air swirling in front of my face. I know the feeling of my hand resting on that slipper, can almost smell the cloying odour of mud and decay. It is so real, so true, an accurate representation of that night. The night I stumbled upon something. Something I shouldn't have. A witness to a heinous act.

I stare at my hand, the sensation of sitting on the wet lawn growing stronger and stronger, settling on me like a heavy shroud. It happened. It was real. The more lucid I become, waking up and tossing aside the fog of sleep, the more I know it actually did take place. They were all out there that night – Mum, Dad, Simon. At least I think Simon was there. It was his slipper: the blue ones with a deep red lining, bought for him by our grandparents, posted to him in a small, cardboard box. I recall his excitement as he opened it, thinking it was a new toy car or the set of motorbike cards he had been hankering after, and then the look of disappointment etched into his features as the contents became apparent to him. Those blue slippers. The ones he was wearing the night he disappeared. They were never found. Everyone presumed he had been wearing them when he left. Or was taken.

I desperately need to call Sergeant Duffield, and yet what would I say to her? That I had a dream I think may have been real? She would think me mad, a raving lunatic. I would lose all credibility. Anything else I told her would be dismissed as unreliable, the ramblings of a crazy woman who is clinging onto the past, refusing to see reason and yet, I don't know what else to do, and I have to do something. Doing nothing isn't an option.

There is a chill in the air as I slip out of bed, shower and get dressed. The house is quiet, the hour still early. Gavin and Gemma are still sleeping. I pad downstairs and make breakfast, the kitchen soon filled with the rich aroma of toast and coffee, the house slowly coming to life.

Everything is still and calm outside. I stand looking out into the garden, thinking back to that night, that dream. The vision that is embedded in my brain: the one of my mother on her hands and knees, scrabbling about in the dirt, the earth still wet after many recent downpours. The police had it in their heads that Simon had wandered, fallen into the river, got washed downstream by the raging current. That didn't happen. He would have been found. People don't just disappear. The river always expels the dead, their bloated bodies washing up on a riverbank, miles away, their clothes snagged by a fallen tree or overgrown shrubbery. It spews them out somewhere. The river swallows nothing. Especially its victims. They resurface once the swell has dissipated, the current slowing down. And Simon has never resurfaced.

So, where is he? I think I know the answer to that question. A sickly sensation sits in my stomach, reminders of that dream nipping at me, refusing to go away. I should do something – anything. I'm just not sure what that something should be.

'Morning. Early start for you after an early night, I guess?' Gavin is standing beside me.

I jump, his voice catching me unawares. 'There's coffee in the pot.

Toast?' I say, opening the breadbin and dipping my hand inside. 'Or would you prefer a full English?'

Even in the midst of impending dread, trapped by the thought of doing the unthinkable, the sight of my son, his voice, the closeness of him, always injects some levity into my life. It's a gift he has, an extraordinary gift of being approachable, genial, permanently cheerful. People warm to him, are attracted to his easy manner.

'Toast is fine, thanks. You sit down. I'll make it.'

He flits around the room, stirring coffee, buttering toast, and I am in awe of how easily he has adapted, slipping back into his role of being a wonderful son with such ease. Warren's face blooms in my mind. It's at times like this I feel his loss keenly. He would have been sitting here with us, discussing Gavin's new role, going through the finite details, advising him, barely able to conceal his delight at the way his son's life is heading.

A fresh cup of coffee is placed in front of me and I have to stop myself from leaning out and grabbing Gavin's hand, asking him to stay with me today, to keep me company and not head off into York to his new office. Today is going to be difficult, a day of fighting off memories, a day of trying to formulate a proper plan. Working out what I should do next. A day of mourning my brother. The brother who, I am now convinced, never actually left this house.

* * *

The day rolls on. I do nothing, wandering about in a haze, too exhausted by everything, too drowsy and lethargic to even think about what I need to do next. I'm stalling. I know that. Stalling and riddled with anxiety. What if I'm wrong? What if I'm unstable, my own memories too wobbly, too damn vague to be trusted? I bite at my lip, nibble at my nails, chew at the inside of my mouth. I'm not wrong. I am certain of this. That's why I am suddenly full of doubt, holding back and using every delaying strategy possible. It's a big thing that I am about to undertake. Huge. And when I go ahead with it, if my instincts are to be trusted, it will open up a whole chamber of horrors and throw up more questions than answers.

My moods, my ability to think clearly, become intertwined, oscillating from hour to hour, minute to minute. I try to do something productive but each time, I find myself standing at the kitchen window, staring out into the garden, to the place where I saw my mother that night all those years ago.

More doubt creeps into my thoughts as the day passes.

Minutes tick by, turning into hours. I am incapacitated, unable to put into action my intentions. Too frightened, crippled by inertia. What seemed possible earlier in the day, is now intolerable: a huge mountain that is too steep to scale.

Gavin and Gemma arrive home sometime before 6 p.m. I am furious at myself for doing nothing, for my lax, slipshod thinking, allowing myself to be held hostage by hesitation and indecision. A day wasted. A day of doing nothing when I could have achieved so much.

We eat, the atmosphere charged with my fear and annoyance. I try to appear normal, to chat and be amiable, but I'm falling apart, pieces of me shrivelling up and coming away, my limbs, my mind disconnected from the rest of my body. A fragmented me, unable to hold it all together. Even having Gavin here isn't enough. Not tonight it isn't. I need something more, something else.

Somebody else.

I wonder if I could have confided in Warren about this new episode of my life? I wonder if it would have happened at all had he still been here. I wouldn't be living back here at Woodburn Cottage. I wouldn't be sleepwalking again. I wouldn't be having the thoughts that I'm currently having, thoughts that I can't supress no matter how hard I try. Thoughts that my parents were in some way involved in Simon's disappearance. Thoughts that perhaps they were the ones who brought his short life to an abrupt and violent end.

**

'You sure you're not coming down with something? You look tired and pale.' Gavin's face is creased with concern, his brow furrowed.

Gemma sits beside him, her eyes narrowed. 'I hope we're not putting on you too much, Grace. You've been cooking our meals and cleaning up after us. There's really no need. We can do it ourselves when we get in on an evening. I'd hate to think you're not well because of our being here.'

I smile, the effort of my rictus grin and forced demeanour making me woozy and nauseous. 'Honestly, it's no bother at all. I'm loving having you both here.' And I am. It's other things; unwanted images, my past catching up with me that is doing the damage, knocking me off balance.

They insist on clearing away the pots. I sit in the living room, listening to their chatter, to the clank of cutlery and dishes, the tap of their feet on the tiles as they scurry about. I let it wash over me, try to clear my head, to rid myself of thoughts I never imagined I would ever have to entertain. Thoughts I don't want to face and yet must.

The evening goes by in a blur of talk about houses and work and the weather while music plays in the background, a series of soft, melodic songs chosen by Gemma. These things should help. They should soothe me, make me feel rested. They don't. I am on edge, my nerves on fire, my flesh burning. I itch to do something, anything. I could crawl out of my own skin, shedding it like a snake, revealing a new me underneath. An invigorated me, less damaged me, all shiny and new and unscathed.

I wait, willing time to pass, willing it be a reasonable hour so I can say goodnight and retire without coming across as rude or unsociable.

It's as the clock strikes 9 p.m. that I stand up, force a yawn and then shiver, telling them that I'm turning in for the night.

'I'm still convinced you're coming down with something,' Gavin says softly.

I try to reassure him, to tell him that everything is perfect, but can sense his eyes as they follow me. I am under his watchful gaze, my every move closely monitored and assessed.

'Honestly, I'm absolutely fine. Just getting older, I guess and in need of more sleep than you youngsters.' My face is tight as I smile. 'See you both in the morning. Sweet dreams.'

I give them a wink and head upstairs, exhausted by the effort of putting on a show, pretending that my life is perfect when in truth, it is on a cliff edge, everything I hold dear on the cusp of falling apart.

30

I am pulling at her, my fingers grasping at the wet fabric of her nightgown. She doesn't seem to see me, to feel me, my presence not noted on her radar even though I am clawing at her, my nails snagging on her skin, catching on the threads of her nightie. She is still crying, her hands and arms working at the soil, pulling at it frantically.

We are wedged down the small space next to the shed. Why are we here? I shuffle closer, almost slipping myself under her arm, trying to get closer and closer. And then I am being pulled away, something – somebody grabbing at my legs. Tugging, tugging, tugging at me, sliding me backwards. My body bucks and writhes, slipping in the wet mud. I scratch and scrape at the ground, resisting. I start to shout. A hand is clasped over my mouth, silencing me.

I am picked up, held tight against somebody's body. I continue to flail about but they are strong. Too strong for me. I use my nails and try to scratch at them, missing and clawing instead at the cool, night air.

Then we drop to the ground, landing on the saturated grass. My back hurts, my eyes are misted over with tears and rain. It's dark. I can't see properly. I start to cry. Loudly. Once again, I am silenced, that big hand pressing down on me. I fight against it, desperate to see my mum. Desperate to know what is going on out here. Another hand catches me on the side of my face. Stars burst behind my eyes. It comes again. Another clout. Hard and vicious. My head snaps back. Pain rushes through me, pounding at my face, my neck, the back of my head.

The strong arms pick me up, carry me towards the house, but it's wet. We slip and slide on the lawn, big feet unable to stay upright, strong arms unable to hold onto me, to fight against the elements. We fall and stagger, air rushing past us, a sense of nothing beneath me forcing me to close my eyes.

I wait for the hit. The ground rushes up to meet us. I feel the crack, the screech of pain across the top of my skull. Then nothing…

* * *

My head spins as my eyes snap open. I remember. I remember that night. My mother digging at the mud with her bare hands, my father trying to drag me away. His arms holding me roughly. Then the hit, his large, open palm striking me. I remember it all. That night. The violence. The night when everything changed. When our little world turned black, the lights extinguished, leaving us floundering about in the thick, unending darkness.

I am outside, standing in front of the shed. I'm wet, the weather inclement. Cold and stormy. I've stopped using the top bolts, hiding the key. That's how I have ended up here, in the wind and the rain. Since Gavin's arrival, I have become lazy. Unthinking. And now it has put me in this position, my lack of preparation. I have been led out here for a reason. To bring it all to an end – the sleepwalking, the flashbacks. Simon's disappearance. Soon, it will all be over.

Above me, the sky is a swathe of black, an expanse of clouds pressing down on me. The weight of the world heaped upon my shoulders. The load of Simon, his vanishing, all coming to this point, this pivotal point in my life when everything changes. When everything breaks under the strain. Over forty years of not knowing, wondering, fearing. And now, discovering, finding out what happened to my brother on that dreadful, fateful evening. I have waited so long, my past cracking open since moving here, my memories returning, a flood of them, forcing me to remember, to confront the past, face it head on. And now it's here. At long last, it's here.

I know now what it is I have to do. Maybe I've always known yet have blocked it out, the truth too painful to face.

I take a trembling breath, a gulp of cold air travelling into my lungs. I stare up at the sky then down at the ground, at the gathering of puddles at my feet. I have to do it. I have to start this thing, this uncovering. And I have to do it now.

My back aches as I drop down onto my hands and knees and scrabble about in the dirt. The rain is pounding against my back, running down my neck and under my clothes, soaking my skin, the fabric of my nightclothes sticking to my flesh like tissue paper and I am crying, snot and tears coursing over my face, mingling with the rain, dripping off my chin and splashing on the floor; not that I can see it happening, but I can feel it – I can feel everything, every whisper of wind, every beat of my heart, every pulse of my body, every drop of rain that falls from the dark sky above and hits me with force – I am hypersensitive to their presence, the impact they have on me and the wet earth beneath me as I frantically search for my brother, for what is left of him after being buried here for all these years. Decade after decade after decade, left out here on his own in the pitch black; season after season, summer through to winter, my dear, beautiful brother exposed to those icy, unforgiving evenings, those long, lonely evenings where the wind rages like a demon and the wild animals prowl, cawing and hooting and growling, their cries and mating calls filling the wide spaces of the village and beyond, a reminder that the darkness is designed for those who do not speak, their language known only to one another, not for us diurnal creatures who shelter indoors in the safety and warmth of our homes. Except for Simon. He has been out here all that time. He has heard the hoots of the owls, the screeching of the wild animals that prowl and hunt and scavenge. He has lain here in the darkness and the silence, waiting to be found.

I stop, my limbs numb and sore, my vision misted with tears. I still cannot quite believe that he was here all the time, in my garden, so close to the cottage, to the place where he was born, spending nearly every day of his short, sweet life playing, sleeping and eating. He smiled, he cried in this house, in this garden, on this patch of lawn. He loved, he laughed, he feared. Oh God, the fear he must have felt...

And now I am up close to his final resting place, to where he lies buried in the loam. He is here, so near to where I am crouching. I lower my head, placing my ear to the ground, listening for him. And I think I can hear it too – his heartbeat. His breathing. The pulsing of his soul as he cries out for me to unearth him, to be exposed once more and taken to a better place, somewhere where he can rest and be free, not lodged under this edifice, trapped next to a dirty wooden shack that is on the point of collapse after years and years of neglect. He deserves better. He deserves to be free.

Fingers numb with the cold, I carry on, clawing at the soil: digging, scooping up handfuls of wet earth, my nails embedded with it, brown crescents of soil, the smell of it filling my nostrils. The rain soaks me, runs down the back of my nightclothes, down my neck, soaks into my skin. It's fitting, I think, that I have come full circle. I am my mother all these years later. I am her, stooped down, crying, scratching, scrambling in the dirt. I know now what it was she was doing that night, who she was trying to find.

'Mum? Mum! What the hell are you doing?'

I don't turn around. If I turn to look at his face, to see the horror in his eyes, I might be forced to take stock, to stop. And I can't stop. I've come too far. No going back now. Just a relentless march towards the truth.

'Mum, stop it! What's the matter with you?' Gavin is next to me now, his arms hooked around my shoulders, his weight pulling me to my feet.

I lash out, knock him off balance, see him in my peripheral vision as he staggers and falls to the floor. I don't stop, don't make any attempt to apologise, to help him back up. I carry on, my arms, my hands pumping furiously, clawing, grasping at clumps of soil, throwing them aside. Trying to find him, to locate Simon. My Simon. He's here. I can feel him, my dearest brother. Our little boy. The boy who never grew old. I can feel him beneath me, can see his arms as he reaches out to me, crying my name. Begging me to help him.

Gavin is behind me again, shouting in my ear, his voice battling against the rain as it lashes against the shed roof, pounds the patio, bashes against the fence. The wind whips up, gaining in speed, pushing at our backs. Gavin pulls at my arm. I shake him free, kicking out at him, throwing him off balance again. He is being gentle with me. I know that. If he really wanted, he could pick me up, carry me off without breaking a sweat and yet he hasn't. That's because he is treading carefully, thinking I'm unhinged, that I have lost my mind. Maybe I have. Maybe I am on the brink of madness doing this, on the verge of a breakdown thinking such thoughts. I don't care. Nothing will stop me. Nothing and nobody. I'll keep going until I find him.

I need tools, a shovel, something that can get me deeper into the earth. The soil is shifting easily. It's wet, malleable, but I need more. I need to get lower, as far down as I can go. I'll go to the centre of the earth if I have to. I am thinking all of this as I work furiously at the mud, knowing that I have to break my pace at some point to go into the shed, retrieve the necessary utensils and finish this job. And then I stop, my hand resting on something. I push farther and farther in, grasp at it, my fingers furled around it, this item I have found. I tug, pull at it, feel it give, a slow loosening as it rises to the surface through the gloop and the mud and the water.

And then it is free. I am holding it close to me, pressing it to my chest, pushing it against the sodden fabric of my nightclothes, this object that I have sucked out of the wet loam.

My son is standing behind me in the pounding rain. A clap of thunder suddenly cracks overhead, the clouds ripping apart, unleashing more rain. Despite all of this, I can hear his voice – gentle, coaxing. Pleading. I can feel the heft of his hand on my shoulder, a tender touch that tries to move me out of this small space, out of the trench I have dug with my bare hands. But I don't respond. I can't. I am frozen to the spot, stuck in a moment. Trapped in a time-warp. Because I know now, what this thing is that is pressed against my shivering body. I can feel its shape, the moulding of the rotten, woollen lining. If I try hard enough, close my eyes and concentrate, I can feel the soft skin that once fitted inside it.

I hold it up in front my face, a scream escaping from my lips, his name repeated over and over and over.

Simon. Simon. Simon.

Simon's slipper. It's here. If his slipper is here, then so is he. So is he...

31

We fall back together on the grass, the muddied, rotten slipper still clutched between my fingers, Gavin's arms locked around my waist. I am nuzzled into his shoulder, tears streaming, my sobs wild, visceral. I don't think I will ever be able to stop now I have started. I will drown in them – over forty years of unshed tears. He holds me close, trying to placate me, to soothe and reassure me. He asks me what is going on. I can't speak, choking on every word whenever I try to explain.

'Mum, please. You're scaring me! What the hell is going on here?'

My body heaves. My head buzzes. I want to explain, to tell him what I have found, but every word feels gruelling. I swallow, try to catch my breath, releasing it from my clutches, waving it in the air between us, spluttering, sobbing. 'It's his slipper, Gavin. It's Simon's slipper. I finally remembered. I remembered what happened that night. I know where he is.'

My face is wet, streaming with rain and tears and snot but I can still see Gavin's reaction, the stiffening of his shoulders, the slight narrowing of his eyes. This is the time, the only time I have, to persuade him, to get him to help me, not write me off as deranged. A woman undergoing a massive breakdown. I won't be shuffled back inside, told to calm down, that I'm not thinking clearly. I have to get him on my side. I have to get him to help me find Simon. It's now or never.

'Please, Gavin. Please hear me out. He's here. I know he is. You can either help me or not but I'm going to do it anyway.'

'Do what, Mum? What're you going to do?' His face is close to mine now, a wall of rain slicing between us, drenching us. Keeping us together. Keeping us apart.

'I'm going to get a spade and find him, Gavin. That's what I'm going to do.'

I am up on my feet and heading into the shed before he can stop me. Which he will. I can tell by the look on his face, he thinks I'm having a mental episode. He will be raking over it in his mind, assuming Warren's death has pushed me over a precipice. He will rush inside, head upstairs, wake Gemma, ring a doctor, ask for help, tell them his mum needs help, needs restraining. And if he does that, it will be over before it's even begun.

Time is of the essence. I can't let any of that happen. I have to move quickly, get that shovel, start digging.

It's dark inside the shed, my feet slipping on the dusty floor. A rack of old tools is stacked high on a metal hook at the back. I take one, turn and see Gavin standing behind me. I flinch, have visions of him grabbing it from me, throwing it to one side, refusing to allow me access to the narrow strip of land between the shed and the fence. A person-sized strip of land. Simon-sized.

He doesn't. He steps forward, hugs me, speaks clearly, softly. 'I'll do it, Mum. Tell me where you want me to dig and I'll do it.'

My son is humouring me. I don't care. He's helping and that's all that counts. It's all I've ever wanted – to be listened to, helped, not turned away, eschewed, told I am overreacting, that my worries are ridiculous. Irrational and unfounded. Finally, somebody is taking my side and I am elated.

He doesn't expect to find anything. I can tell by the look on his face, the faraway expression, his slow, deliberate movements as he takes the spade and begins to carve away at the ground, pulling weeds aside, slicing at the soil, unearthing great clumps of it and throwing it over his shoulder. It lands, a rising mound of mud, weeds and rubble. Over forty years' worth of debris. We have a lot of work to do. These are the thoughts that are rumbling around my head as Gavin shifts the wet soil, digging, digging, digging. So much effort. So much work to do. Except there isn't and we don't. After only a matter of minutes he stops, drops to his knees, starts pulling at the ground with his hands, tearing at it, panting and gasping.

And then it happens. He turns to me, his face crumpled, his eyes wide, brimming with tears. 'Mum,' he says, an element of panic creeping into his voice. 'We need to call somebody. Go inside and get the phone. Please. Do it now!'

And then the world begins to spin, the heavy night sky lowering, crushing me; the clouds, the stars, the weight of each raindrop pinning me to the ground, pushing my face onto the wet grass, pressing me hard into the loam.

I don't reply. I can't. Gavin waits, watches, then steps over me, heads back inside, leaving me out here alone. I scramble up, crawl on my hands and knees to where he was digging. The place he dug to try and mollify me. The place where he has found something that scared him, made him bolt for help.

Water has begun to fill the hollow, that wretched dark space next to the fence. I scoop it out with my hands, so much of it. Freezing, dirty water. And then I stop, my fingers landing on a solid object. A cold, hard length of something. I don't need to lift it out, to inspect it. I trace the shape of it with my fingertips, knowing what it is. I shriek. Fall backwards. Let out a muffled howl, relief and misery, years and years and years of it escaping in a long, deep moan.

The length of bone is grimy, covered with compacted dirt, but nothing can disguise what it is. I hold it in front of me. My hands are trembling, my body shaking.

He's here, he's here, he's here.

All this time and he was so close by, calling out to me. Waiting to be found. Our connection was never truly severed. I knew it. I just knew.

I sense Gavin's presence behind me, can feel his fear, his growing disquiet. I turn, look into his eyes, water half blinding me, hold the bone up into the air, clutching at it as if my life depends on it. 'It's Simon, Gavin. Simon is here. He was here all the time.'

* * *

The hot tea fails to warm me. Every inch of me is like ice, my body aching as I shiver, my teeth chattering, my legs knocking together like ninepins. Gemma's arm is around my shoulders. She is pulling me towards her, trying to comfort me. She thinks I'm upset. I'm not. What I am is relieved. Relieved that it is finally all over. Except it isn't. We're not quite there just yet, at that elusive finishing line. There are lots of unanswered questions – questions that may never get a proper, satisfactory response. How can my mother possibly recall the events of that night? She is the only one left who would know the truth, the events locked in a cell deep in the recesses of her brain. A brain that no longer functions as it should. And if she can't tell us, then how will we ever know what happened?

Outside, a team of police officers battle against the elements as they head towards the grave. Simon's grave. His final resting place. I don't need to wait for the results of any DNA test or forensic investigations to confirm my suspicions. It's him. My lovely brother. My Simon.

Before me sits Sergeant Duffield, a look I can't quite fathom evident in her face, the way she is watching me, assessing me. Everything I do and say is being noted and held under a microscope for closer scrutiny. For now, all I want to do is wait here until they find the rest of him. I'm not leaving this cottage until their search is complete.

'We need to contact your sister. Can you give us her number so we can call her?' Sergeant Duffield's voice is soft, gentle but I know for certain that this is an act. She is on duty, watching for chinks in our armour, waiting for us to collapse under the strain, to fall apart and for all our secrets to come spilling out. We're all suspects and guilty until proven otherwise.

Gavin is on his feet, handing over his phone for her to see. She scrolls through it, notes down Kim's number and excuses herself, disappearing into the relative privacy of the hallway. We hear her voice, a whisper in the silence of the living room, as she speaks. I can hear snatches of the conversation, stray words filtering through to where we are sitting.

Discovery.
Forensic investigation.
Questions.

I wonder if it's Kim or Greg she is speaking to. I wonder what they are thinking, what their expressions are as they listen to Sergeant Duffield, whether they are wide-eyed and incredulous or are thinking this is a sick prank. A false alarm perhaps. Somebody pulling a horrible stunt. Maybe Kim has waited for this moment and is steeling herself, waiting for the inevitable body blows that this investigation will bring.

Greg's car pulling up almost an hour later breaks into the uncomfortable silence that has settled on us. It's an interlude in our anxiety, a welcome break from our collective uneasiness. They head into the living room, the pair of them, hair tousled from sleep, eyes dark and baggy. I smile as Kim seats herself opposite Sergeant Duffield, Greg squashing himself next to his wife, their bodies pressed together for protection. Kim is nervous. I can tell by her lack of eye contact, the way she locks and unlocks her fingers, pushing them down into her lap to stem the fidgeting. I wonder what she is hiding. Exactly how much does she know about that night?

They speak when spoken to, Greg's voice rough and throaty, Kim's a whisper, scarcely a noise at all: a baby breath, soft. Innocent. I want to go over there, sit myself between them, all of us huddled together for comfort. It's alien watching them being questioned. I don't like it. I am still trying to come to terms with the recent restructuring of our relationship. Is this something we need to reveal to the police? Lying solves nothing, that much I do know. What if they find out? It will surely arouse their suspicions, make them think there's more to discover, that we are hiding the truth from them. Maybe we are.

I shudder. Everything is fragmented, an unfixable mess. I am suddenly fatigued, a wave of exhaustion hitting me side on. My eyes are heavy. I close them, rest my head on Gemma's shoulder and wish it all away.

32

THE NIGHT HE LEFT

John Goodwill stirs in his sleep, a noise waking him. He sits up, his skin prickling with annoyance. He doesn't like noises at night and he doesn't like being woken abruptly. This is his house, his rules. Nobody breaks them. Nobody.

He flicks on the bedside lamp. Sylvie's not there. Her side of the bed is smooth and cold. His annoyance quickly turns to anger: full-blown, white-hot fury. She has no right to be up wandering at this hour. Where the hell is she? That woman causes him no end of problems. All he asks is to be left to do his own thing and to sleep soundly at night. He's the bread-winner of this family. He deserves a little respect. And if they don't show him any, he will be forced to do stuff he doesn't like to do. They know this, this weak-willed family of his, so why do they continue to rile him, ignoring his rules, bending and breaking them as if they are nothing of note?

The floor is cold beneath his feet. He searches for his slippers, decides to find his boots instead. Slippers appear softer, less edgy. And right now, he is very edgy indeed. He wants to come across as authoritative. Tough. Somebody to be reckoned with.

A distant noise stops him as he rummages at the back of the wardrobe for a thick sweater. He turns, listens, his scalp crinkling, the skin on his neck puckering. Voices. He can hear voices. Another step, then another. He is standing next to the window, listening. They're coming from outside, the voices.

He moves the curtains to one side, squints. And sees them. Anger, panic, dread course through him. He thinks he knows what's going on here. She threatened him with it last week. He laughed, told her to shut her mouth, that she was making things up, had an overactive imagination. A filthy mind. That's what he told her she had, to be thinking such thoughts. To accuse him of such things. A filthy fucking mind.

'You've cooked all this up to spite me!' he had shouted.

She had cowered. Damn right she cowered. With a mouth like that. With ideas like that. Who the hell did she think she was talking to?

He heads downstairs then thinks better of it, stepping back up and peering into his eldest daughter's room. She is lying there, a still mound under the bedsheets. No sound of her breathing. No noise at all. 'Kim? You awake?'

No response. Just a drawn-out silence that speak volumes. She's awake. He knows it. She knows that he knows it. They've been lying to each other their entire lives. You can't kid a kidder. Maybe she's in on this little scheme, this plan his wife has cooked up. This secretive, fucking little plan that will split his family apart. He can't let it happen. He won't. She's probably been down there already, joining in with whatever is going on.

He backs out of the room, heads downstairs. His head thumps. He didn't know Sylvie had it in her. The fucking gall of that woman. The fucking gall of her!

At the bottom of the stairs stand his shoes. He pushes his feet into them, ties his laces, a rough attempt with clumsy fingers that makes him cross and sweaty. He gives up, shoving the laces down the side of his boots. Too long. Everything is taking too damn long. It could be over by the time he gets out there. They could be gone. And he can't allow that to happen. This is his family. He can do whatever he likes with them. Nobody takes them away from him, least of all that fucking woman and her interfering old hag of a mother. She'll be involved somewhere along the line. He just knows it. Silly cow. He never did like her and the feeling, he knows, is mutual.

He never could understand why they're still so close, his wife and her mother. They're both adults, have their own lives and should have cut the cord a long time ago. What is it with that family and their need to constantly be in touch with each other? He broke away from own parents years back. They taught him discipline, how to be independent, not ruled by his emotions. It's the only way. He's tried to instil it in his own kids, teach them that being soft gets you nowhere.

She fought against him, Sylvie, bucking back every time he laid down the law. She soon saw his point of view once he showed her who the man of the house was. He didn't enjoy using his fists but what else could he do? If she had done as she was told, taken his words of wisdom, it wouldn't have happened. Things would have been smoother, easier. All of their problems are her doing.

The back door is ajar. He rolls his eyes, lets out a deep, irritated sigh. She doesn't even have the common sense to shut it, to cover her tracks and stop him from following her. Stupid bitch. She could have locked it, trapped him inside. But then, she knew what would happen next. How it would end. Maybe she's not a stupid as she makes out. His house, his rules.

It's cold out; the rain has just stopped. The ground is spongy under his feet, the lawn slippery as he heads over the where the noise is coming from.

He sees the boy first, his crop of hair bobbing about. They're at the bottom of the garden. He's still in his pyjamas and slippers, for God's sake. What the hell is she thinking? John marches over to them, grabs the boy's hand, pulls him away. Sylvie turns, glowers at him then ducks, her hands covering her head. She's expecting something, his fist connecting with her face. A slap, maybe. Or a solid punch that will knock some sense into her. Not now. Not here. He'll wait until they get back inside before he deals with her. Then she'll know. Then she'll regret what she is trying to do, wish she hadn't even attempted it.

'Nobody takes my kid from me. Nobody. Understand?' His voice is a whisper. This is a private moment. He needs to get them back inside. Prying eyes and all that. That miserable old bastard next door might see them. He can't risk that, have Ted Waters blabbing his mouth all around town.

She nods, her chin wobbling, eyes wide. She thought she could get away with this. Is she mad? Has she not learned by now who it is she is dealing with? The lengths he will go to look after and control his family?

Then she grabs at Simon again, pulling at the lad's arm, trying to get him close to her so she can take him, salt him away somewhere: probably at her mother's house. That'll be her plan – drive him up to Northumberland, thinking he'll be safe there. He won't. Simon is his boy, his property. He stays here, in this house with his family. It's where he belongs, where he will always remain.

A tug of war ensues, Sylvie pulling the boy one way, his father pulling him another. The youngster starts to cry. Great big sobs, his chest heaving. John needs to shut him up, show him how to behave properly, like a man, not a big baby. He won't have any child of his growing up a sissy. He should have been tougher with him over the years, shown him how to stand up for himself, not let him whimper and moan like a big, blubbering idiot.

He doesn't hit Simon hard: no more than a light slap. Barely a touch at all. Sylvie staggers backwards, the lad's hand still clutched in hers. They stumble about together, unable to stay upright, the momentum of the tug of war, the hit, sending them reeling. The boy lets go of his mother's hand, his feet unsteady as he slips on the wet paving slabs and slams head first into the brick coalhouse. A sickening crack. He falls to the floor. Unmoving. Still. A crumpled heap.

It all happens so suddenly. John rounds on Sylvie, hisses at her, telling her it's all her fault. She was going to drive him to her parents' house, take his son from him. This is on her. She shouldn't have grabbed him, shouldn't have tried to fight him, to go against his wishes. If she hadn't taken him from the house, snatching him out of his bed in the middle of the night, none of this would be taking place.

Sylvie is down on her knees, cradling her son, whispering his name over and over. His body is floppy, unresponsive, his eyes open, no sign of life there.

'This is your fault, you stupid bitch. You did this. You killed him. You murdered your own son...'

33

Kim was asleep when he looked in on her. She had already been down there but came back to bed, terror coursing through her. It's her default emotion. Her whole life, one big rollercoaster of panic and dread.

They're out there right now, arguing. She saw them earlier but ducked out of view for fear of being seen. This is her fault. She did this, speaking to her mum, telling her what was going on. Not that her mum didn't already know. She knew. She definitely knew.

Kim's words caused something inside her mother to snap. She was able to see it in her face, the way her eyes turned dark, her face draining of all colour. It was the final straw. Something had to be done, it's just that Kim didn't know what that final thing was going to be, how it would look. As a family, they have so few options, nowhere to turn. Nobody to step in and help. She guesses that Mum was trying to take him to Grandma's house, somewhere away from here. Somewhere he would be safe. But it looks as if that's not going to happen. He woke, their enemy. Her father. He has intercepted her plan. Stopped her.

Kim kneels on the bed, pulls the curtains aside, sees them down there, their body movements jerky and aggressive. Her heart is battering like a drum. Something awful has happened, she can tell. Something worse than what takes place in this house day after day, night after night. As if anything could be worse than that.

Her father picks up Simon and carries him across the garden. Her little brother isn't moving. Oh dear God, he isn't moving.

The room spins and slopes, everything warping, sliding away from her. What's wrong with Simon? Where is he taking him?

She lies back on the bed, chest tight, breathing shallow. She's too frightened to look out, to watch what he's going to do next. Everything is a whirling vortex, her tiny, damaged world spinning out of control. She thought things couldn't get any worse. She was wrong.

Time is an empty concept, a painful, immeasurable thing. Nothing makes any sense. Or maybe it does. If she's going to be honest with herself, it makes perfect sense. Something was always going to happen. Just not this. She never anticipated this.

They're still out there. She is back up on the bed, peering out into the darkness, half hidden in the shadows. There's movement down the side of the shed. Her father appears, his face veiled, his expression unreadable. Down on her knees beside him is her mother, her hands spread out on the ground. And then something else – a smaller shadow walking towards them. A child. She sucks in her breath. Her throat tightens. It's Grace. She's out there again, making her way towards them. Sleepwalking. Again. And no Simon. Oh God. No Simon. Where the fuck is Simon?

Terror pulses through her. This is all too much. Out of control. Their damaged, dysfunctional family is unspooling, falling apart, all their badness and wickedness fighting its way out into the open where everyone can see it.

Feet unsteady, her breath ragged, she races downstairs and sees him. He's carrying her through the kitchen, Grace. Her sister. Her child. She is slumped in her father's arms. Is she asleep? Unconscious? Kim swallows, pushes her fingers through her hair wearily. Is she dead? Their dad is capable of doing this. She knows it, he knows it. He is capable of anything. Anything at all.

She grapples with him, pulls Grace from his arms, feels the weight of her as she wraps herself around the child's body, snuggling her in. He doesn't resist. For once. For once, she has the upper hand, can move away from him without a fight.

Kim takes her child, her sister back up to bed, tucks her in, hopes that by the morning this will all be over. Whatever *this* is.

34

NOW

The DNA results didn't take long to confirm what we already knew – that they were the remains of Simon, our beautiful, beautiful boy. The boy we lost all those years ago. The boy who vanished from our lives, from this house, without ever actually leaving home.

The investigation is still ongoing, Kim providing them with as much information as she is able. And she hasn't held back. Everything has been fully disclosed, our family's dirty linen hung out for all the world to see.

It was a relief in the end, she said. A relief to unburden herself, to open up and let it all out. She had lived in a world of filth and murkiness for most of her life, she said afterwards, always creeping around, worried about being found out. Deceit is a festering wound. It never heals, infection after infection setting in, rotting the surrounding areas of flesh, charring and scarring, ruining and corrupting forevermore.

I only know what she has told me. Sergeant Duffield has been careful, discreet, keeping our conversations separate. I have had to rely on Kim for information but am sure that it won't be long before everything is revealed. I am looking forward to it and dreading it in equal measure.

Gavin and Gemma have been unbelievably supportive. And then yesterday, a visitor arrived. Lucy standing in the living room as I came downstairs after a mid-morning shower was enough to stop my heart.

Relief and love bloomed within me. All together. My family was all together. A poor set of circumstances in which to meet, but we are all here under the same roof and that is enough for now.

Later today, I am going to be interviewed at the police station. I will tell them all that I know. Not that it is much. Fragments of a disordered childhood is all I have: snatches of a past blurred by time and distorted and dulled by somnambulism.

But before that happens, I am meeting up with Kim. She insisted we speak beforehand. There's something she wants to tell me. Something important. She wants me to hear it from her rather than from a stranger in a police station. I am all out of ideas as to what it can be. I'm not sure I have any more room for nasty surprises but I will do my best to not react disproportionately, to try to keep my emotions in check and not cause any further upset. We need to stick together, us Goodwills, not do something that will drive a wedge between us. All we have is each other.

I tell Lucy and Gavin that I am going to be a couple of hours, that I am meeting Kim to discuss the case and that time dependent, we will visit Nana afterwards. I pray they don't try to accompany me and am more than a little relieved when they nod and wave me goodbye, the three of them sitting at the kitchen table, talking, chatting, drinking tea and eating cake. It's a fine old sight and makes me as happy as I can recall feeling for the longest time. A splash of colour in my life. No more shades of grey. Only rainbows and sunshine after a long and powerful storm.

Kim is sitting at our usual table. She gives me a cursory wave and a warm smile as I enter and head towards her. She stands, takes my hand in hers when I sit down and it's then that I know this is going to be serious. I brace myself, sucking in chunks of air in readiness for what I am about to hear.

I think I'm prepared for this, after what we have endured over the past few weeks.

I'm not.

Once again, she blindsides me, knocking all the air out me, leaving me faint and breathless.

'Grace, what I'm about to tell you isn't easy. All I ask is that you don't get up and walk out of here without hearing the whole story. When I said you needed protecting from yourself, it wasn't an insult. You've always had an active mind, been inquisitive. You have always been keen to get to the bottom of any situation and I was scared that you would probe a little too far, discover things that were best left undiscovered.'

I shake my head, jut out my bottom lip to indicate my mystification at her words.

'Our dad was an abusive man. A horrible, cruel man.' She looks away, her eyes filling up at the memory, her mouth and chin trembling.

'He wasn't my dad really,' I say, hoping to distance myself from his actions. Hoping to distance myself from him. I am almost certain now that Sylvie did nothing wrong, that he was the one who did the damage, that he was the one who killed Simon. She was trying to save him. It was him all along. It was always him.

Kim glances back at me, her expression veiled, anxious. My insides tighten. I don't want to hear this. I promised I wouldn't walk out. I have to keep that promise. I can't keep on running from the past. It will chase me for forever if I don't stay and face up to it.

'That's the whole point, Grace. This is what I wanted to tell you. He *was* your dad. And he was my dad too. He raped me. I was thirteen years old; a naïve, quiet teenager and he raped me. His evilness, his depravity knew no bounds. I am so sorry, my darling. I am so very, very sorry.'

I feel no rage, no desperate, growing anger. Instead, a deep sense of calm settles within me. Maybe I've always suspected this, since Kim first told me about our real relationship, about who we really are. I don't need to get up and walk out. I don't need to do anything at all. Nothing has changed. I am still me. My identity hasn't altered. My provenance isn't something of which I am particularly proud. I won't be shouting about it from any rooftops, but it doesn't alter who I am. It's experience that shapes us. Experience and being loved and nurtured. And despite growing up with somebody like him in our household, I was both. You can't kill love. You can try, but we hung onto ours. Even amidst the terror and the trauma, we always knew that our mother loved us even if he didn't. Regardless of his physical strength and all-encompassing temper, her bond, the wealth of love she had for us was always the greater, more powerful force, as was Kim's. She tried. She really tried. She was strong mentally. He was stronger physically. It wasn't her fault.

Kim stands up, moves around the table and puts her arms around me, holding me close. We stay like that for the longest time until she sits back down, dries her eyes and smiles at me. 'I wish I could say that's all there is to say but unfortunately, there's more.' She takes a sip of her coffee. 'I know that you're robust enough to stomach it. You have the tenacity and strength of a thousand-strong army and to be honest, it's a huge relief to speak openly. I've had years and years of staying silent, not speaking, being terrified of letting it all out.'

I reach across the table and place my hand over hers. The café is almost empty. Two elderly women sit in the corner, their conversation loud and rapid. We are not in their line of vision. They are too engaged in their own talk to take any interest in ours.

'Mum tried to take Simon away because of the abuse. She couldn't prove that Dad was actually abusing Simon, but I saw him sneaking into his bedroom on more than one occasion and did what I could to protect him, hiding him in my bedroom with me. He'd abused me for years. Simon wouldn't have been immune to it.'

She stops and I swallow, thinking back to those memories – Simon skulking under Kim's bed, the terrified look on his face. I feel a stab of dread, a knife twisting in my gut. That vile man. That poor, poor boy.

'She was going to take him to Grandma's house in Northumberland but he caught her. She panicked, made mistakes, made it too easy for him to catch her out. She knew that he had raped me and feared for Simon. Even if he wasn't abusing him sexually, Simon certainly met with Dad's fists on plenty of occasions, as did Mum. That monster had no redeeming features or qualities, certainly none that I can recall. An odious little man through and through.'

'And he is our dad.' I rub at my eyes, my shoulders hunched, a streak of misery roaring through my veins.

'But we're not him, Grace. You are part of me and I am part of you and that is all we need to know. We've survived thus far. All we need is each other.'

'And Mum,' I murmur, smiling as I think of her sweet, little face, her tiny, frail body perched in a chair at the care home as she watches out of the window, waiting for our visits. The past rearing its head in her poor, demented mind, continually biting at her.

'And Mum,' Kim replies. 'She has always been there for us.'

'How did—'

'How did she get away with passing you off as her own child?'

I nod, tears building, a lump wedged in my throat. I want to weep for an eternity – tears for me and Kim, tears for Simon and tears for the mother who sacrificed everything for her children. We owe her so much. A thousand kisses, the promise of an eternity in heaven wouldn't be enough for the woman who risked her life to save ours.

'As soon as she realised what had happened, she packed me off to Grandma's house under the pretence that I was asthmatic and had bronchitis, saying the clean air would do me good. She hardly ever ventured out of the house, lying low and then pretended that she had given birth, telling anyone who asked that she didn't realise she was pregnant until she was six months gone. I think there were those who suspected – the likes of Janine Francis – but nobody could prove anything. Things were different back then – no visits from the midwife or health visitor. It could be done and *was* done. You're living proof of that.'

'And this is why you didn't want me to move back into Woodburn Cottage?'

She shrugs and smiles. 'Maybe. I kind of guessed what had happened to Simon and that was why Mum would never sell the place. I couldn't prove anything and would never have attempted to. Mum would have been tried as an accessory to murder when all she had tried to do was save her son from a monster. That night, after it all happened, Dad made sure everything looked normal in the garden, no obvious disturbances to the soil. He cleaned the patio down, both he and Mum bathed, washed their clothes and went to bed, then the next morning – well, you know the rest.'

Something jars in my head, a distant memory. A memory of Kim peering out of the window and pointing to Mr Waters' house. I don't ask her her reasons for doing such a thing. She was young, frightened, wanted to deflect the blame elsewhere, away from Mum. She didn't want to admit that so many terrible atrocities could happen in our own family. She had an image of Mr Waters as an abusive man when all the while, the monster lurked in the heart of Woodburn Cottage, the place we called home.

'After Dad died, why didn't Mum go to the police? Tell them what had happened?' I bite at my nails feverishly, a habit I thought I had shaken.

'Because how could she prove that she hadn't done anything wrong? She was put in an impossible situation. Damned if she didn't and damned if she did. At least we've now got Simon back and Mum is too ill to recall what went on. It's the best way really. The only way.'

'The only way,' I murmur, nodding my head sagely. 'Did you always suspect that Simon was buried there?'

Kim sighs, blinks back more tears. 'I wasn't sure what to think. I was terrified and knew something awful had happened to him.' She lets out a trembling sigh, swallows hard. 'I went through loads of dreadful scenarios about where he was and then had to block it out of my mind. I didn't see what actually happened, so even if I'd told the police, it would have been my word against his. He was such a strong man, both physically and mentally: overpowering and insidious. Imagine the beatings we would have all have had to put up every single day if I had done that?' More deep breaths. More tears flow. 'We had so much to hide, so much to be scared of. I feared that if I spoke too freely, they would start to dig deeper, find out about you and then take you away from me. I just couldn't risk that happening. Social services would have got involved, seen the signs of abuse and what remained of our family would have ceased to exist. You would have been sent to a foster home and we might not have seen you again. So we learned never to question anything, instead hiding it all away, going about our daily lives with our heads down, too frightened, too traumatised to do or say anything at all.'

I screw up my eyes, cocking my head to one side. 'Signs of abuse? What do mean, signs of abuse?' A clock ticks in my head, a countdown to an exploding bomb. I wait for it to detonate, for the shrapnel to embed itself in my brain, to tear at my flesh, leaving me in ruins, a shell of the woman I used to be.

'We did what we could to keep you safe and as far as I am aware, it only happened once or twice in the months following Simon's death, but that was enough. We knew then that things had to change. We had to do something.'

I can't breathe. It comes to me in a flash – a memory of him coming into my bedroom at night, lying next to me, the heat of his body pulsing beneath the cool cotton sheets. Oh God. Oh dear God, it happened to me too. I blanked it out, all that horror and suffering. All that abuse. I blanked it out and now it's back. It has somehow managed to slither its way back into my brain, a latent memory reawakened. Moving back to Woodburn Cottage, the sleepwalking, it stimulated dormant memories, breathed life back into them and allowed me to see the truth. The truth about Simon. The truth about what sort of a man my father really was. The truth about my damaged childhood. He was a violent abuser, a villain. A demon.

'What changed?' I ask, perspiration breaking out on my back, my neck, under my arms. I am hot, cold, shivery at the same time. 'What did you do?' But even as I am saying it, I already know.

I rest my head back on the surface of the wall, the feel of the cold on my burning flesh a welcome sensation. I already know. I didn't have to ask. I know exactly what she is going to say.

35

I tell them what I know. The police don't want to hear about dreams. They don't want supposition or guesses or embellishments. Just plain and simple facts. The plain and simple facts are that I remember very little. I was a young child. I was out there that night.

My memory of my mother scrambling on her hands and knees on the mud is a fact. The truth as I remember it. I recall running to her, desperate to reach her, then my father picking me up. I recall struggling against his hold, being slapped, hit. Punched. Then nothing else. I tell them how he was so devious that he even left those bolts off, ready to implicate and blame his own son for disappearing. Apparently, they told the police at the time that it must have been an oversight, leaving them off. So many lies. So much hurt and deviancy that we were practically buried alive. Lies heaped on top of more lies, more dirt thrown on top of already compacted dirt.

I tell them about my sleepwalking, how it blurred my memories, blotting out great chunks of my childhood, dreams and reality merging and combining until I could no longer tell them apart. They listen hard when I get to the bit about my memories of that night coming back to me, why I was out there by the shed. How I unearthed Simon's body. Why I have started sleepwalking again as an adult. How my newly acquired therapist has told me that the move to Woodburn Cottage and Warren's death were possible triggers for it.

Were.

Because since finding Simon, it has all stopped. I have slept soundly and safely in my own bed every night. No more nocturnal wanderings around the garden, no further trips out into the street half naked. Just peaceful slumbers occasionally fringed with even more peaceful dreams. I am beginning to feel half human again, my thoughts once more neat and orderly. I can speak clearly and coherently as I sit in the local police station, telling them about a man so grossly abusive and violent that my mind blocked it all out, the events of my childhood so shocking and disturbing, I was able to act as if they didn't actually happen.

'Thank you,' I say as I stand up, my legs weak, my mind clearer than it has been for months.

'Don't forget to get in touch if you remember anything else.' Sergeant Duffield says her goodbyes and a young fresh-faced constable leads me out to the main desk.

'Do you have a family, PC Warwick?'

He nods, his face flushing red as I speak. 'Two brothers, a sister and a stepdad. My real dad died when I was little and my mum passed away last year.'

My heart tightens for this lad, this inexperienced slip of a boy who is young enough to be my own son. 'Think of them often. Talk to them, watch out for them. Love them. They're irreplaceable.'

I don't wait for his reply, turning instead to leave, the swish of the automatic door the only sound to be heard as I step out into the light.

* * *

It's a small affair, Simon's funeral. Private and brief. We wanted to keep it low-key, keep the media and grisly onlookers at bay. Because they are out there, the voyeurs, the gossipmongers, those who would wish us harm for being ruled by an abusive father. For being the offspring of a man who cared only for himself. We are at fault apparently for having not spoken about it, for keeping it secret for most of our lives. They have no idea, these people. No idea of the damage it causes, the long-term effects it has on the minds of the abused.

And then there are those who have shown us nothing but love and pity, sending cards and flowers, words of love and affection written there for us to see. They are so welcome, those words, obliterating the hatred and the disbelief and the general consensus that we as a family brought it on ourselves. It has helped me to believe that not all people are bad, that there are good, thoughtful people out there who care for others. Not everyone is a monster. Warren was a good man. My children, my nieces and nephews are decent, kind individuals. I have to remember that, not let the chill of the shade block out all the light.

We gather in Kim's garden afterwards, a handful of family and friends, drinks in hand, their relief at it all finally being over evident in their smiles, their body language, how they chat animatedly; voices, whispers, laughter mingling in the air around us.

'So, you will come and see us then?' Carrie says, her eyes resting on mine. I have so much affection for this woman. The woman who has shown us nothing but consideration and kindness in the past few weeks.

'I definitely will.' And I mean it too. I have plans, lots of them.

I have plans to travel to Scotland to stay with Carrie and her family. I have plans to visit Lucy once she goes back to Oxford. I definitely have plans.

'Will you be staying at Woodburn Cottage?'

My answer is swift. Steady and solid. 'Absolutely. Why would I want to live anywhere else?'

Carrie smiles, relief in her eyes. 'That's good to hear. I'm not sure Dad could cope with new neighbours at his age. He likes routine and familiarity. He likes you.'

We talk for a short while before I move on, trying to thank people for coming. It's kind. They are kind. That is my new mantra, my new way of thinking. People are good and kind. It's just the odd rotten apple that spoils the rest.

Kim and I will visit Mum once everyone has left. She doesn't know about Simon or the funeral. We discussed it with Amanda and decided the best thing to do was leave things as they are. Mum wouldn't understand. The mention of his name would unleash too many demons, too many unpleasant memories. We will leave her be. She is peaceful lately – happy and content. For how long is anybody's guess. Dementia is a heartless disease but we will cherish the moment while it lasts.

The police also made the decision to not question Mum. She is a vulnerable person and any witness statements she makes, unreliable. The case is still ongoing but with mine and Kim's statements, they are piecing it all together, forming the picture of beastly, violent man who treated his family as if they were his property, doing with them as he saw fit.

They decided to not investigate his death, putting it down to an accident. We agree.

36

JOHN GOODWILL

It's been months. The worst is over. The police didn't suspect anything. Why would they? This is his family. He takes care of them, directs what happens under his roof. Do they have any idea how hard he works to bring in the money that feeds and clothes this family? He doubts that they do. Nobody seems to care or understand. Nobody, least of all his wife and children.

Spring is on its way. He opens the bedroom window, inspects the sill for flaking paint and stops, the cool breeze wrapping itself around him. Outside, it's still. No birdsong, very little noise at all. This is a nice village. Everyone keeps themselves to themselves. No nosey parkers pushing their sticky beaks into business that doesn't involve them. Exactly as it should be.

He prises the lid off the paint tin, picks up the brush and drags it across the outside sill. If he kneels, doesn't lean too far out, he can just about reach the far end.

Behind him, he can hear Kim and Sylvie as they mill about in the bedrooms, tidying up, doing whatever it is they do with their time, their voices irritating him. He wanted peace and quiet. He wanted to be left alone with his thoughts while he improved this house. Their house. The house he pays for. Is there no respite from their whining? Nowhere he can be free of the constant, tinny grumbling of their voices?

Frustration and annoyance jab at him, burning beneath his skin, putting him on edge. That's his default position, it would seem. Always clinging onto the precipice of exasperation. His head aches, his jaw is set in place, tension rippling through him.

He grinds his teeth as he thinks about the last few months, about what happened. What she made him do. And now everything has changed, their lives irrevocably altered, their family fragmented. He wonders what the future holds, whether he can keep things together. She has threatened to leave him on numerous occasions. It won't happen. Where would she go? He would always find her. She's his wife and this is where she belongs, for better for worse. Silly bitch, thinking she could have got away with it, taking his child away from him.

This is all on her head, and he's told her so often enough, told her that if she ever opened up to anybody about that night, he would give them the full story, relate how he was carrying the kid back inside when she grabbed him, pulled him to the ground, smacked his head open. She always was the nervous type, too timid to think beyond the superficial. Too lacking in confidence to see the obvious.

They got questioned by the police afterwards. Of course they did. That's standard procedure, but he held it together, was ready for them, kept to the story whilst appearing distraught. He was a reliable witness whereas she was a nervous bloody wreck, constantly fidgeting, stumbling over her words, flicking her gaze around the room. He knew who they would believe and told her so. So she kept quiet, kept her head down, didn't put a foot out of place. As it should be. She is the housewife. He is the man of the house. The breadwinner, worthy of respect.

He reminds her constantly of what she did, chiselling it into her mind. She needs to remember that it was her idea to kidnap the boy, send him away. She set the scene. Made it all happen. No jury in the land would find him guilty. He knows it. She knows it. They are bound together. Never to be apart.

He flexes his muscles, grits his teeth, leans out and drags the brush across the stretch of wood. The voices in the other room continue to chatter. Not so much a chatter as an incessant drone, like nails being dragged down a chalkboard. First Sylvie, then Kim. Then Kim and next Sylvie. Difficult to tell them apart. Cut from the same cloth they are. Always full of self-righteousness, always plotting and scheming, conspiring against him. Sometimes, he feels like a stranger in his own home, locked out of their conversations, their witchy little ways. Have they learnt nothing in the past few months? Do they not realise what he will do to keep them here? What he is capable of?

He goes over it all in his head: that night, their family, how it all got to this point. He is so caught up in it, he doesn't hear the footsteps behind him, the creak of the floorboards, the opening of the door. He isn't sure who it is, doesn't have the time to turn around to find out, but feels the rush of air as it happens. He feels the push, the weight of the hand, that final, fateful push and the terrifying sensation of floating, of nothing beneath him, his limbs flailing, clutching at thin air, his head spinning, eyes bulging. And next, the sickening crack of bone as he hits the concrete patio at speed, headfirst. Then blackness. An eternity of nothing.

In the house, a woman's voice cries out, a practised scream that disguises the relief as John Goodwill lies sprawled on the concrete, blood pooling, eyes wide open. No movement, no breathing. Nothing at all.

They are free. At long last, they are all finally free.

ACKNOWLEDGEMENTS

A huge thank you to Boldwood Books for taking on this book and republishing it, giving it a much-needed makeover and finding new readers for what was once a much unloved and unread story.

I loved writing *While She Sleeps*, and although I don't suffer from sleep-walking, I do suffer from many other nocturnal issues such as night terrors and sleep paralysis so it was inevitable that I would at some point write a story that is centered around a character who takes to the streets at night, unaware of who or where she is.

As always, my thanks go to the staff at Boldwood Books, my family and friends for their ongoing support and my small but strong network of author friends. You all know who you are. Keep on being you.

Thank you to all the bloggers and reviewers who take the time to read and review my books. Every review counts.

I can be found on social media, hoping for somebody to contact me so I can prevaricate a little more instead of focusing on my writing.

Facebook.com/thewriterjude
Twitter.com/thewriterjude
Instagram.com/jabakerauthor

ABOUT THE AUTHOR

J. A. Baker is a successful writer of numerous psychological thrillers. Born and brought up in Middlesbrough, she still lives in the North East, which inspires the settings for her books.

Sign up to J. A. Baker's mailing list here for news, competitions and updates on future books.

Follow J. A. Baker on social media:

- facebook.com/thewriterjude
- x.com/thewriterjude
- instagram.com/jabakerauthor
- tiktok.com/@jabaker41
- bookbub.com/authors/JABaker

ALSO BY J. A. BAKER

Local Girl Missing

The Last Wife

The Woman at Number 19

The Other Mother

The Toxic Friend

The Retreat

The Woman in the Woods

The Stranger

The Intruder

The Girl In The Water

The Quiet One

The Passenger

Little Boy, Gone

When She Sleeps

The Widower's Lie

The Guilty Teacher

THE *Murder* LIST

THE MURDER LIST IS A NEWSLETTER DEDICATED TO ALL THINGS CRIME AND THRILLER FICTION!

SIGN UP TO MAKE SURE YOU'RE ON OUR HIT LIST FOR GRIPPING PAGE-TURNERS AND HEARTSTOPPING READS.

SIGN UP TO OUR NEWSLETTER

BIT.LY/THEMURDERLISTNEWS

Boldwood

Boldwood Books is an award-winning fiction publishing company seeking out the best stories from around the world.

Find out more at www.boldwoodbooks.com

Join our reader community for brilliant books, competitions and offers!

Follow us
@BoldwoodBooks
@TheBoldBookClub

Sign up to our weekly deals newsletter

https://bit.ly/BoldwoodBNewsletter

Milton Keynes UK
Ingram Content Group UK Ltd.
UKHW040717080724
445163UK00001B/5

9 781835 612460